The Lucky Ones

The Lucky Ones

LIZ LAWSON

DELACORTE PRESS

This is a work of fiction. Names, characters, places, and incidents either are the product of the author's imagination or are used fictitiously. Any resemblance to actual persons, living or dead, events, or locales is entirely coincidental.

Delacorte Press is a registered trademark and the colophon is a trademark of Penguin Random House LLC.

Visit us on the Web! GetUnderlined.com

Educators and librarians, for a variety of teaching tools, visit us at RHTeachersLibrarians.com

Library of Congress Cataloging-in-Publication Data
Names: Lawson, Liz, author.
Title: The lucky ones / Liz Lawson.
Description: First edition. | New York : Delacorte Press, [2020] | Summary: "In the aftermath of a school tragedy, May and Zach struggle with grief, survivor's guilt, and the complex emotional impact of the event, learning how to heal and hope in the face of it all"— Provided by publisher.
Identifiers: LCCN 2019011208 (print) | LCCN 2019020245 (ebook) |
ISBN 978-0-593-11851-1 (el) | ISBN 978-0-593-11849-8 (hc : alk. paper) |
ISBN 978-0-593-11850-4 (glb : alk. paper)
Subjects: | CYAC: Grief—Fiction. | Guilt—Fiction. | School shootings—Fiction. | High schools—Fiction. | Schools—Fiction.
Classification: LCC PZ7.1.L38444 (ebook) | LCC PZ7.1.L38444 Lu 2020 (print) | DDC [Fic]—dc23

The text of this book is set in 12-point Dante MT Pro.

Interior design by Stephanie Moss

Printed in the United States of America

10 9 8 7 6 5 4 3 2 1

For my parents: thank you for always believing in me.
(And, Mom: sorry for all the cursing in here.)

And if you're still breathing, you're the lucky ones
'Cause most of us are heaving through corrupted lungs

—Daughter, "Youth"

CHAPTER ONE

May

I bolt across the lawn, squinting through the inky black. The streetlamp behind me casts a pool of light, but it's weak. Clouds block the moon.

As I run, I wipe my hand across my forehead, and it comes back wet. It's hot as shit out here, even though it's January in Los Angeles and that's supposed to mean something. It's been like this for weeks—hot and still. Earthquake weather, Lucy's grandmother claims, even though I keep telling her it's been scientifically proven that you can't predict an earthquake.

I'm alone; Lucy ditched me after our late-night dinner. I guess I can't blame her for going home; it's after midnight and we have school in the morning—my first day at this new school since I was kicked out of the old one almost ten months ago. I probably should have gone home too, but I couldn't without coming here first. It's not like I sleep anymore, anyway.

Lucy would have a fit if she knew where I went after she left.

Ever since we figured out that Michelle Teller installed motion-sensitive lights on the side of the garage, Lucy's been so much more cautious—all *Dude, May, I love you but we need to be careful, messing with that shit*—which I get for her—I get it, I do—but for me, it's different. For me, it's worth it. She disagrees, but as much as I love Lucy and as much as I tell her about what's running through this fucked-up head of mine, I don't tell her everything.

Like, tonight. When I called her, late, and asked her to meet me at the diner for some food—I didn't tell her why.

This afternoon I checked the mail for the first time all weekend and there was another one, waiting for me in the box.

When I saw it, my insides froze. I grabbed it, went upstairs, stuffed it under my clothes way in the back of my closet, and then went into the bathroom and threw up. After, I lay down on my bed, head pounding. But from across the room I could feel the thump of its presence, like a fucking telltale heart. There are so many now, hidden around my room, haunting me at night from my desk drawer, from my closet, from every nook and cranny in my bedroom where I shove them. If I actually fall and stay asleep, like a normal human being, they creep into my dreams, turning them into nightmares.

I couldn't stay still. I jumped out of bed and started cleaning my room but couldn't concentrate enough to do much more than pace back and forth across the cluttered carpet.

Hence the call to Lucy. Hence not going home when she did. I need this—it's the only thing that will smooth the sharp memory of those letters.

I finally reach the garage door, but as soon as I get to it an image pops into my head, distracting me, of my twin brother Jordan's body sprawled on the jazz band room floor, thick, bright crimson pouring out of him, soaking into the ratty gray carpet. I'm thrown for a moment, before I take that image and shove it down out of my head, down into the depth of my belly, and I step too close to the side of the house. I know not to; over the past months, I've gotten to be an expert on the layout of the Tellers' driveway and the system of lights they hooked up, but as usual I screw things up.

A spotlight blasts on, and for a split second I'm like an animal caught in headlights, one of the idiotic ones that always get mowed down. I freeze.

After a few long seconds, I finally get it through my dumb head that standing here in the middle of a bright circle of light is not a great idea, and I force myself to move. I dart around the corner into the blackness of the backyard and press my body up against the stucco of the house. I'm gripping the can of spray paint so hard that my fingers turn white, standing out against the black of the night. I suck in breaths like Dr. McMillen, PsyD, taught me, one long inhale for four counts and one long exhale for four, and my heart begins to slow.

I try to think of what Lucy would say if she was here, other than the obvious—*Be more careful, May, you dumbass.* Would she tell me to go home? Yell at me for being a pussy? Normally she'd be out here with me, the two of us charging through the night together, but over the past few weeks she's been doing this more and more—ducking out and leaving me to come here on my own.

My breath calms me enough that I can think about moving again. I need to pay more attention, stop letting memories distract me, remember what I read in *The Art of War,* which I found buried in Jordan's room in a pile of his clothes a month after he died.

In the midst of chaos, there is also opportunity.

That guy, Sun Tzu, was pretty smart. It's how I first came up with this thing—a way to show the asshole lawyer who took that psychopath's case that what she's doing isn't okay. From that book. I figured it was a sign or something, finding it in Jordan's stuff.

I'm pretty sure the night I found it was the first time any of us had been in his room since it happened. Even now, eleven months later, my mom still refuses to go in there, refuses to sort through his things, and sometimes—on the rare occasions when my parents are both at home—I hear her and my dad arguing about it, late in the night when I can't sleep.

Darkness settles back over the driveway, and I decide it's safe to shake the can just enough to prep it, even though each time the hard ball hits the bottom it sounds like a cannon going off. You'd think, it being the twenty-first century and all, someone would have invented a quieter way to do this, particularly since, in my experience, no one ever uses spray paint for activities that are . . . let's just say . . . *totally legal.*

Although, I'd argue that the purposes I use it for are right in line with my moral code, and that everyone is getting what they deserve.

I'm out in front of the garage finishing the last letter, paint still dripping red down the door, when there's a rustling behind me. For a second, David's face flashes through my mind, and even though I know—I *know*—he's secured behind bars at the Twin Towers Correctional Facility in Downtown LA, I leap about twenty feet into the air and whirl around so fast that I trip over my feet. I land hard on the driveway, scraping my palms, and the goddamn spotlight flicks on again, blinding me from above. My heart's beating a million miles a minute, and tears prick at the edges of my eyes. I'm squinting at the sudden glare, trying to scramble to my feet, generally having a massive heart attack, when I hear a soft *mew,* and something brushes against the back of my leg.

Fucking hell. It's just a stupid cat.

I collapse back on the driveway in the center of the spotlight to catch my breath and stop my insides from sprinting away from my body down the street. I don't even care if someone sees me. My limbs feel like they've been filled with lead. The cat, unaware that it almost killed me less than ten seconds ago, walks up onto my chest like it owns the place and starts to knead my sweatshirt.

"Jesus Christ." I can't help it; I start to laugh and have to squeeze my lips together to keep the sound from bursting out of my mouth into the night. "Kitty, you scared me half to death, no joke." I reach out and run a hand along the side of its fur, only realizing after that I've left a faint red line all the way down its back. I glance at my arm and see that it's streaked with paint from fingers to elbow. I must have sprayed myself when the cat freaked me out.

This last part of the night is *not* going as planned. I'm definitely going to give Lucy shit for abandoning me. Tired, my ass.

Whatever, the cat will just have to deal with its new color. A little red paint never killed anyone, right? (I actually have no idea if that's true, but I'm going to go ahead and believe it for the time being, otherwise I could potentially end up washing a cat in the dark.)

I'm still lying here in the driveway with a cat nudging at my face when the spotlight goes out, leaving me in dark.

CHAPTER TWO

Zach

BITCH.

That word, still slightly wet, dripping red paint onto the asphalt of our driveway, is the first thing I see as I leave the house to head to school. First day back after winter break—what a great way to start the semester.

The letters are huge—massive, in fact—tearing their way across the garage door.

When I see them, I stop in my tracks.

Gwenie slams into my back and screeches, "Zach, what the hell?" Her curly blond hair is a mess, all unruly and tangled, and I make a mental note to find her a better brush. File under *yet another thing a parent should do for their daughter that I'll be doing instead.*

My sister thinks she's so grown-up this year, what with her cursing and the belly-button piercing she got without permission at some shady place down near the Venice Boardwalk. She's convinced that entering high school has made her a full-fledged grown-up. What she doesn't know is how little she still is. How much she should always want to be little. Playing on her swing set in the backyard, ignorant of messages like the one that's been spray-painted on our house, yet again.

Instead she's standing behind me, glowering at my back.

"Gwenie, go inside." I turn and try to shove her back through the front door so she doesn't see, but she's too quick. She darts under my arm and stops at the corner of the porch.

"What is it?" She's squinting; she doesn't have her glasses on, and the contacts she normally wears have been retired for the time being, until she can remember to take them out at night. "They were here again? In our driveway?" Her voice is rising, her breath coming out in short bursts.

"Go back inside." I'm trying to stay calm, but my voice comes out like a growl, and her spine stiffens.

"It says *bitch*!" Her voice squeaks; she sounds like another version of herself, the one that would follow me around constantly when we were younger, trying to get me to play with her.

I sigh. "Gwen. It's nothing. Just the same stupid crap that people have been doing ever since Mom took this case, you know?"

"But . . . it's on our house. *Again*. They keep coming, Zach. When we're sleeping inside! They're out here, and we don't even know it." A sob escapes her mouth and she turns back to me, tears gathering at the corners of her eyes. "We should get Dad."

I run a hand through my hair and tug at its ends, trying to think. Our dad's still asleep upstairs. It's *my* job to drag Gwenie out of bed in the morning; my job to drive her to school, to make sure she has dinner, to make sure she gets all her homework done and handed in on time. Over the break, that's all I did—drive Gwenie to the mall, order dinner for the two of us, stay on top of her to finish the reading she needed to do for her new classes.

I don't know when I became my sister's keeper. Was it when my mom took this stupid case and my family became a fixture in local gossip? When this fucking vandalism started, escalating from mean notes left in our mailbox to graffiti marking the house and salt killing our front lawn? When Gwen started waking up in the middle of the night from nightmares? Or did it begin way before any of that? It's not like our mom was ever here much—it's not like our dad's been present in years. Not since he was laid off five years ago and instead of looking for a new grown-up job decided to pursue a career as a musician at the ripe old age of forty-five. Surprising no one, except maybe him, his career didn't take off, and six months ago he collapsed into a useless heap of skin and bones. I'm sure the total lack of support from my mom's end these past few months didn't help matters; she basically ignored the entire situation, per usual, and, from what I can see, has started to treat him like her third child. A role that he's readily adopted, a role that's overshadowed his identity as, you know, a FATHER. Gwen and I are *so* lucky.

"Dad's sleeping." I glance up at his dark window. "C'mon. Let's just get to school. I'll text him so he knows what to expect when he goes downstairs today."

If he goes downstairs today.

"We're just going to . . . leave that word? Sitting there? What if the neighbors see it?" Gwen asks.

Considering it's light out and I can see the kids down the block waiting for the school bus, I'm pretty sure that ship has sailed, but I'm not going to tell her that. Not to mention, I think the neighbors are used to it by now, although I wouldn't know because they ignore us just like everyone else.

"It's fine, okay?" I hoist my heavy backpack farther up on my shoulders and walk over to where she's standing, frozen, a statue made of ice and fear.

I put a hand on her arm. "Gwenie. C'mon. We're gonna be late if we don't leave."

"I don't care if we're late. I hate that place." She mutters this so softly that I almost miss it. I grit my teeth and turn away, pretending that I didn't hear, pretending that the hot, blustery Santa Ana winds snatched up her words before they could reach me.

I walk by her motionless figure to my car and beep it unlocked.

Behind me there's silence, and then the sound of her footsteps, running to catch up.

* * *

We pull into the parking lot at school, and it's all I can do to remember how to find my space. I've been driving us to school every day since senior year began, but I still can't seem to wrap my mind around this labyrinth of a lot, which they opened this year when all the Carter kids were transferred here. If I didn't know any better, I'd say that it changes shape and size every night after everyone goes home.

After an embarrassing amount of time, I remember that we need to take a left at space 355 instead of a right, and moments later I'm parking.

As I turn off the ignition, a Volvo pulls in a few spots over. I glance over without even meaning to: the white of the car's paint catches the sun, and it's like I can't help looking.

And there she is.

My ex, Rosaline.

I usually time this better. I usually get us here early, because I know Rosa, and if there's one thing you can count on with her, it's that she's always, always late. But that stupid word on our stupid garage door threw me off schedule this morning, and now we're stuck.

Gwenie opens her door and then looks back over at me, because I'm sitting here, immobile. She must spot Rosa through my window, because she sucks in a breath.

"Shit. Zach . . ." She trails off.

"I know." I squeeze my eyes shut and count to ten to steady myself, like the school counselor told me to do last time I was in his office, after another nasty note was left in my locker and a teacher found me slumped against the door.

"What are we going to do?" She sounds scared.

"I don't know." I glance back through the window at Rosa's car and find myself looking directly into her eyes. She looks as surprised as I feel, and for a split second I think I see something cross her face that doesn't look like the normal revulsion she directs toward me and my family, but then it's gone, replaced by the mask of anger and contempt she's worn nonstop since last fall.

Unlike my sister and me, she doesn't hesitate to get out of her car. As I watch, unable to tear my eyes away, she pulls off her seat belt and throws open her car door in one oddly elegant motion.

My heart is ripping in two inside my chest. Gwenie and I are trapped like rodents in the car, and I don't know where to direct my eyes. I'm sweating; my shirt's gonna be a mess. And we haven't even gotten out of the car yet. This is a fucked-up way to start the new semester, but fucked-up is pretty much par for the course these past few months, thanks to our lovely mother.

I glance in the rearview mirror and see Rosa, her back rigid, walking quickly away. A small hand slips into mine, and only then do I realize that I'm trembling something fierce.

Gwen and I sit there silently in my car, trapped, waiting for the coast to clear.

CHAPTER THREE

May

I'm fucking sore.

And tired.

Tired and sore. Biking home from the lawyer's house took way too long last night.

And now I'm driving to school. For the first time in almost a year.

Not Carter, of course. They closed that building down a few months after, because the air inside was full of ghosts. Bad ghosts. Pained ghosts. My brother's ghost.

No, I'm driving to some other high school in the Valley—a school we used to play in sports occasionally, I think. I never knew anyone who went there. It was too far away, and Los Angeles traffic is beyond shitty. This morning it's taken me over forty minutes to get here, and it's less than ten miles away. *Quincy Adams High School.* It sounds so bougie. So fucking lame. Lucy says it's been weird—all the Carter kids keep to themselves, and the QA kids let them. She says it feels like they're afraid of us. Like we're infected by what happened. Apparently, last semester the administration tried to force interaction by doing stupid assemblies where they would do team-building exercises and shit. That went over about as well as you'd expect.

Last year, for a few months right after the shooting, they tried to keep us at Carter, which was an extremely stupid idea if you ask me. Toward the end of the semester, things got so bad, with breakdowns and fights and people dropping out left and right, too afraid to go back to that place, and they finally decided a fresh start was better for everyone.

Hence, their decision to transfer half of the leftover kids from Carter here at the beginning of the new school year and half to Miller, the next closest high school in the Valley. This is where I ended up when my parents and Dr. McMillen decided homeschooling wasn't working out. Wasn't working out . . . so *sue* me if I couldn't take that whimpering homeschool teacher seriously as she sat in front of me, clutching my textbooks in her aging hands, barely able to hold them up. Couldn't take her seriously as we both sat there ignoring the ever-present ghost of my brother, which draped itself over everything in the house, over furniture like ill-fitting slipcovers, over conversations like a heavy fog, over *every fucking interaction* like an anchor pulling us down, down, down to the bottom of the ocean.

Last fall, the Executive Decision (vom) was made that it

would be better for my *mental health* (again, vom) if I was around people. Not homeschooled, since my parents couldn't (read: *wouldn't*) be there with me to make sure I was, you know, actually *doing* stuff and not just ignoring the teacher they'd brought in, who had failed at her "job" pretty miserably.

Principal Rose-Brady somehow convinced the school board to let me back in, even though I'm pretty sure she had to field several angry phone calls after that decision from parents of kids who I may or may not have punched in the face at some point in the past. Honestly, though, how could those parents fight my reenrollment? The fact is: *I'm a SURVIVOR.*

I'm the leftover.

The *lucky* one.

The only one in that room who lived.

And now I'm back in school.

It sucks.

I don't know where to park, so I spend far too long trying to maneuver through the stupid maze of a lot, one hand on the wheel and the other clutching the hand-drawn map Lucy gave me last night to try to alleviate my anxiety.

I'm so exhausted that the lines of her drawing keep twisting together like ropes, crossing in imaginary places. I didn't get home until almost two a.m.; I stayed on that driveway for almost an hour, lying there with that stupid cat, just breathing.

Feeling like the sky was pressing down on my head, like the stars were going to pop like old lightbulbs any second, leaving the world black.

I finally find my space and turn the car into it with enough force that for a second I'm afraid the brakes will fail and I'll go slamming into the car across the way. I'm used to Jordan sitting next to me, reminding me to slow down. Even toward the end, when we weren't talking much, when our silences could swallow entire car rides, his hand on my arm could calm me. Now there's an empty seat next to me: a reminder that I'm alone.

Once I'm parked, I head across the sidewalk to the main building.

When I reach the front door, I remember what I forgot.

The sight of the metal detectors slams me in the stomach. They look like something out of a sci-fi movie, something that I should see in a place that is dangerous and frightening, not in a school building, but of course now they are one and the same, the frightening places and the daily places, and my mouth tugs downward and my stomach plummets through the asphalt into the center of the earth.

Then, because I have no other option, no other choice, I push through the doors and put my school bag on the conveyor belt and walk through the detector. Out of the corner of my eye I see a uniformed guard patting down another late arrival, gracelessly poking at his pockets and around his ankles.

On the other side, I come face to face with a giant placard

displaying the names and faces of the other people who were in the band room that day—my favorite teacher, my friends, *my fucking brother.* Why they insisted on putting up this disgusting memorial at all the high schools in our area is beyond me. The shooting didn't happen here. It's like they're just trying too hard—trying to act like they care—trying to act like they understand.

Like they could ever understand.

Thank god Lucy warned me or I'd probably puke all over it.

Before I can explode into a thousand tiny molecules of fury, my friend Chimera is on me like white on rice. She clamps her slender fingers around my arm, and I almost jump out of my skin.

"May, oh my god, I am so glad to see you. Do you have an extra tampon? I just got my period. It's like a fucking bloodbath down there. . . ." She trails off and her face goes scarlet. My heart's beating at a thousand ticks a minute, and I'm breathing in and out, trying to calm myself down. Chim glances over at Jordan's face, which is staring at us from the bullshit display on the wall. "Oh god. I didn't mean that. Oh my god, I am so sorry . . ." She drops my arm and puts her hands to her mouth. This is such typical Chim. Haven't seen her in three months, and in the first twenty seconds I'm reminded why.

Since I got kicked out of school last year, I've tried to learn how not to react. How to control my face and my emotions like a fucking Zen monk. It's an art form, I swear. One I'm not very good at, especially around Chim, who reminds me of who I used to be—a person I'd rather forget.

I force a smile and rummage around in my purse with shaky fingers, finally locating a tampon. I hand it to Chim and she smiles, all grateful. I manage not to roll my eyes directly in her face. She's wearing a skullcap that's totally inappropriate for the eighty-degree day, and the ends of her hair peek out from under it. She's chopped it since I last saw her three months ago, and apparently dyed it pink. She looks cute, I guess, if you like that sort of thing.

We start down the crowded hall together, into the black hole that is this fucking school, toward lockers and classrooms and all the things I hoped to never have to deal with again. We have to push by people to get through; Lucy warned me how overstuffed it is here, but I didn't really expect it to be this bad. I should have, though, I guess, since there are now so many students enrolled here that we have two principals: Rose-Brady, who came with us from Carter so we'd have a *familiar face* in charge (eye roll), and Kalb, the original QA principal.

The walls around us are papered with flyers talking about dances and tryouts and all the normal crap, but I see the other ones too—the ones talking about grief groups and counselors and how to deal with life after death. I want to tear them all off the walls and throw them in the toilet and flush them far, far away from here—from me. Rose-Brady made me go to one of those grief groups last year, before Carter closed, but that didn't turn out so well. At all. So now I see a private therapist. Who tells me shit like *It gets better.* I used to have to see her multiple times a week—luckily, since last fall I've managed to avoid going outside of the once-a-month sessions that Rose-Brady and the school board made known were a requirement to even *consider* my reenrollment.

"Chim. Please stop. It's fine; you know it's fine. Now that I'm back you cannot start tiptoeing around me. You know I hate that shit." More accurately, I hate having to have conversations with people whose eyes are so full of pity, who don't see *me* anymore, just a reflection of Jordan's ghost.

Chim, who never used to get embarrassed by her big mouth around me, blushes an even deeper shade of red. It's impressive.

"No, I really am sorry. I have to start thinking before I speak; my mom keeps telling me that. I'm always saying stupid stuff, and I know I need to be more sensitive around you. . . ." She's babbling, all nerves and tongue flaps, and my chest tightens. We've known each other since kindergarten—she was my first real friend outside of Jordan, actually—but ever since last year it's been hard for me to stomach the sight of her. It's not fair, I know that, but it's like I just can't let myself relax when I'm with her—we can't seem to find the rhythm of our friendship since Jordan died.

We reach her locker, and she's still talking. I am so tempted to slap her to get her to just *shut up* (am I really supposed to just stand here and listen to this incessant chatter?), when a warm hand clasps my arm.

"Ladies." I turn, and there she is—my savior, Lucy, the only person I want to see these days; the only person who seems to be able to see *me* through the haze of what happened last year. She smirks like she knows exactly what I was just thinking—knows that she stopped me from smacking Chim across her lovely, annoying face.

"How are we this morning?" Lucy, as always, is wearing black on black on black: a T-shirt of some obscure local band who will be famous by next year, and ripped leather pants. The administrations of all the local public schools outlawed that sort of clothing last year when they instituted a strict countywide dress code, but Lucy is apparently the exception to that rule. She usually is.

She hip-checks me and lays her curly brown head on my shoulder. My heart rate slows, and I remember how to breathe as some of the tension drains out of my body. My hand unflexes by my waist, and Lucy slips in a roll of Girl Scout cookies. Thin Mints. My favorite—pretty much the only thing I ate last spring after Jordan died.

I love Lucy.

"Good to see you here," she whispers into my ear.

"Luce!" Chim's eyes light up. Chim's had a crush on Lucy since I can remember, which is cute when she's not following Lucy around like a lost little puppy dog.

"Hey, Chim." Lucy nods at her. "Thanks for coming out

Saturday to see the band. Sorry we sucked. I think I might quit. I'm actually gonna go check out another band tonight; I need something new."

"You *so* did not suck." Chim's voice is an octave higher than normal. She's been going to Lucy's shows since forever. I don't think she's missed one. In fact, I'm pretty sure she skipped her cousin's bat mitzvah in order to make one a few years ago.

Jordan and I used to go to them, too, which was fine, until it wasn't. Sometime during sophomore year, I started resenting the fact that Lucy always invited both of us. That my friends were *our* friends. Like he didn't have enough with his perfect grades and his perfect hair and all the attention our parents poured on him. So, at Lucy's shows, instead of hanging out with him, I would ditch him as soon as we arrived and spend most of the rest of the night out back with Chim, drinking and smoking and getting fucked-up. Basically, doing everything in my power to avoid him and his judgmental looks and making Chim come along for the ride. He started bringing a few of his friends along soon after.

I push the thought out of my head, far out, try to erase even the imprint of it from my mind.

"May." Lucy squeezes my hand again. "Yo, the bell rang. It's time to get to class, *chérie*."

I'm startled out of my reverie. I glance around the hallway, realizing for the first time that it emptied while I've been deep in my own memories, obsessing.

Chim freaks out when she hears the bell. "Shit. I'm going to be late for chem again. Not that it matters; I'm basically failing."

Lucy rolls her eyes. "So, what, you're getting a B right now?"

"Whatever. I gotta go." Chim takes off down the hallway, and I wave to her back, wiggling my fingers like *Good to see ya, friend.*

"Dude. You are harsh." Lucy grabs my hand and holds it down near her hip. "She means well, you know that."

I yank my hand out of her grip. "Yeah. I know. I get it. But, man. Sometimes I want to slap her so bad."

Lucy snorts. "No shit. I saw you earlier. You need to chill. She loves you—she just doesn't know what to say." She considers me. "And you're lucky that I got here when I did, or it woulda been detention for you, no matter who you are. You know what Rose-Brady said when they agreed to take you here: *best behavior.*" She taps me on my head between my eyes.

I flare my nostrils. "I know what she said," I say. *I just don't care.*

She leans in and brushes the hair off my forehead. "Hey. You look exhausted. Are you okay?" I nod, cross my arms tight against my chest. Lucy pauses, bites her lower lip, clears her throat. "May. You're flying under the radar right now, but barely. You know this. I know this. You have to be careful. They aren't going to keep giving you chances—even with Rose-Brady in your corner—if you can't control yourself.

Okay?" She glances down at her watch. "Shit. I gotta run. I'll see you at lunch."

I chew on the inside of my cheek, silent as she walks away. Repeat over and over in my head one of the many mantras the school-appointed therapist, Dr. McMillen, taught me last summer: *You are safe. You are safe.*

It's not working. It never works. My heart pounds in my chest and it's like I'm back there, in that tiny closet at Carter, sitting wrapped in a ball with my hands over my ears, trying to block out all those screams. My brother's screams. And then after what seemed like an eternity but was probably only a minute, the screams stopped and the silence began, and it was the thickest, most suffocating silence I've ever heard.

The last bell rings and I jump. It's loud and it's sharp and I swear to god that my eardrums start bleeding, that I can feel the blood trickling down my cheeks, but when I go to wipe it away, I realize that it's nothing more than my own tears.

CHAPTER FOUR

Zach

I walk into third-period history, which is held in a bungalow behind the school. It sits on the field where the JV baseball team used to practice, before everything here doubled in size and space became impossible to come by. There's no more JV team. They've been axed, just like half of the other shit at this school the administration decided wasn't important enough to salvage when the Carter kids came. I've heard people talking about it in the halls, moaning how unfair it is that we have to suffer just because those kids needed a new place to go.

Which should tell you something about my classmates and how wonderful they are. Just so, so wonderful.

As I move through the room toward my seat, everyone avoids making eye contact with me, per usual. From the far corner, I hear whispers and giggles. The hair on the back of my neck pricks and my skin goes hot. I don't have to turn around to know who's talking, or that they're talking about me.

I've begged my counselor only about a thousand times

to get me out of this class, but she keeps telling me that it's impossible, that with the influx of kids from Carter, every classroom is filled to the brim. I suppose it's an appropriate punishment, in a way, that I'm now stuck in a room every other day with my former friend, Matt, who hates me and, to slam that cherry on the top of the disaster that is my life, is now dating my ex-girlfriend. Which, to be perfectly honest, is sort of my own fault.

I hear more giggles and force myself to keep moving toward my seat. I slump into it and train my eyes on the white board at the front of the room. I just *love* coming to school, to a place where people used to greet me with high fives and now turn their heads in disgust when I walk by them in the halls. It's amazing how fast people will turn on you, even after you've known them practically your whole life.

Thankfully, Conor slides into the seat next to me a moment later. My shoulders start to drop away from their position near the top of my head. Conor's the only one who stuck around; the only one who acts like my mom's decision hasn't somehow infected me. In part it's 'cause he wouldn't know what to do without me, and in part because he knows better than most that the choices parents make sometimes suck a big fat D. About eight years ago, his dad got back from Afghanistan all messed up in the head and his mom decided she couldn't deal and split. Left Conor living alone with his mostly unemployed, generally drunk dad. He started staying at my house a bunch after that.

Point is: he gets that parents are bullshit. Mine, his—them all.

"'Sup, dude." I nod in his general direction.

"Hey." He slouches down in his chair and splays his legs out in front of him. I see one of the girls behind us glancing over once, twice, nudging another girl with her elbow and nodding our way. I flush and duck my head. Most likely, she's thrilled to be back at school after break so she can stare at Conor. Girls love him, even when he's not onstage singing. Always have, always will. It's been this way since we became friends in third grade and has gotten even more annoying since freshman year, when he started booking shows with his band.

It's just gotten a little disconcerting since everything went down with my mom. Since then, people have started staring at me, too. And unlike Conor, I don't revel in the attention. Unlike Conor, it's not 'cause girls think I'm hot or mysterious or talented, or whatever they think about him. I'm just . . . whatever. Normal. Average. I used to be invisible. I miss those days.

The bell rings, and at the front of the room, Mr. Ames clears his throat. Rules and teachers and authority have never deterred Conor, and he immediately starts talking to me.

"You comin' tonight? To our practice? We're auditioning new drummers, since f'in' Lockett went AWOL last week. What kind of monster does that? We have our first gig at the Orion next week, man, and he just up and leaves us 'cause he needs a job or some shit?"

I slide down in my seat as far as I can go without melting

onto the floor. Why does Conor always have to draw attention my way? Ames is sending death glares at us as he begins to drone on about whatever the hell is on the syllabus today in dead-European-white-guy history.

I mutter my response under my breath as quietly as I can. "I thought he got his girl pregnant. That's why he needs a job, no?"

Conor's basically deaf, since he refuses to wear earplugs at his shows, so he has no idea what I just said and makes a confused face in response. I shake my head and mouth, "Never mind," all exaggerated, but there's no stopping Conor, not when he really wants something, and he says at top volume, "WHAT?"

Maybe he doesn't really shout, but it sure as hell sounds like a cannon going off to my ears, and Ames appears to agree. He interrupts himself and marches over to our seats, bending down so he's at eye level.

"Want to share whatever it is you're talking about with the class, Simonsen? Since it's apparently *so* interesting that it can't wait?" Ames always sounds like he taught himself how to speak to students by watching crappy 1980s sitcoms.

Conor leans back in his chair and folds his arms across his chest, while I wish to god that the floor would open up and swallow both my desk and me whole. I know Conor way too well, and I know he never just shuts up because a teacher tells him to. . . .

"Not really, *sir.*" Conor's voice is a full-on smirk.

Yup, I know Conor.

He'll never just shut up.

Ames rolls his eyes at the ceiling. "Conor, it's a new semester. A whole new year, *amiright*? I thought we agreed that you'd can the attitude come 2020? Guess that resolution didn't stick?"

The class laughs, in part because they know Ames and Conor secretly love each other, in a they're-so-alike-it's-creepy kinda way.

"And." He turns to me, and I pray again that the floor will swallow me. "You."

I raise my eyebrows at him and try to channel Conor's IDGAF attitude. I'm sure I just look constipated.

Ames shakes his head. "Zach, get better friends."

The class roars. Ames walks back to the front of the room and Conor smirks.

As the noise quiets, I hear Matt whisper behind me, "Good luck with that," and I want to die.

I'm walking out of the room after class when someone grabs my elbow. I know it's Conor because no one else touches me these days—and I mean that both literally and figuratively.

"So, you comin'?" He nudges my arm with his elbow. Someone across the hall shouts to him, and he waves halfheartedly without even looking to see who it is. Oh, to be so cool and semifamous that you don't even care who's screaming your name.

I cock my head and shoot him a sideways glance. "Coming where?"

He lets out a sigh of exasperation, way dramatic, and replies, "To my *practice,* man, remember? *Hello?* I told you about it in class?"

"Oh, right. Yeah, I dunno." We reach my locker and I swing my backpack around to do a quick book-related pit stop. Conor props himself against the adjoining locker, shooting me exasperated looks as I unzip my bag, unlock my locker, and start switching out books.

"Man, c'mon!" He puts his foot on top of my bag so I'm forced to stand back up and meet his eyes.

"Dude, I'm gonna be late for class. Get your foot off my bag." He's starting to really annoy me. He is not great at not getting his own way.

"Just say you'll come tonight, and I'll move along. K?" He smirks.

I roll my eyes. "I don't know why you even want me to come. No one else does. I mean, the one time I went this year, Matt spent the whole time you guys weren't playing shooting me death glares and making out with Rosa. It wasn't super fun."

"Oh, who cares—*fuck* Matt. Don't let that a-hole control your life. You know the only reason he's still in the band is 'cause the other guys outvoted me, although you have to admit he's a bomb guitar player. He's basically Hendrix, like, reincarnated into the body of a suburban teenage white kid. . . ." He trails off and gets a faraway look in his eyes, and I know I'm about to be subjected to some long diatribe about music and his band, so I interrupt.

"Fine, fine. Whatever. Fine. But we have to drive Gwenie home first. She's had a shit day. I'm not making her take the bus." I fill him in about this morning's spray-paint incident on the garage.

"Jesus. Gwen saw that shit?" He shakes his head. "All right, well, we know your dad hasn't done anything about it." I shrug. Can't argue with that. "So we'll stop off at the hardware store to get some paint. We'll just put a quick coat or two over it before we take off, okay? And then we'll roll out to practice and you can watch these auditions?"

This is why even though Conor can be really self-centered, he's still kinda great. He's pushy and irritating and ignorant to the rest of the world, but he always comes through in a pinch. No one else would voluntarily offer to paint my garage door with me. It doesn't exactly qualify as a fun after-school activity.

"Cool. See ya later." Conor slaps me on the back of the head and I give him a tired nod. He retreats down the hall.

I sigh, slam my locker shut, lean back against it, and close my eyes, trying to motivate myself to get through the day.

Coming to school didn't use to be like this—utterly draining, a void filled with white noise and Conor's voice. I used to have friends. A girlfriend. A life.

* * *

I slide into drama class late. I was forced to sign up for this elective after I procrastinated and didn't register for classes until the last possible second this past fall. I had other things on my mind, like, you know, my girlfriend of a year telling me she needed a break because I was shutting her out of my life, after which, in a fit of total stubbornness, I told her, *Sure, SURE—go ahead and say yes to my absolute dickhead of an ex-friend who asked you to fall formal, what do I care.* Oh, and everyone in school except Conor hating my guts.

Fun stuff like that.

The teacher is already at the front of the room, manically waving her arms as she speaks, her crazy-curly brown hair loose and flying around her head. She's a total cliché of a drama teacher, and I can't help but snicker to myself as I watch her. A girl sitting a couple seats over must hear my dorky laugh, because she glances at me with a crooked little smile.

I've never seen her before in my life, but that smile . . . it melts my heart. Not only because no one ever smiles at me anymore, but also because I recognize something in it that's super smart and knowing—something that makes me think, *Wow, someone gets me.*

Something I rarely feel these days.

CHAPTER FIVE

May

I'm in the middle of my fourth class of the day and I could not give less of a shit. The teacher is a total wack job. She's up in the front of the room, flinging her arms around, and it's like, *Honey, could you please go run a brush through your hair?* She's riding a fine line between I-haven't-washed-my-hair-in-five-days hipster and, like, straight-up homeless. I reach for my phone to text Jordan about it before I realize what I'm doing.

The chairs in here are super uncomfortable and really close together, even though we're in a theater. You'd think that someone out there would've considered that it might be an issue. How the fuck are you supposed to get out of here if something goes wrong? There's no way to escape.

My hands are trembling in my lap. A big part of me is thinking, *Can I just get up and go home now, please?* The day is going by so slow and feels so pointless. There's something about the shrill ring of the bell; the classrooms with these tight rows of seats; the piercing, rabid laughs of the kids in the hallways that's just too much. I have a headache.

I'm considering leaving—class, school, everything—when this tall, gangly kid flies in late and slams his body down into a nearby seat. I glance over, and even though he just got here, he appears properly awed by our teacher, like Jordan would have been. He laughs to himself and then glances at me for some reason, and I can't help but smile in response. Everyone else in the room is so serious, and fuck if I wasn't afraid I'd be the only person in this room who isn't all *Rah rah theater blah blah blah.*

Random laughing kid looks surprised that I'm smiling, like he thinks I'm making fun of him or something. My cheeks heat up, and I wonder what I've just done wrong. I haven't socialized much in the past eleven months; Lucy is like my second brain, and my parents . . . God knows if I even know how to interact with people anymore. Probably not.

I drop my eyes back to my lap and two thoughts pop into my head simultaneously: coming back to school sucks even more than I thought it would, and that random laughing guy is kind of cute.

I make sure to leave drama well after Laughing Boy, because I've already embarrassed myself enough for one millennium.

When I hit the hallway, I run smack into a wall of flesh. I

flinch. My heart starts pounding. I want to take a hot shower and burn off the feeling of another human's body on my own.

And then, when I see who I smashed into, I want to throw up: Miles Catalano. My ex-boyfriend. Literally the last person I wanted to see today, the person I hoped I'd never have to see again, except of course I knew he goes to this shitty school, and now so do I.

His eyes widen when he sees it's me. He freezes mid-walk, and someone slams into his back, pushing him closer to me. His face is inches away.

God*dammit*.

"Crap. God. Hi." He pushes his wild curly hair off his face. "Jesus. May. Hey."

If it were any other person or any other set of circumstances, I'd enjoy the monosyllabic nonsense falling out of his mouth, but right now I just want him to shut the fuck up and move on.

"Yep." I take one step back from him and then another. "It's May. Good to know your eyesight's intact. K, cool, gotta go." I swing around to escape, but the hallway is beyond crowded, thanks to all of us they've jammed in here from Carter, and I barely make it a foot before his hand clamps down on my shoulder.

"May. Wait." My skin crawls at his voice.

"What!" I spin around, and I don't care that I'm getting in his face or that I just screamed at him out of nowhere. I want him to let me go. If he was going to hold on to anything—

any*one*—couldn't it have been *mother*fucking David Ecchles the morning of the shooting, when he walked by Miles on his way into the band room, carrying that big black duffel bag, and Miles glanced up from his locker and thought, *That's weird, he's not in jazz band,* but did nothing. Miles told me about that moment, sobbing, a few days after, the night of Jordan's funeral.

I broke up with him on the spot. Told him the sight of his face made me sick.

That was when he decided to be an even bigger prick than I thought he could ever be. His eyes narrowed and he said that I was an idiot. That I had done so much worse. That he'd seen me talking to David Ecchles at Adam Neilson's party the weekend before the shooting. He claimed we were sitting out by the pool, David's head leaned toward mine like we were deep in a serious conversation.

I was so wasted that night I barely remember anything between getting to Adam's house with Miles and waking up in my bed the next morning. I do remember that when we got to the party, Miles ran off with some of his soccer friends, leaving me alone. I remember that I found Chim in the kitchen doing shots and joined in. After that, my memory is beyond blurry—it's a black hole. And I know that if you get too close to the edge of a black hole, it'll pull you in and you'll never escape.

Somehow, I allegedly made my way outside and was sitting by the pool when David found me. At least, that's the

Gospel According to Miles. But I don't believe him. I would never have talked to David Ecchles. And Miles never bothered to mention it until that night, after I broke up with him. There's no way David Ecchles would have been at *any* party—especially one at Adam's house. Adam had always teased him mercilessly—basically made his life a living hell. David Ecchles didn't go to parties. He didn't get invited. There were always all these rumors about him—about the creepy poem he wrote in English class, about his home life, about the tattoo of a gun he had on his stomach. Sometimes I'd catch him starting at me in the halls. Something in his eyes always creeped me out—they had this flat, empty look in them, like he was part zombie.

In front of me, Miles has an expression on his face that's something akin to pity. "Jesus, May. Relax. I'm just surprised to see you. I knew you were back, but . . ." He's so uncomfortable. *Good.* I want nothing to do with him or with any of this. My hands ball into fists.

Over his shoulder, a security guard watches us. I force my hands to relax.

"Okay. Good talk." This time I'm ready. I push past him into the crowd and let the flow of people take me farther and farther away.

It's finally lunchtime, and all I want is to grab on to Lucy like the life raft she's become and never let go. I walk through the swinging doors into the cafeteria to find her, but before I can get more than a couple steps inside, I'm hit by a cacophony of noises. There are people everywhere. Most I don't recognize; they must be the original QA students. The ones who belong here. The ones who fit.

A person brushes by me and I find myself looking into the eyes of one of Jordan's best friends, Brian Ramirez. Brian was in jazz band, too, but wasn't a section leader. Wasn't in practice that day.

Which is why he's here, in front of me, instead of . . . not.

Brian and I lock eyes for a second and I freeze. My stomach turns as he opens his mouth to say something and I just can't . . . I can't . . . I can't . . . and before he can get out any words, I duck behind a group of people who are coming in through the door and bolt across the room to the other side and don't look back.

I need Lucy. Now.

I dig through my bag and find my phone at the very bottom.

I text her furiously, *WHERE THE HELL ARE YOU* with at least seventeen exclamation points and several *I CANNOT DEAL WITH THIS SHIT*–type emojis. Then I slump against yet another wall to wait.

Across the room, I see Steve Irmen. His girlfriend, Britta, died that day. She played the clarinet.

Steve is laughing, his arm around another girl.

"Girl, what're you doing hanging out by the trash cans?"

Chim saves me from total loserdom/a complete emotional breakdown/freaking out and getting kicked out of school all over again. I offer a silent apology to the universe for almost slapping her earlier.

I shrug. There's nothing much I can say back, because it probably does look like I'm chilling by the trash cans, of all places.

She shakes her head, a worried look in her eyes. "May. It's going to be okay. I promise. C'mon." She motions for me to follow her as she walks off into the depths of hell (aka the cafeteria). I sigh and follow her, because my other option is to scream and run out of school and keep running and never stop. And while that's tempting, I'm pretty sure security would catch me before I got anywhere close to off campus—and oh, also, my parents would commit me or force me in to see McMillen. Which would be super not-fun (understatement of the century). If I do anything too fucked-up right off the bat, I'll be back to how it was right after everything happened—going to her once or twice a week, sitting there silent, wasting my time and hers.

Chim leads me to a table filled with people I recognize from Carter, most of whom I have no desire to see—now or ever again. A girl with bright red hair waves at me from down at the end: Juliet Nichols's best friend, Hannah. One of those people who would come up to me during the few weeks we were back in school before I got kicked out, all *May, I'm having a rough day. I miss Jules so much. How are you doing? Do you want to come do yoga with me after school?* And I'd want to scream in her face, scream and maybe never stop screaming, but instead I'd somehow force the word *no* out from between my lips. (Who knew that two letters could take a thousand years off your life?)

This isn't our normal lunch crowd. In the past, it was always just me and Chim and Lucy and sometimes Jordan and Brian and his other best friend, Marcus, and then Miles and some of his soccer guys after we started dating. Sometimes a rando girl or guy—Lucy's flavor of the week—but that was it. Hannah should be eating with Juliet at their table filled with other kids who played in the wind section of the band. Not with us. Not with me. Not without Juliet.

Not instead of Jordan.

I can't do this. I start to turn and head back toward the cafeteria doors, but a hand grabs my arm. That hand belongs to—thanks be to Baby Jesus—Lucy. I start to let out a whimper of relief but manage to stop it before it leaves my mouth.

I'm pathetic enough as it is.

I slide into a seat next to Lucy and lay my head on her shoulder. I mumble into her shirt, "I saw Brian and he tried to talk to me, and I just couldn't, and I ran away." I let out a choked sob, and Lucy puts her hand on my arm.

"Oh, honey. Brian . . . You still haven't talked to him?"

I shake my head without lifting it off her shoulder. She knows how many times he called me over the first few months after the shooting, trying to talk about Jordan, to remember him, but I sent him to voice mail every time.

She strokes my hair. "I'm sorry, May. I promise. It's gonna be fine. Half the day down, only . . ."

"A trillion to go?"

She laughs. "Always so dramatic. More like a hundred twenty-five and a half days."

"Your ability to do math like that in your head is just wrong."

"It's easy."

I snort. "For you, maybe."

"So, tonight—wanna hit the house?" Lucy's smart. Talking about our extracurricular activity is a surefire way to make me feel better.

I nod, my face still pressed into her shoulder. No need to mention I was just there last night.

"But before that . . ." She pauses for a beat and I look up at her. She smiles. "Well . . . like I mentioned earlier, I'm actually going to audition for a new band."

I squeeze her arm. "That's awesome!" I force enthusiasm into my voice. It's not an emotion that comes easy these days.

"Soooooooo . . . will you come with me? Please?" Lucy begs.

My stomach drops. I haven't done anything remotely social in almost a year, and this sounds like it falls square into the events-that-take-place-outside-of-my-bedroom-and-with-strangers category. Which I am not into. At all.

But it's Lucy, and Lucy has done everything for me these

last eleven months and asked for almost nothing in return. So I nod.

"Of course I'll go with you." I glance at the other faces at the table and catch Chim's eye. She's down at the other end, flirting with some girl I vaguely recognize. She shoots me a quizzical look, and I shake my head and bury it in Lucy's shoulder.

Lucy says, "Thank you. Look, I know it's hard. Coming back to school. Seeing these people. It was for me, and for you . . ." She trails off. "I know you hate this, but I have to ask. How are you doing?" She sounds so concerned, and I feel the immediate need to pretend. Pretend, pretend, pretend it's all okay—that's what my parents taught me; that's what I've always been good at.

But when I pick my head up to meet her eyes, I just want to cry.

Stop it.

I look down and study the top of the table, drum a rhythmless beat on my jeans, repeat the phrases that the therapist told me would help—*calm calm, safe safe, blah blah kill me blah* (well, that's a modified version of them, at least).

"You hungry?" Lucy knows better than to push the mushy stuff, thank god. She holds a pretzel in front of my face. I take it and start nibbling.

I shrug. "Not hungry. Just want to find a corner and curl into a ball and disappear."

She shakes her head. "Seriously, May. It'll be over before you know it."

"The day?"

"The day, the year, everything. I know this isn't what you want to hear, but try to take it day by day, at least for the next few weeks."

I can't help but smile. "Don't think I don't know what you're doing. Trying to indoctrinate me with all your AA slogans. *A day at a time,* et cetera, et cetera, et cetera."

Freshman year was not Lucy's finest moment. Apparently, she inherited the drinking problem that her dad dealt with when we were younger. It was like drinking did one thing to most of us—Chim and I became louder, more obnoxious versions of ourselves, which wasn't ideal, but at least wasn't destructive—but Lucy . . . went dark. Super dark. It was like she turned into a whole other person. Thankfully, after a year and more scary nights than I'd like to remember, she decided to follow in her now-sober father's footsteps and attend AA meetings with him. She's been so much better since.

I, on the other hand, should have quit drinking when she did—should have quit partying, quit thinking I was so fucking cool. Doing dumb things. Acting like I was indestructible, like my actions didn't matter. I should have listened to Lucy—to Jordan. Maybe things would be different right now if I had. Maybe he would be sitting next to me, instead of lying in a hole in the ground. . . .

All of a sudden, my breath is coming out in fast, jagged

bursts. The fluorescent lights are getting brighter. They're burning my pupils.

"Lucy." I grab her shirtsleeve, gasping. "Lucy."

She takes one look at me and drops the sandwich that's midway to her mouth. "Okay, okay. It's okay. *Shhh* . . . breathe." She puts her hand on my back. "Put your head between your knees. Yeah, like that. Good." She's rubbing the small of my back and my head is between my knees and the fuzzy sound in my ears is subsiding, the noises of the cafeteria becoming clearer.

I'm trying to slow my breathing and she's whispering in my ear—soft, kind things—until I feel semi-okay again. Not like I'm going to vomit all over everyone at our table. Not like my brother's ghost is going to spontaneously materialize out of my head and start shouting accusations at me.

I straighten up and wipe my eyes.

Everyone at the table is staring at me like I'm a total freak.

Not that I can blame them.

'Cause really, that's what I am.

CHAPTER SIX

Zach

I can barely lift my arms high enough to stuff my textbooks into the top of my locker as I wait for Conor and Gwen after school. Apparently, that's what I do best: wait. Wait for them to show up, wait for the day to end, wait for graduation day to arrive. All the colleges I applied to are far, far away, where no one knows my family, where I can walk down the hallways and not feel like half the student body wants to spit in my face.

Today was the longest day in the history of the known universe. Like, I'm pretty sure that if scientists measured every minute today, they would discover that each one had at least eight more seconds than normal.

All I want to do is go home and lie on my bed with all the lights off and try to pretend this year has already ended.

"Dude." Conor's voice breaks me out of my reverie. He walks up to my locker. "What's up?"

"What?"

"You look like shit, man." He stops next to me and swings his satchel to his other shoulder. On anyone else the bag would be mocked as a man purse, but once Conor started carrying the thing at the beginning of the year, they caught on, and now they're all the rage. It's amazing to me that I'm not still considered semipopular, since Conor still associates with me, but I guess that just goes to show how shunned I really am. "You look miz."

I roll my eyes. "First of all, please stop with the abbreviations. You sound like a seventh grader. I can't take it. Second, I don't want to talk about it. Let's just find Gwen and get outta here. I'm beat."

He shakes his head. "You better not be trying to use that as an excuse to skip out on my band thing tonight. You did that the last four times I asked, and it's getting a little lame, dude."

I heave a sigh. "No. I'm not. Get off my back. I'm coming." Great. Blew my one shot at flaking. I slam my locker shut.

"Good." He makes a motion with his fingers like *I'm watching you* and all I can think is *Yeah, I'm quite aware you're watching me—you and everyone else in this prison.*

Before we can get deeper into our bickering, Gwen stomps up and collapses onto the door of my locker. "I could hear you guys arguing from down the hall. Can you please stop? This day has been crap; I just want to go home."

"You too?" Conor nudges her leg with his boot. "Jesus, you Tellers are such grumps." Gwen and I swing toward him and shoot him death glares. "Whoa, whoa, all right, sorry, guys." He holds his hands up in front of him and starts backing down the hall. "Peace, man. Let's GTFO of here." He turns and strides away with the confidence of someone who knows he's going to be followed.

"Abbreviations!" I yell at his back. He started using these abbreviations last year, after he briefly dated a freshman, and for whatever reason, they stuck. Thankfully, the girl didn't.

He shoots his middle finger in the air. Gwen and I roll our eyes at each other but do what we always do—trail after Conor as he walks away.

I pull into our driveway after a quick stop at the hardware store for white paint, and sure enough, there it is, still streaked across our garage door in red: *BITCH*. I swear it's gotten bigger since this morning.

I love that it's still there. Just *love* it. If Gwen hadn't already seen it this morning, she couldn't miss it now.

I sit in the car for a beat too long after Gwenie's hopped out. Conor notices.

"You okay, man?" He pauses with his hand on the door, looking at me with eyebrows raised.

I grunt affirmatively, shoot him a half smile, and reluctantly get out of the car. I thought I'd learned to temper my expectations of my parents long ago. The fact that my dad hasn't done shit about this all day shouldn't be a surprise, but for some idiotic reason it *is,* and that pisses me off more than anything. How dumb can I be?

"Whatever." I lean against the driver's-side door of the Jeep and rub my eyes. "Expected this, right? It's why we got the paint."

Conor nods and I think I see a flash of pity run across his face, but it's gone before I can figure out whether it was actually there or if it was just a figment of my imagination. He walks around to the back of the car and unloads the paint.

"Let's get to it."

It takes us about an hour and a half to paint the garage door. Gwen comes out with a couple bottles of water for us, which is pretty sweet of her. It's been hot as balls this month. By the time we're finished, my arm is aching and I'm sweating my ass off, but I still haven't heard a peep from my dad. I know he must be inside; his car is in the driveway. I can't work up the energy to ask Gwen if she's seen him.

It wasn't always this way with him. When I was little, he was a whole different person. I don't know what changed, whether he became a shit dad when he lost his job and started trying to make his lame garage band a serious thing, or if it was a few years after that, when he started to realize his dream was never going to happen. Usually I don't even think it matters which came first—the fact is, he changed. It's too late, and I'm over it.

"Want to go inside and grab a bite before we go?" I ask

Conor. I'd much rather head out to anywhere but here, but I need to change out of my paint-splattered clothes, and unfortunately, I don't have a spare outfit in the car. Conor's the one person I still allow inside my house—not that anyone else is beating down the door.

Conor shrugs. "Sure."

We make our way inside and it's dead quiet, as usual. After a moment, I hear faint music start to play from Gwen's room upstairs, but there's no sign of my dad anywhere.

In the kitchen, Conor swings a high stool between his legs and rests his elbows on the counter. "Man, my arm is sore. Practice is gonna be a bitch."

I rummage through the pantry and start tossing random shit in his general direction. "Pretzels. They're only, like, a couple weeks old. Potato chips . . . might wanna check the expiration date before you eat 'em. What else?" I stick my head farther into the cabinet. "Oh, sweet. Some old Goldfish. Probably stale as fuck."

Conor sighs. "What the hell have you guys been doing for food since your mom took this case?"

I snort and turn to face him, leaning back against the fridge, arms crossed. "Since she took *this* case? Meaning, before this case we were just bursting with fresh fruits and, like, gourmet meals every night?"

He rolls his eyes. "No, but at least before, she was around sometimes. Like more than now . . ."

I shrug. "Yeah, I guess. Whatever. You know, I grab something for me and Gwen on the way home from school. It's not like I have anything to do most nights, so I've been trying to learn how to cook. . . ."

Conor lets out a huge laugh. "You? Cook? No fuckin' way, man."

I shake my head at him; I'd be embarrassed if I were talking to anyone other than Conor. "Yeah. I'm trying. Get over it." I should have kept my mouth shut, but I hated the way Conor was looking at me, like I'm some poor orphan boy who needs to be rescued. He has no room to talk. It's not like his home life is a *Brady Bunch* episode. His dad barely knows he's alive.

"I'm gonna go change."

"All right, man, I'll be here, just chowin' on these pretzels. . . ." He sticks one in his mouth and starts coughing. "Dude, these are stale AF. Are you kidding? Are you trying to kill me?" He jumps off the stool, runs over to the sink, and starts lapping water from the faucet.

"You're an idiot. You've been here a million times. You should know to expect a certain quality of food. That said, feel free to eat whatever; just, you know, watch out for mold. Be right back." I smirk at him on my way out the door.

In my room, I throw on some clean clothes, and then I head back downstairs, grabbing my wallet off the front hall table as I pass by. As I approach the kitchen, I hear a bark of laughter. I walk in, expecting to find Gwen and Conor giving each other a hard time, but instead what I see is my dad perched on the stool next to Conor's, sharing the stale pretzels—which Conor is still eating, for some ungodly reason. My heart almost stops.

"There he is!" My dad's smiling, and dressed in a real, grown-up, appropriate-for-the-daytime outfit instead of the pajamas he's normally still wearing when we get home from school. He must be having one of his good days, when he gets out of bed, speaks to people, leaves the house. Amazing that even on a *good* day he can't do what any other parent would—remove the goddamn graffiti from the garage. I mean, who cares what the neighbors think, right?

Moreover, wouldn't a normal parent have called the cops to try to figure out who keeps doing something so shitty to their property? This incident isn't the first by a long shot. I tried my best to stop the vandalism; I called the cops. They told me to have one of my parents go down to the station to file a report, but *shockingly,* that never happened. So I dragged Conor over here a few months ago and we figured out how to rig a light to the garage. It goes on when it detects motion. Big help that's been. I've been asking my dad to set up cameras for months now, but has he done it? No, of course he hasn't. Of course.

I realize I'm squeezing my wallet so tight that it's cutting off the circulation to my fingers.

"Come join us, kid." My dad motions for me to take the

seat next to him at the counter. "We were just discussing Conor's band. . . ."

"Nah, I'm good." I stand in the doorway to the kitchen and cross my arms. "We gotta go anyway. We're running late because we had to paint the entire garage. Not that you care."

His face falls, and because I'm a dumb fuck of a pushover I feel bad for a second, but I quickly come to my senses.

"Ready to go?" I sound impatient. I am impatient.

"All right, well, next time." My dad's voice is all woe-is-me-ish. Fuck that noise.

Yeah, Dad, next time. Sure. Next time Conor's here, you'll probably be locked in your bedroom, per usual. Actually, Conor's the one person my dad seems to want to communicate with on the rare occasions he wants to communicate at all—they talk about band stuff, commiserate on how hard it is being a musician. The first couple years after my dad decided to pursue that shit as, like, an actual career, he'd corner Conor in the kitchen every time Conor was over here, asking him about equipment and whether he'd listened to whatever dumb band Pitchfork was talking about that week. All that bullshit stuff that means everything when you're my age but should mean less than nothing when you're an adult with two kids and a mortgage. It was fucking embarrassing.

That's when my mom started working so much—in part because money got tight, I think, although it's not like my parents sat down and discussed finances with me, more like because every time she was around my dad, her face would get pinched and narrow as he talked and talked and talked about his music. I know he played when they first got together in college; I know because years ago my own mother told me, sounding proud. But I don't think she expected him to try to make it his actual *profession,* decades later. I don't know—but I do know that these days, I can't tell who sucks more: my dad, who hangs out in his pajamas all day, or my mom, who is never home.

I nod and give my dad a tight-lipped smile.

"C'mon," I say to Conor.

His head is bouncing back and forth between me and my dad like he's watching a tennis match he wishes he could figure out how to turn off, and when I address him, he hops right off the stool.

"Yup. Yeah. Ready. Let's go."

"Gwen home?" My dad's still trying to engage with me. "I haven't seen her."

"Upstairs." I point to the ceiling, like maybe I can magically beam him up there, away from me. "Gotta go."

"All right, well, see you later? Don't get home too late."

I roll my eyes, because the last time either of my parents actually cared when I got home was back in eighth grade. I could disappear off the face of the earth and they probably wouldn't notice until Gwen needed something and no one was there to help her. I shoot him a sarcastic thumbs-up and walk out of the kitchen.

As I put my hand on the knob of the front door, I hear him

call softly down the hall, "Love you, kid." I flare my nostrils and pull the door open so fast that it shakes on its hinges.

I look back at Conor. "Let's get the hell out of here."

He nods, and for once, he follows me as I walk out the front door.

CHAPTER SEVEN

May

I'm sitting in the kitchen of my house waiting for Lucy to pick me up to go to this dumb band audition, when it happens. I hear the garage door grind open and the hum of a car engine, which shuts off a few moments later. I glance over at the clock on the microwave: it's only five p.m. Way too early for my mom to get home. But unless a stranger has obtained the remote to our garage, it has to be her . . . or my dad. My stomach twists into a knot and I push away the bagel I just toasted. I'm tempted to bolt back up to my room, but Lucy will be here any minute, so instead I bury my face in my phone and pretend to be fascinated by my Instagram feed.

The door from the garage to the kitchen opens, and I hear loud voices, arguing. I'm so surprised to hear two voices instead of one that I look up, and there they are: both of my parents, together. I have no idea what in the fuck is happening; I haven't seen them together in approximately six months. My mom comes home still, but late, usually after I've gone to bed.

We don't really talk. My dad . . . I barely see him. Six months ago, my parents sat me down and told me that the latest show my dad was producing was filming out in Palm Desert and he was going to need to spend some time out there for a while. *A while* . . . that's dragged on, and on, and on.

And on.

I don't know if he's still living there. And I really don't care. All I know is he doesn't come home.

I can't make out most of what they're saying; I just catch some angry words from my dad: "We *need* to talk about potentially moving forward with a suit. I need you to get on board, Joan, before . . ."

I drop my head back down. I try to make myself as small as possible, hope that maybe a hole will open up and suck me into the pits of hell.

Hell couldn't possibly be worse than what's happening in this kitchen.

Their voices quiet; they must see me. I hold my breath, praying that they'll walk right by, act like I don't exist like they normally do. My skin prickles. I can't help myself; I look up again just in time to see my dad's back, walking away. My mom's standing by the stove, leaning against the counter, shoulders hunched. Even from across the room, I can see that her eyes are bloodshot and swollen. I swear that over the past year she's shrunk.

I don't know where she went, the person who was our mom for all those years. The busy, successful financial advisor, who was a decent mother until pushing Jordan became more important to my parents than anything else. She was always seemingly on board with my dad's plans for him—all the early testing and the AP classes when he was a freshman and sophomore, all the night classes and the weekend activities to round out his college applications. Until my dad started talking about his grand plan to have Jordan apply to college our sophomore year. My mom dug her heels in and wouldn't hear it. After that, I would hear harsh whispers from their bedroom as I came up the stairs at night, and I knew it was about Jordan and his future. I think Jordan did, too.

I'm digging my fingernails into the base of my thumb so hard I'm leaving marks.

My mom and I lock eyes, and she gives me a wobbly smile. The effort strips ten years off her life. I don't know what I'm supposed to do. I'm sitting here in the same room as my mother, but it's like we're a thousand miles apart. I don't know where her grief is—whether she still thinks about Jordan, whether she still cares. At his funeral, she could barely walk down the aisle to the front pew. But now she's a shell and she's hollow and it's like my dad has almost fully eclipsed her, even though he's almost never here.

Just as I open my mouth to say something—anything—to break this fucking god-awful silence, my dad walks back into the room.

"Joan, I'm serious, I'm done. . . ." Voice firm, face beet red, he looks like a giant bull as he opens the fridge and pulls out a beer. My mom shrinks back against the counter, into herself, and a memory flashes into my head: my mom, years ago, driving Jordan and me to some summer enrichment camp, back when they'd sign both of us up for that stuff. We were all in the silliest moods that day, and I started making up my own lyrics to one of the songs on the radio, and Jordan joined in with his own version, and my mom laughed and laughed and laughed—so hard she started crying and had to pull over to the side of the road.

Now, I swear to god, I can see through her. She's fading away.

My dad catches my eye, and for a split second he looks . . . ashamed? But then I blink, and the expression is gone, and there's no way I really saw that, because if I know anything about my father, it's that he never second-guesses himself. His lack of self-reflection is something Jordan and I always joked about.

My dad has stopped talking, and my mom's sniffling again; the tension in the room is making me sick. They still haven't spoken to me, but I don't care.

I don't.

I don't.

I look at my phone and see that Lucy's texted; she's outside. My escape. My liberator. I try to force myself to stand, but the weight of everything presses down on my shoulders. I'm frozen.

My dad clears his throat like he's going to speak, and all

my energy slams back into my body at once. I bolt out of my seat, surprising us all, and start to babble. *Gotta run, Lucy's here, blahblahbblah*—I don't even know if I'm forming words or just making sounds. I can't hear my voice over the heartbeat thumping in my ears. I grab my bag off the counter beside my mom, give her a smile that might actually be a grimace, and hightail it over to the kitchen door. As I pull it shut behind me, all I hear is a deafening, sickening silence.

Lucy's taste in music is . . . eclectic, to say the least. More than half the time when I'm in her car, I have no idea what band is playing, what era they're from, and whether anyone other than Lucy and the lead singer's mom thinks they're decent. I don't care, though; I'd literally listen to a human scream for the next hour if it meant I didn't have to be in that house with my parents.

The first time I saw Lucy, in third grade, she had just moved to the States from Haiti with her dad and grandmother. She was sitting on a swing on the playground wearing these awesome Mickey Mouse headphones. When I got up the nerve to ask her what she was listening to, she silently handed them to me. Later, I learned that it was a band named the Velvet Underground, which didn't sound anything like Katy Perry or Taylor Swift or any of the other music I loved back then, and that they had a badass female drummer. Lucy's always listened to music outside of the crap on the radio, and all the stuff she gravitates to tends to have women behind the drums. Jordan and I always loved when she'd introduce us to bands—we shared a Spotify account, and it was always a fight over who would get to use it on nights after she would turn us on to someone new, because we knew without a doubt that the rest of the school would be talking about them a few months later.

Right now is no exception. Whatever she's playing in her car is simultaneously making me nauseous and causing my leg to bounce in time with the beat. I want to hate it, but for some reason I don't.

"What in the hell is this?" I reach out and turn down the volume so she can hear me over the noise. "I've only heard one song and I already hate-love it. It's, like, disgusting, but I want to dance to it anyway."

She laughs. "That's awesome. I'm telling Conor that when we get there. He'll love it, I bet."

I have no idea who she's talking about. She's great at saying a lot without saying anything at all.

She catches my stare. "Oh right—sorry. Conor—the guy singing this song. This is Proper Noun and the Noun, the band I'm going to audition for. So you get to hear this stuff in person." She shoots me a side smile. "Maybe you'll start dancing. Or singing, even."

I snort. "Yeah. I'm definitely going to break into song in the middle of some rando band practice. I'm good, thanks."

She scrunches her mouth as we pull up to a stoplight. "You

know, I remember when you used to dance all the time . . . when you used to sing. 'Member that time I caught you dancing to music alone in your bedroom, and then Jordan came down the hallway? Jordan and I started dancing too . . . and you started singing . . . and Jordan went and grabbed his guitar. We didn't even *need* the background music. I could have watched the two of you making music together for hours. Honestly, May." She sniffles, and I can feel her eyes on me, but I deliberately turn away, look out the window.

She shakes her head. "I really miss hanging out, the three of us. You singing, Jordan playing guitar, me on drums . . ." She glances at me, sees my hardened expression. "I know it's hard, but talking about him isn't going make the world end. Maybe it'll even help. . . ." She trails off as my expression morphs into a glare. "Or not."

I'm silent for a beat; then I ask, "How many cans did you bring?"

"Cans?"

I squint at her. "Yeah. Cans. Of spray paint? For later?"

She shrugs. "Oh right. That. I was thinking . . . maybe we could just skip it tonight."

I tense. "What? You promised. You already bailed last night. I was attacked by a cat and. . . ."

She gives me a look like *What the hell are you talking about, May?* and I interrupt myself, since I know she wouldn't be down with me going to the lawyer's alone.

I clench my teeth and concentrate on the view outside my

window. "Fine. Whatever. But you're the one who brought it up, you know."

"Yeah, I know. I felt bad; you were freaking out." I can hear her drumming her fingers on the steering wheel like she does when she gets nervous. "And about all this . . ."

"All *what*?" My voice is steely. Then my lower lip trembles and I bite down hard to stop it. Look back at her. Her face is drawn.

She continues, "It's just . . . with college. Scholarships. I don't think I can do it anymore." She pauses. "I thought about it a lot today, after lunch. You know I started off really into what we were doing. It made sense—it was retribution. It felt like we were doing something *good*. Like we were doing something important to remember Jordan. But now . . . with David's parents moving to god knows where and this obsession you have with his lawyer . . . I don't feel right about it. Especially with college . . . If my chance of getting a scholarship is taken away because they catch us . . ." She shakes her head. "Dude, I'd be so screwed. You know I can't afford to go anywhere without one. I've worked too hard for it all to be ruined, and it would destroy Grann. I'm sorry."

My insides collapse on themselves, but there's no way I'm going to let her see it. I don't ever want to hurt Lucy's Grann, who is one of my favorite people in the entire universe and the only person other than Lucy I could bring myself to speak to right after Jordan died. But it's *Michelle Teller*. Lucy doesn't feel right about what we're doing to her? So, what, it's *right* that she sleeps at night, safe and secure, after spending her days defending the piece of shit who killed my brother? It's not a fucking *obsession*. It's my pathetic attempt to force the universe back into some semblance of balance.

I dig my nails into my palms. Bite down even harder on what's left of my shredded cheeks. They start to bleed again.

It doesn't matter.

I'm made of stone.

I don't have any feelings left to hurt. Any tears left to cry.

I grit my teeth so hard I think they might break.

"It's fine. You gotta do your thing. College or whatever. Moving on."

She grimaces. "I'm sorry, May. But don't you feel like we've done enough? For Jordan? For his memory?"

I nod—a total lie—because what she doesn't understand is that it's *never* going to be enough. I could avenge every hurt human living on this planet, every human who will ever live, and it will never make up for the fact that I stayed in that closet like a coward. It will never make up for the fact that I am the only one David left alive.

"It's fine. Like I said. Whatever. You do you." I turn toward the window, and we ride the rest of the way to the audition in silence.

By the time we get to the warehouse, I'm a ball of fury. This is one of the reasons I got kicked out of school—oh, *sorry*, asked to "take a leave of absence." Last year, before she said those words, Rose-Brady told me she'd given me second . . .

third . . . *tenth* chances (her words, not mine), but they just couldn't risk letting me stay in school. I was a loose cannon (again, *her* stupid words); I was going off on people too often. Plus, every time I took a test, sat through a lecture, walked by that fucking boarded-up entrance to the band room . . . *every time,* I felt another little piece of what was left of my soul die. The hilarious part is, I got asked to leave only a few weeks before the administration decided that Carter was too full of anger and ghosts and shut it down forever.

Lucy and I walk into the warehouse and find ourselves in a long, narrow hallway lit by bright overhead fluorescent lights. The noises of instruments pile on top of each other, creating a cacophony. It's the first time I've heard live instruments since that day. I haven't played my trumpet. I don't even know where it is. The last time I saw it was in that room, before I got up to find an extra music stand, leaving it behind. Leaving so much behind.

I don't know what they did with it, and I haven't asked. I don't want to know.

"Where are we going?" I put my hands over my ears to block out the sounds. It's so loud in here I can barely think. I want to punch the wall.

"This way." She takes off down the hallway to the right. I stuff my hands into my pockets and follow her, head down. About halfway down the hall, something hard hits my shoulder and I'm thrown off balance. I look up and see some kid with one of those annoying hipster haircuts. He's lugging a trumpet case—a fucking *trumpet* case—which must be what hit me. We make eye contact, and every atom of my body clenches tight. A bolt of anger shoots through my gut. What the fuck? Who the hell does he think he is, hitting me and then taking off without an apology? There's no way I'm going to let him get away with that shit.

I turn to him as he's passing me and shove him face-first into the wall without a second thought, every ounce of fury I've buried over the past week—the past month—the past YEAR—bubbling up fast and hard, white and hot and blinding.

"Hey!" The kid's voice is high and squeaky, and I realize he's a lot younger than I thought, maybe thirteen or fourteen at the most. His face is baby fat and pimples. "What're you doing?" He sounds scared. Of *me*. Like I'm a monster; something that might hurt him, someone I wouldn't recognize if I looked in a mirror. Our faces are only a few inches apart, and I see tears spring to his eyes behind his thick glasses. My breath hitches.

"May." Lucy's hand is on my shoulder, pulling me back from the kid. "May, what the fuck are you doing?" She leads me a few steps away. The kid stays frozen for a second and then takes off down the hallway at a sprint. As he's about to leave the building, he calls over his shoulder: *"Psycho!"* My jaw clenches tight and I back up against the wall, against the solidness of the building, trying to ground myself, *psycho* ringing in my ears.

Lucy tightens her hand on my shoulder. I realize I'm shaking hard. Even with the sturdiness of the wall behind me, it feels like the world is shifting: rising and falling with my every panted breath, knocking me farther off balance, dizzy and confused. The pressure of Lucy's hand doesn't help, not this time.

"What was that?" Her voice is calm but has an edge to it that's all too familiar.

"Nothing." I shake her hand off and drop to a crouch, head in hands. "Nothing! He hit me. I . . . He . . . should have apologized." I can barely get the words out; they stick hard in my throat, and once they're out of my mouth, they sit in the air between us, heavy and wrong.

Lucy drops to her knees next to me and brushes a stray hair off my forehead the way she used to during all those months I would barely leave my room.

"Hey." I don't want to look at her. "*May.* Look at me, please."

I finally concede.

She cocks her head. "Dude. I haven't seen you get this aggro in months. What's the deal? Is it being here? Coming to see a band play? I'm sorry. I didn't even think about that when I asked you. . . ."

I take a couple deep breaths, try to slow my racing heart. My hands are balled so tight that I wonder if all the tiny bones in my hands might break. "No . . . it's nothing. I'm fine. I'm sorry." I drag myself up off the floor and she follows. I'm trying to shake it off and be normal and not ruin her entire night, like I've done more times than I can count over this past year.

"I'm fine," I say again. Lean back against the wall for a moment.

Lucy knows I'm lying, I know I'm lying, but what else is there to say? I don't know what my deal is. The sound of instruments? Starting school again? The fact that my parents suck? The looming anniversary of That Day, which is in just over a month? Everything and nothing, balled together into one giant shitty mess?

She sighs. "You know you can talk to me, right? Look, I'm sorry about earlier, in the car. I know you're pissed at me for ditching you. . . ." She runs her hand through her curls. "You have to understand, though: I *need* to get a scholarship. I gotta get out of here, you know? My dad's been acting weird again these past couple months, and his new girlfriend isn't helping matters. . . ." She trails off. "Just know that it's not personal, okay? I love you, obviously."

"I get it." I feel like a self-centered bitch. "I'm sorry. I love you too."

"I know." She glances at her watch. "I hate to cut this short, but I gotta get to the thing, okay?"

I nod and motion for her to lead the way.

CHAPTER EIGHT

Zach

I've been trapped in this room for about ever with Conor, Matt, and fucking Rosaline, who apparently now goes everywhere with Matt. When I walked in with Conor earlier, Rosa's eyes opened so wide I'm surprised they didn't pop right out of her head. It's been thrilling thus far, sitting here, watching my best friend make nice with my ex-friend and my ex-girlfriend make out with the same ex-friend. It's like one of those stupid CW shows Gwen likes so much come to life, and one of the main reasons I haven't been to one of these practices in months. I'd rather be at home, listening to my dad's TV blaring from his bedroom upstairs, eating a frozen dinner alone, than here. I'd rather be anywhere but here.

Matt's being a total bag of dicks too, big surprise. Whenever I remember how once upon a time I was under the impression that we were friends, it makes me feel like a moron, not to mention question why I even *wanted* to be friends with him in the first place. He's a tool who's currently kissing his girlfriend with his eyes open and glancing at me to see if I'm watching. The whole thing is creepy as fuck. Rosa really picked a winner there.

I'm gathering my stuff, getting ready to tell Conor that I'm bailing, when the door to the room creaks open and this beautiful girl pops her head into the room. She does a quick survey of the setup, which, let's be honest, is a total mess and super–amateur hour, and then her eyes fall on me.

"Hey." She waves from the doorway.

I raise my hand in a halfhearted hello in response.

"This the band audition? For the drummer of Proper Noun and the Noun?"

I nod.

"Nice!" She pumps her fist and walks into the room, then glances behind her. Another girl trails in a second later. She's dressed in tight black jeans and a ratty-looking T-shirt and is clutching her bag in both hands like it might defy gravity and take off into outer space at any moment. Her dark hair hangs in front of her face, but when she blows it off and glances around the room, I realize it's the girl from drama class earlier today. The one with the great smile, who made me feel like a human being for a minute. What is she doing *here*?

The first girl comes over to me, all confident and oozing sex, and sticks her hand out.

"Lucy," she says.

The couch I'm sitting on is so old that it takes me a few seconds to struggle my way out of its bent coils and stand so

I can properly greet them. I glance at the second girl to make sure she didn't witness my complete lack of coordination, and of course she's staring right at me. We lock eyes, and she raises an eyebrow and smirks. I bite my bottom lip and look away as fast as humanly possible.

"Hey. Zach." I shake the Lucy girl's hand, which is weird because I haven't shaken another kid's hand, like, ever, but I'm barely concentrating on her even though she's a total smoke show. I can't help glancing over at her friend again, hoping she'll make a move to introduce herself.

"So . . . this is the band, huh?" Lucy surveys the room and doesn't seem too turned off, which is a miracle. If I were her, I'd make a break for it. All the guys in the band are just milling around, ignoring that someone is, you know, actually here to audition. On the other side of the room, Matt and Rosaline are making out again. My stomach turns. At least this time he isn't trying to catch my eye while his tongue is smashed inside her mouth.

"Yup." I don't really know what to say, per usual, and I'm still distracted by her friend, who's now slumped against the wall next to us with her arms crossed. "Umm. You're here to audition? I assume . . . ? Or . . . ?" I do an awkward nodding thing in the direction of her friend. "Is she?"

Lucy glances over at the other girl and smiles. "May? No, not her. I wish. Every band needs a badass trumpet player and backup singer." The two of them appear to have some weird private conversation with their eyes, then May drags herself over to us, like she'd rather be anywhere else. I know the feeling.

We're all silent for a beat, and then Lucy smirks. "Okaaaaay . . . cool, cool. I'll do all the talking here. May." She points to her friend. "This is . . ." She pauses. "Shit, sorry, what'd you say your name is again?"

"Zach."

"Cool. May, Zach. Zach, May. Okay, you guys talk. Or don't. Up to you. I'm going to go talk to whoever's in charge here." She pauses, appraising me. "You're not in charge, right?"

My cheeks flush. Is it that obvious? I shake my head. "No, that'd be the guy over there. With the microphone and the Justin Bieber haircut?"

"Gotcha." She looks at her friend. "You're okay?"

May nods.

"Great. I'll be back soon."

She leaves May and me standing by the couch and strides across the room, all long legs and bouncy hair. Conor's going to have a freaking heart attack when he sees her.

For lack of anything better to do with my body, I take a seat on the arm of the stupid couch; then I force words out of my mouth. "You're in my drama class, right?" I groan silently. *Cool line, bro. Totally cool.*

"What?" She's watching me talk like I have two heads.

I swallow and clear my throat. "I said, I think you're in my drama class?" This time it comes out louder but squeaks up at the end like I'm just hitting puberty. I knew I should have stayed home.

"Oh. Yeah?" She arches a perfect eyebrow at me, and I'm embarrassed because obviously when we made eye contact in class it meant nothing to her and everything to me. I wish I could learn to shut the fuck up.

"Yeah. I mean, I think so. Or maybe not? I go to QA. . . . I just thought . . . you kinda seemed familiar. . . ." I trail off.

She looks out into the room for a minute, quiet, and then back at me. "No, I think you're right. Ms. Kowalski? Fourth period?"

I nod, trying to be cool. "Yeah. Kowalski. With the hair?"

Her mouth twitches. "Oh, yeaaah. Her hair. Chick's never heard of a hairbrush. Should be an interesting class."

I shrug. "I guess."

That same twitchy smile. "Not a drama person?"

"Not really. It's more like I didn't sign up for classes in time, so they stuck me in there."

Now I get an actual almost-full smile. We make eye contact, and that same electrical bolt I felt earlier today in school zaps my heart and takes my breath away.

"Ha. Ditto." She nods at the band. "So, this is more your scene?"

I look over at Conor, now deep in conversation with Lucy, and shrug again. "Yeah. Well . . . it used to be, but not so much anymore. My friend over there"—I point at Conor—"he sort of forced me to come. I was about to take off, actually, when you walked in. . . ."

"Oh." She folds her arms across her chest and leans against the wall. "Cool. Gotcha. See you around."

I'm thrown; she went from almost friendly to dead cold in a split second. I stutter, "N-no—no. I mean . . . I was thinking about it, but Lucy seems like she might be fun to watch, so I think I might stay." My heart's beating fast and I don't even know why, except she's making me super nervous, and I want her to think . . . I don't know what I want her to think. That I'm cool? That I'm someone worth talking to? She seems like someone who doesn't bother with people unless she really wants to. I want her to want to bother with me. However, considering I can't even manage to form a coherent sentence in my brain, nevertheless out loud, that's probably unlikely.

She furrows her brow at my spluttering nonsense. "Oooookay."

I mentally kick myself.

"Anyway." I force myself to take a long breath before I continue. "Is Lucy any good?" *There you go, Zach; finally got those words out of your mouth. Jesus.*

At the mention of her friend, a real smile crosses her face. It's as awesome as—maybe more awesome than—the one earlier today in class. "Lucy? Lucy isn't good. Lucy is *amazing.* Just wait."

"Nice. Conor's going to be stoked. He's wanted to get a

female drummer for the band since forever. Thinks it'll help their image."

She rolls her eyes.

I laugh. "I know."

Across the room, someone knocks over a snare drum and it crashes to the floor, loud, reverbing off the walls. When I look back at May, her eyes are wide.

"You okay?" She looks super spooked, like she might take off running out of the room. Her breath is coming out all choppy and weird, and her face has lost most of its color.

She doesn't respond. Instead, she stands there pressed against the wall, unmoving and silent for about a minute. I'm starting to think maybe it would be a good idea to grab her friend Lucy, because she doesn't look right, but as I start to rise off the arm of the couch, May coughs and jolts back to life.

She looks around the room, slowly, and then focuses on my worried face. She blinks like she just remembered that I'm here.

"Hey . . . are you okay?" I don't want to come off like her mom, but I don't think that was a normal reaction to a falling drum.

She shakes her head. "Yeah, of course. Sorry. I'm fine. I was just thinking about Kowalski's hair." She laughs, but it sounds forced. She licks her lips. "Do you think she even owns a hairbrush?"

I pause before I reply, because she's sort of repeating

herself with the hairbrush joke. But I don't want to call her out or make her feel weird, so I just laugh again. "Probably not."

She grunts. "Yeah."

Silence falls over us. I'm racking my brain trying to think of witty, cool things to say, when I realize that her eyes are fluttering and she's leaning against the wall like it's a life raft.

"Hey, do you want some water?" I bend down and reach under the couch and rustle around until I find my backpack. "I brought a couple bottles. . . . I know it can get super claustrophobic in here sometimes."

Her eyes open wide, like she's surprised that I noticed. "Yeah. Thanks." She takes the bottle from my outstretched hand and gulps down half of it in one breath. She sits down on the couch and I take a seat on the other end.

"Impressive drinking skills." I groan to myself, because, like—worst dad joke ever?—but her face relaxes and she smiles at me. A real smile this time—one that touches her eyes.

I want to see her smile again. And again. We settle in on the couch to watch Lucy.

May was right; Lucy is a badass drummer, like beyond Lockett or anyone else who's ever played with the band. All of them—especially Conor—are blown away.

However, good as she is, I can barely concentrate on the music, because it's like all of my molecules are being pulled toward May. I swear I've never been so aware of another person in my life. The couch is small, and her arm presses against me every time she moves, making the hairs on my arm stand on end. When the band breaks between songs, we start talking. Sometimes at the same time, about the same thing. The first time it happens, May pulls her head back, surprise passing across her face like she's reminded of something she'd rather forget.

Lucy's audition ends a short while later, and she starts gathering her things. Conor circles her like a hawk. May is stirring next to me, and I panic, trying to figure out a way to make this last longer. Moments when I feel comfortable with another person are so rare these days.

"Are you guys taking off?" I struggle to keep my voice casual, to keep the desperation out, and only sort of succeed.

May looks up at Lucy, who's standing next to the band's drum set, holding her sticks, head thrown back, laughing at something Conor said. May turns to me and rolls her eyes.

"Yeah. Whenever she's ready, I guess."

I swallow, trying to think of something that might make the moment last longer, but before I can, Lucy's walking toward us.

"May, you ready to head out?"

May peeks at me out of the corner of her eye and I swear there's a question there, but as usual, I'm mute. She turns back to Lucy and shrugs. "Yeah, let's go."

She stands and I push myself off the couch, struggle to

come up with something entertaining to say, something that will make her stay, but the words that come out of my mouth when I'm finally upright are "Cool to meet you, you know, officially. See you in class."

And then they're gone, walking away, and I'm left beating myself up for being such a wimp.

Auditions end a little while later. Watching some of the other drummers play after Lucy is like having the insides of my ears cleaned with a jagged metal pin.

I head over to Conor. "So. Obvious who you're going to pick for the band, huh?"

"Dude. That girl . . ." He shakes his head. "I've never been so turned on in my *life*."

I roll my eyes. "She was pretty fantastic, for sure."

He nudges me with his elbow. "Hey—I saw you talking to her friend. What's her deal? She looked a little . . . angry."

"Nah, she's cool. She's in my drama class."

"No shit? I didn't even know they went to our school until Lucy said something. Why have we never seen them around?"

"I'll tell you why." Matt appears at Conor's elbow, wearing his shit-eating grin. My entire body tenses. "They transferred in from Carter last semester."

My face flushes. There's only one way he can be heading

with this line of conversation: to jab me yet again with some snide comment about my mom.

Conor shoots Matt a vicious glare, but Matt's undeterred, per usual. "Awkward, huh, Zach?"

I shrug; try to play it off, like I already knew. "Nah. Why would it be? It's fine." My stomach is sinking into my knees, though, and I know it's not fine. It's not fine at all.

"Oh really?" Matt smirks. "Well, how about this, then. Do ya know who the girl is you were talking to?"

I hate to be one down in Matt's presence, so I shrug. "Yeah, her name is May. We have drama together. She told me she used to go to Carter." Total lie, but to a shark like Matt, cluelessness smells like blood. And he's already circling.

He snorts. "Doubt that."

I give him a dirty look. "Why? She did. It's not a secret, is it?"

He lets out this mean little laugh. "Probably not, but I'd wager she wouldn't bring it up in casual conversation." I'm silent, waiting for the other shoe to drop. With Matt, there's always another shoe waiting to drop on my head and crush me into a million pieces. He continues, "Did she happen to tell you her last name? Or her brother's name?"

The pit in my stomach grows wider with each word that leaves his mouth.

"No." It comes out as a mumble.

"Didn't think so, man." He snorts. "That girl is May

McGintee. I assume you've heard of her brother? Jordan McGintee? That super-genius kid who died in the shooting? He got a perfect score on the SATs as a seventh grader or some shit. Pretty sure your mom knows who he is; maybe you should ask her."

Something squeezes deep in my chest.

Fuck my life, so hard.

"Yo! Dude. Leave him alone." Conor is finally inserting himself into this torturous conversation, but it's too late. Damage done. "You're such a dickhead. Seriously, just get outta here." Conor's up in Matt's face, and per usual, I'm frozen like a statue.

Matt snorts and backs away from Conor with his hands up. "Whatever. You guys are such little bitches. I gotta run anyway." He motions to Rosa, who's still sitting over on the ratty sofa in the corner, playing on her phone. She looks up, sees us all in a tight clump in the middle of the room, and grimaces. She stands, pulling her bag up onto her shoulder.

Matt walks over to her and gives her a kiss on the cheek. What a fucking sociopath. He goes from soul-crushing jerk to sweet, caring boyfriend in the blink of an eye.

Rosa pulls away slightly, just for a second, but then he throws his arm around her shoulders and she relaxes back into him. She whispers something into his ear, and he rolls his eyes but nods along to whatever she's saying. As they pass by Conor and me, Matt mumbles, "See you guys," like he didn't just wreck my world.

Conor clamps a hand on my shoulder. "Dude. He is such a prick. I wish he wasn't such a good guitar player; I'd kick him out of the band in a heartbeat. You okay?"

I nod, trying to shake off Matt's assholeness and the info he just dumped on me. "Yeah. I'm fine. It's whatever."

"You know you aren't your mom, right?" Conor sounds serious for once. "That girl, she'll understand."

I shake my head. "Nope. I bet you she won't. Doesn't matter anyway. If you guys decide Lucy's the right person for the band, I'll stay out of the way. After tonight, I don't really have a desire to be in public ever again."

"C'mon, don't be like that. You can't let Matt get to you. You know he loves pissing you off."

"I don't get why he has to be such a dick."

Conor shrugs. "Jealous, probably."

I snort. "Of what, exactly? My stellar home life? All my adoring fans?" I motion around the empty room.

Conor smirks. "Nah, man. Ever since eighth grade, he's been trying to nudge his way between you and me. He's already managed to do it with you and Rosa. . . ." He trails off when he sees my expression.

"He can have her," I mutter under my breath, like I don't care. Because I don't—mostly.

Conor sighs. "The thing that gets me about all this is how nobody seems to remember your mom's cases from before. Like how she stepped in when my dad got those DUIs and kept him out of jail. She helped keep me out of fucking *foster care,* man." He sets his mouth in a hard, tight line. "It's messed up that nobody remembers that shit."

"Yeah, well. She only did that 'cause I forced her to," I protest. "I'm surprised she even took the time—"

Conor levels me with a glare. "I know you have some beef with your mom, but lay off her just this once, okay?"

"Fine." I turn away from him and keep packing up his shit like the obedient little boy I am.

When we leave the room, Conor's back to trying to convince me that everything with May will be all right, but I know it won't be. It never is.

CHAPTER NINE

May

I'm chased by nightmares the two nights after Lucy's audition. The kind of nightmares the meds McMillen put me on last fall are supposed to stamp out. The dreams are brought on, I'm sure, by the fat envelope that was waiting for me in the mailbox when I got home on Monday night, which I stuffed next to the last one, in the back of my closet. I've never gotten two back to back before. They're usually separated by weeks, with just enough time between their arrivals that I start to let my guard down.

It's been a while since I had a nightmare this bad, where I wake with a jolt, panting, bathed in sweat, on the verge of screaming, David's face flickering on the edge of my brain. Right after the shooting, I had them every night—dreams about walking into that closet, about the noises I heard coming from the other room, the realization that Jordan was still out there, the ache of my arm muscles squeezing hard against my legs, the pain from the scream held tight inside my throat, and then there's a bang and I jolt upright out of bed.

Both nights I wake up confused, disoriented, brain scrambled, bathed in sweat, arms aching. The only way I manage to pull myself back to reality is with the grounding techniques that McMillen taught me over the summer, where I list everything I see, touch, smell, feel, hear, and finally my brain is back in the present moment and out of that closet.

My mom doesn't notice, of course. The first morning, she's gone before I even come downstairs, and the second, she's actually here, full of logistics and formality. That's the way my family has always communicated—through our weekly schedules. It used to make sense: when Jordan was around, my parents had to juggle work and his various activities, all the details of who was driving him where, when. Back before things got really tense between us, Jordan used to joke that without all his extracurriculars, our parents wouldn't know what to do with themselves, and I'd reply, *Also they wouldn't know what to talk to* me *about,* which was funny at the time but really not funny at all when I think back on it. Now, on the rare occasions when we run into each other, there's always this brief moment of confusion on their end like *Wait a second, who is this strange girl in our house?* before they remember who I am and that I still exist.

It turns out that now that all his stuff isn't on their calendars to think about, work has easily expanded to take their place, almost like Jordan was never here.

This morning, after my mom leaves me in a wake of stale perfume, I collapse into a chair at the kitchen table and pour myself a bowl of cereal. I take a bite, but it tastes like cardboard. I used to love cereal, but so did Jordan, and these days I can barely choke it down.

I push the bowl away and put my head down on the table for a second, wondering just how bad it would be if I skipped school. I haven't been out with my spray can in a couple days now, not since Lucy handed in her dumb resignation, and my fingers are itching to light Michelle Teller's house up with color.

Two days back at school, and I'm already sick of it. This year cannot end fast enough.

On the way home from her audition the other night, Lucy told me that she talked to Zach's friend Conor, the lead singer, and he said she was a shoo-in for drummer. I was unsurprised, of course. They would have been idiots not to pick her, since (a) (the dumb guy reason) she's totally hot, and even though she doesn't normally swing his way, it's not like he knows that yet, and (b) (the actual, real reason) she's legit the most badass drummer since John Bonham died (swear to god). I'm excited for her, even if I can't manage to show it properly. Also—and this isn't like an actual *thing* I've been thinking about, because I have no interest in boys or dating right now or ever again—that kid Zach seemed pretty cool. And he was even cuter close up. The other night, sitting there with him after I almost freaked out for the dumbest reason ever . . . I almost felt safe.

I haven't felt safe in so long.

We have drama today, so instead of letting my head sink farther into the wood of the table, I pull myself up and out the front door.

I get to school and it's the same shit as the past few days, except seeing the photo of Jordan's face hanging at the entrance isn't as shocking. The memory of it is already there in my brain, a negative of a photo, just out of reach, taunting me. I force myself past the seven photos, the faces smiling down: reminders that we're still here and they aren't.

That I'm still here and he isn't.

As I make my way down the hall, my heart is beating a thousand times a minute. For a brief moment, I consider calling Dr. McMillen's office to see if she can squeeze me in after school, but I remind myself how pointless those appointments are and how they're obviously not helping, and how Rose-Brady is forcing me to go, like I'm a child. Resentment boils in my belly. No one thinks I can handle anything on my own. I swallow hard. *They're wrong.* I clench my fists and keep walking toward my locker, head down, pulling my phone from my bag.

Lucy's been texting me all morning; she's officially in the band. Her first show is coming up next Friday, which is, I guess, why they were so desperate for a drummer. She's like

May, I know it's going to be hard, but if you don't come I will kick your ass. The girl certainly talks a lot of shit, considering she's gone all Mother Teresa on me over the past few days. I text her back as I walk, tell her I'll consider it.

Maybe.

Probably not.

I don't know.

I can barely concentrate on anything other than the deafening thrum of my heartbeat in my ears.

As I'm about to reach my locker, I'm jostled from behind. I whip around, heart still pounding, even faster now, and why don't people get that they should STAY THE FUCK AWAY FROM ME, and now I'm face to face with Lee Brothers, the guy who was the president of the vocal ensemble at our old school.

He reaches out to steady me. "Whoa, May. You okay? I guess you're back." He pushes his glasses up on his nose and gives me a strained smile. "I heard from Miles that you were." He looks everywhere but at my eyes—down the hallway, at the posters on the wall beside us. We used to be friends. Used to go to the same parties. Now he can't even look at me.

"Yup." I dig my nails into the palms of my hands, try to get a fucking *hold* on myself, try to take those deep breaths that McMillen always goes on and on about—try to stop the fucking *hammering* of my *heart*—but nothing works, so instead I plaster a giant obnoxious smile on my face. Swallow the dread into my belly. Pretend to be okay. "I'm baaaaack. Lucky me, huh?" My voice sounds like nails scraping down a blackboard, high and piercing and raw.

"Yes." He gives me a weak smile. I can tell he's not sure I'm serious; he's doing this bemused mouth-twitchy thing he used to do in meetings when he was nervous. That's right: I attended those meetings, because I was the secretary. I thought maybe it would impress my parents, the fact that not only was I singing, I also held an office position in the ensemble. But of course, they barely noticed.

"Well. . . . errr . . . it was good to run into you." He's about to walk away but then pauses and touches my arm, his voice oozing with sincerity. "By the way, I hope you saw the memorial? We worked hard with the student governments and administrations of all the local high schools to put them up. . . ."

I go cold. This conversation was going *so* well too. "Yes." My voice is flat as a pancake. "I saw it."

"I'm so glad. When we all got transferred here, me and a few other choir and band members came up with the idea. We all miss them." He clears his throat. "I'm sure you know this, but before . . . everything . . . Jordan and I had gotten to be pretty good friends. He wanted to play the guitar for one of the vocal ensembles, so we started talking. I miss him a lot. . . ." He trails off. I glare at the poster about the spring formal that's taped to the wall behind his head. There's a beat of silence, which I'm sure some people would describe as awkward, but I don't care enough about this conversation to feel awkward about any part of it. Lee barely knew Jordan, except through me. I don't even know what he's talking about, saying they were *friends*.

Lee starts talking again. "Anyway. Yeah. With the memorial—we thought we shouldn't forget, you know? We were like, this is important. . . . You know, that day, when it happened, I was in the cafeteria. We were all *so* scared. . . ." He keeps talking, but it sounds like a buzz in my ear, not like actual words.

"May, you okay? You look a little pale. . . ." He reaches toward me, but I smack his hand away.

"DON'T!" It comes out much louder than I intend it to, and all of a sudden the kids passing us in the hallway are taking notice. Everyone is staring. *I'm a freak, I'm a freak, I'm a freak.* I reach down deep inside myself and slap tiny imaginary me in the face—tell her to get her shit together, take a huge breath.

"Sorry." Plaster on another fake smile. Pull my body off the wall. "Sorry, just tired. Not used to waking up this early."

Lee nods like *Sure, May,* but he lets it go, because who wants to push the subject with an obviously emotionally disturbed person? Not most people, and definitely not Lee Brothers, Master of Emotion and Propriety.

"Anyway, good to see you, May." He's backing away as he talks, like he can't get away from me fast enough. "I gotta run. . . . Good to see you." He already said that, but whatever.

I wave.

At his back.

Fourth-period drama, and Ms. Kowalski's hair whips around like it's powered by an invisible tornado. You have to give it to her: she truly does not give a fuck. I can respect that.

Today she starts class late because a couple drama freaks have been talking her ear off in the front of the room—a bizarrely animated conversation full of dramatic gestures and mock fainting.

Zach slips in late again, halfway through her roll call, and my heart leaps at the sight of him. He looks surprised that class hasn't started yet, since when he got here last time Ms. Kowalski was already teaching. He's wearing headphones around his neck, and I make a mental note to find him after class and casually ask him what he's listening to.

"Hi there!" As Kowalski greets him, the glasses she has perched on her head slide down her forehead and land on her nose. "Oh, my glasses! I've been searching for them for hours." She chuckles to herself and then turns back to Zach. "Sorry. I don't think I got your name last class?"

Zach looks super annoyed that she isn't just ignoring him like last time he came in late. I try to catch his eye to commiserate, because I agree—this is *drama* class, who cares if you attend at all?—but he holds his gaze steady on the front of the room.

He mumbles something under his breath.

"Please speak up! Drama is all about learning to project your voice!" Kowalski booms. She has no issues with projection.

"Zach." He's still mumbling, but this time he puts a little more energy behind his voice. He still hasn't acknowledged me. Probably mortified to be put on the spot.

"Zach." She scans the class roster. "Ah. Gotcha! First time in a couple years that you're the only Zach in my class!" She smiles. "Zach Teller, I presume?"

My heart stops beating as he opens his mouth to answer. It opens and closes with no sound.

Teller.

Now he looks over at me.

And I can't look away.

His last name is Teller.

There's no way this is a coincidence. All the lightness that crawled into my being when he entered the room leaks out, replaced by nothing.

CHAPTER TEN

Zach

This goddamn teacher just won't leave me alone. I can't bring myself to look over at May. I got here late to try to avoid this—the roll call, the reading of last names. I would have skipped class entirely, but what was I going to do? Skip for the rest of the year? Fail out? All in order to keep May from learning my last name? Conor keeps insisting that my name does not make me, no matter what everyone else seems to think. That's easy for him to say. He's not the one living with it.

"Zach Teller, I presume?" At the front of the room, Ms. Kowalski's waiting for me to answer.

I nod. The air around me feels heavy, like molasses. I can barely get my head back up. "Yes. Zach." I swallow. "Teller."

And then I force myself to meet May's eyes.

The fury in them makes me want to die. Something inside me recognizes how inevitable this moment was.

Now that she's ruined my life, Ms. Kowalski moves on in her roll call.

CHAPTER ELEVEN

May

I can't breathe.

CHAPTER TWELVE

Zach

May's face has turned red. She's shaking.

The anger in her eyes is drilling a hole through my skin. I swear I can feel it burning me on my insides.

"Are you okay?" I mouth at her, even though I am more than certain that she wants nothing to do with me, now or ever again. She drops face-first on her desk and wraps her arms around her head. This is not good. Ms. Crazy-Hair at the front of the room blabbers on like nothing has happened.

I start to stand but hesitate. If I go over there, I might make things worse. Considering I'm the dickhead who caused this to happen.

I'm halfway out of my chair when Ms. Kowalski finally takes notice.

"May, are you okay?" May's head is still buried in her arms.

Another student raises his hand. "Ms. Kowalski? Not to freak you out, but I don't think she's okay. It sounds like she's panting."

"Yeah," a girl in front of me chimes in. "She did *not* look good before she wrapped herself up like that." She pauses and then in a bad stage whisper says, "I mean, you know who she is . . . right?"

Ms. Kowalski does not look like she has the faintest idea who May is, or what she's supposed to do. She glances around at us, head bobbing back and forth, panicked. "Can someone please take her to the nurse?"

Everyone just sits there, silent. Apparently, no one wants to get involved, which is so messed up, considering that just about every assembly we had last semester was about how we need to speak up if we see someone in pain, how we need to support each other. Way to go, fellow students.

I finally raise my hand.

"Great! Mack, was it?" She points to me.

"Zach." I manage to resist the urge to scream.

"Right, right, Zach. Please escort her to the nurse's office, okay?"

May's head starts to shake back and forth, but her back is rising and falling way too fast, and I doubt she'll be able to get a sentence out of her mouth to protest. I know I should leave her alone, but I want to protect her, even if the thing I'm trying to protect her from is me.

I stand and walk to her side. "Can you get up?"

Her brown hair shakes faster, back and forth across the desk. I reach out to try to help her up, but she jerks away. I pull my hand back as quickly as I can.

The teacher is at my side now. "May, Zach is going to take you to the nurse. It's going to be okay. Can you get up on your own?"

May sucks in a shaky breath and then pushes back her chair and stands. Her head is down, hair curtaining her face. I reach out to help her, but she edges past me and heads for the door. I grab our bags and run to catch up.

CHAPTER THIRTEEN

May

Who does this guy think he is? This *Teller.* Trying to touch me. Trying to help me?

I can hear his footsteps behind me as I rush out of the classroom, and I want to grab him, punch him, kick him, SCREAM into his stupid face, but I barely have the strength to push open the double doors.

"May!" He has the audacity to say my name, like he thinks he has the right. "Hey! May! Wait up."

I am just going to ignore him. I'm not sure where I'm going—definitely not to the nurse's office, which is always the most useless place in every school—but wherever it is, I need to figure it out, fast, and get the hell away from this shit. I'm trapped in a hallway of lockers that's just like every other hallway of lockers in every other goddamn hellhole high school on the planet. You'd think before they sent us here, they could have at least attempted to make this place look different from Carter. You'd think that, but you'd be wrong, because the public-school system doesn't give a shit what happens to you when you're a leftover.

"Hey! I have your bag." Zach's behind me, panting.

I whirl around, hair whipping out, and grab my bag from his outstretched hands. "Great. Thanks. Bye." I turn and keep moving down the empty hallway.

"Wait." He's still here, breathing down my neck. He's really testing the limits of my self-control right now. "I want you to know. When we met the other night, I didn't know . . . who you are. Not that I wouldn't have talked to you, but, like, I wasn't trying to trick you into liking me. Or being nice to me. I didn't know . . ."

"So instead you tried to sneak into class late? So, what, I wouldn't figure out who your mom is? Who you are?" I stop myself from continuing. This guy isn't worth my words.

He groans. "No. I mean, sort of, I guess, but I wanted . . . I thought maybe if you got to know *me* instead of my last name . . . I had a good time with you the other night. I haven't had fun talking to another person in so long. . . ."

"I don't care." Why won't he leave me the fuck alone?

"And you obviously figured it out now. That I'm . . . that my mom is . . . the lawyer. For the guy."

I stop in my tracks. Rhetoric matters to me, even if it doesn't to him. "'*The guy*'? You mean the shooter? You mean David fucking Ecchles, the psychopath who killed my brother and five of my friends and my favorite teacher? Who murdered them all for no reason?"

Zach's face falls. Good.

I'm up in his face now, breathing hard. My hands are balled into fists. "He's not *the guy,* you asshole. He doesn't even deserve to be called a guy—it makes him sound too human."

"Yeah . . . I know. I'm sorry. I wasn't . . . I wasn't trying to play it down. Who he is. What he did. I know . . ." He runs a hand through his hair. "No. I don't know. I can't imagine. And my mom . . ." His face shuts down. "My mom is not someone I like to think about."

"Good for you, that you have that privilege. I think about her. I think about her *every. single. fucking. day.* Every single day, and every single night as I try to sleep. I dream her face. Hers, and Jordan's, and the face of that fucking psychopath. Sometimes they all get mixed together. Sometimes Jordan's face isn't his . . . it's one of theirs. Those are the worst." I swallow hard. I'm trembling. I'm saying way too much, more than I've said to my therapist, more than I've said to Lucy. Why do I suddenly have diarrhea of the mouth?

He shakes his head. "No—no—that's not what I meant. I don't like to think about her, but I still have to. Of course I do. She's my mom. And she ruined my life." He pauses, like he's trying to decide whether to continue talking. I start backing away from him. "No, please wait. You have to know—I'm not my mom. We might share the same DNA—the same last name—but I'm not her. I don't agree with her choices. I'm not responsible for her actions. I never asked for this."

My heart clenches. I shake my head. "Fine. You didn't. But neither did I." I spin on my heel and take off down the hallway without so much as a glance back.

CHAPTER FOURTEEN

Zach

I pull into the driveway after the most disastrous day ever and find my worst nightmare waiting: my mother is home. Her car's bumper sticks out of the newly painted garage, and my stomach drops at the sight. She hasn't been here for dinner in weeks, and *today* is the day she decides to come home? Great. Please excuse me while I go puke.

Gwenie, on the other hand, squeals, "Mom's home!" like it's the most exciting thing that's ever happened to her, instead of a reason to flee. I do not get her. She's had it almost as bad as me this year, but she still *likes* our mother. Gwen logic makes no sense.

As soon as I park, Gwen jumps out of the car and runs toward the house. I put my head down on the steering wheel, where it seems to reside far too often these days, and give myself a pep talk before going inside.

My earlier conversation with May runs through my head—the fact that she accused me of having the luxury to not think about my mother strikes me as particularly ironic, given my current situation.

When I finally get inside, my mom's chopping vegetables and my dad's sitting at the counter. They're chatting about the weather. It's all so weird and *Twilight Zone*–y that my head is about to explode. What is happening with my life today?

"Hi, Zach." My mom nods in my direction, but I ignore her. Instead, I watch my sister make a fool of herself, like she normally does when my mom appears in our home. She might as well be hanging off Mom's back, she's so up in her face, acting like a neglected puppy that's finally getting some attention. I love my sister, but she really needs to work on keeping it together and playing hard to get with our life-ruining mother.

I grunt in response.

"Zach! My man. You eating here tonight?" My dad tries to give me a light punch on the shoulder like we're buddies, but I step aside at the last moment and his fist whiffs through the air. I shrug.

My mom glances up from her chopping. "It would be nice if you did. I came home from work early so we could all catch up."

"Yeah, sure," I mumble. "Whatever." Not like I have anywhere else to go.

"Great. Set the table, please." My mother only speaks in imperative sentences.

"Already?" It's four-thirty.

She looks at me over the rim of her glasses. "Yes, thanks."

I flare my nostrils and consider saying no. I think about running out of the house and never coming back. Moving in with Conor or something, even though I know Conor's home life is as shitty as mine, just in a different way, not that anyone at school would ever guess from how he dresses or carries himself. I decide it's not worth it—the conflict, the drama of arguing with my lawyer mother—so I sigh and pull the silverware out of the kitchen drawer and start to set the table without a word.

When I'm done, my mother comes over to inspect my work, because god forbid I did it *wrong*. My shoulders tense as I wait for whatever criticism she comes up with, but she gives me a small nod and a pat on the shoulder, and I guess that means I'm dismissed until dinner is ready. I sprint out of the kitchen and up to the relative safety of my bedroom.

The safety is temporary, of course. Two hours later I'm back downstairs, sitting at the dining room table with my family, wishing I had the ability to speed up time so this could all be over and I could be back in my room.

"How's school going?" My mom passes the salad to Gwen, asking the question like she thinks she can trick us into believing she cares about the answer. If she really cared, maybe she would spend more than three evenings a month at home.

"It's great!" Gwen is practically drooling on the table from the attention. "My history teacher told me today that my term paper from last semester was one of his favorites . . . and I'm thinking about trying out for cheerleading next year!" I shoot her a glare when I hear that. "Also Emery Lambert invited me to her birthday party next week, which is so cool because she's never spoken to me before, so I obviously have to go." She pauses to take a breath, and my mom cuts in.

"That's great, Gwen." She turns away before Gwen can say more, and Gwenie's face drops. I try to catch her eye, but she's staring down at her plate like it's the most interesting thing in the world. My dad is silent at the other end of the table.

"What's happening at school for you these days?" My mother turns her attention to me, but I ignore her. I'm still trying to get Gwen to smile, or at least meet my eyes. "Zach. Hello? I asked you a question."

I finally turn toward her. "Why are you even here?"

I've caught her off guard, and she tilts her head back for a beat. "Excuse me?"

"I said, why are you here?"

She looks around the table, at my sister and my father. "I live here."

"Could have fooled me." I stab at a piece of meat on my plate so hard that the table shakes.

She clears her throat and gives me a tight, fake smile that doesn't reach her eyes. "I know I haven't been around much. . . . This case has been ramping up, and—"

I cut her off. I don't want to hear her lame excuses. "I don't think you get it. You can't just show up here whenever it suits you and think things are going to be normal."

Her eyes widen, like she thinks I'm out of line. Like she thinks I'm the one who has something to be sorry for. "Excuse me? '*Show up here*'? I sleep here every night. And I'll remind you that I'm your mother, so watch your tone." I can tell she's getting ready to go full lawyer on me, and all the fight drains out of my body.

"Sorry." I'm back to mumbling. Across the table, Gwen looks like she's about to cry. I swallow hard.

My mom sighs and runs a hand through her hair. "It's okay. I don't want to spend our time together fighting. Now, can you please tell us how school is?"

I look around the table before answering. Gwen's still hunched over her plate, my dad's fading into the wallpaper, and my mother has bags under her eyes that look like they've become permanent fixtures on her face.

This is our family dinner.

CHAPTER FIFTEEN

May

It's late. It seems like it's always late, like the days just slide by me and the nights are the only times I can hold on to. I'm standing in my bedroom, staring at my white walls, where posters used to hang. Posters of bands I went to see with Lucy and Chim and Jordan, art museums my parents took Jordan and me to when we were younger, all the bullshit stuff I used to be interested in before I realized none of it matters. I took them down after Jordan died.

Now the walls of my room are bare.

The thick envelope clutched in my hand is unopened. I know it's another letter from him. It says so right on the postmark: *Los Angeles County jail, Twin Towers Correctional Facility.*

I only know one person there.

David Ecchles.

The boy who killed my brother.

* * *

I usually leave these letters unopened. I opened the first one, and after that I knew better. I stuff them under my mattress, around my room, try to forget they exist. I can't throw them out; in some perverse way, they're my last connection to Jordan. Everyone else around me has healed, moved on, put up memorials, but these letters are my reminder that nothing will ever be the same. And I deserve to be reminded. Punished.

It's my payment for surviving.

That first one arrived shortly after David was incarcerated and denied bail. I got home from school one afternoon, a month after everything, and found an envelope in the mailbox addressed to me. I never got personal letters in the mail—I don't live in the fucking Dark Ages—so I was curious. I literally did not think he could write to me from in there.

I was stupid back then.

I didn't know about all the ways you can get to someone from jail. The forwarding services that can be used to route letters to places they aren't supposed to go. The prisoners willing to send other inmates' mail, for a price.

I opened that envelope a naive kid who thought she was safe. I read the first lines—*I hope you're okay, May. I was so worried about you that day*—and my insides froze, and I grabbed the pages and stuffed them under the clothes way in the back of my closet.

And then another one came, and another. And now it's been months and I haven't told anyone and I'm not *going* to tell anyone because they can't protect me.

They didn't protect me from the first letter.

They didn't protect me at all.

I'm considering opening the letter that's lying on my lap. Something inside me shifted today in the hallway, facing off with Zach. All the shit I've been trying to ward off has started to sneak back in, and now the envelope is heavy in my hand, burning a hole through my palm.

I stare out my bedroom window into the dark night for a while, brain blank, body frozen, and then rip the top off in one violent motion.

Inside is a handwritten letter. It's pages and pages long. I read the first couple lines: *It's lonely in here, May. Have you ever felt darkness pressing down on your head so hard that you think your neck may break? My parents moved away. They don't visit or call. You haven't come to see me either. Why not? I told you, I have something to tell you about that day.* I drop onto my bed.

I'm shaking. Hard. I wrap my entire body in a blanket, bury my head into it too, and lie, motionless, arms wrapped around my legs, like somehow, if I manage to hug myself tight enough, I might cease to exist. Sometime later, I drift into a restless sleep.

I'm jolted awake by the slamming of a car door. Heart

racing, brain still half-asleep, I jump up and peer out my bedroom window to the driveway below. My mom, home from work. She looks tired. I glance at my clock: eight p.m. Early for her, these days.

I hear her downstairs slamming kitchen cabinets, and then heavy footsteps on the stairs. A few seconds later, her bedroom door slams shut with a bang. *Nice to see you too, Mom.*

I lie back down on my bed and stare at the ceiling for a few minutes, but I'm restless now. I flop to my side, and the fucking letter falls off the bed onto the floor, its pages spreading across the carpet like a stain. I jump up. That's it. I can't lie here any longer with this bullshit contaminating my space.

I bend down and gather the pages, trying not to think about what might be written on them, trying not to breathe. I crumple them together and head downstairs and outside. When I get to the garbage cans on the side of the house, I start tearing the paper into confetti. It's getting all over the ground, but I just want his words gone. I want to erase their existence. Tear them out of my mind. Scrub them from my brain.

By the time I finish, my fingers are bleeding and my face is on fire. There's no way I'm going to get back to sleep. So I grab my backpack from behind the old refrigerator in the garage, where I stuffed it the other night, and take off down the driveway on my bike.

About thirty minutes later, I pull up on the curb outside the Tellers', panting and drenched in sweat. The night air is thick and heavy on my skin. The house in front of me is dark. I sling the backpack off my shoulders onto the ground, tucking it and myself behind a bush in the front yard.

Now that I know Zach lives here, it seems different. Before, it was just a building, a place that houses a woman I despise. For a second, I wonder which window is Zach's bedroom, but I force the thought out of my head. *Concentrate, May.* Since when do I let boy-related bullshit seep into my thoughts when I'm supposed to be focused? When I broke up with Miles after everything, it was a clean cut. No sentimentality—I dumped the few gifts he'd given me, the dried-up flowers I'd saved, the old T-shirt I'd borrowed from him one day after we went swimming. Threw it all out in one fell swoop. Deleted his text messages.

He was gone.

I felt nothing.

With that final thought, I pull a spray can out of my backpack and stand up, set my jaw. This time I won't trip the spotlight on the driveway. This time I won't end my night making out with a cat.

I tighten my grip on the can and start across the front lawn. It's hot as shit out here, just like last time.

I'm almost to the house when a light comes on upstairs. I dart to the side, back into the darkness, heart pounding. This has never happened. I glance at my watch and realize it's only nine-thirty—still early. I forgot to check the time before I left; it's not like me to screw this up. This is the one thing I normally get right. I'm so done with this day, this week, this year. This life.

I clutch the side of the house, hiding in the shadows, watching the light. I'm trying to catch my breath, calm my heart, which I swear to god you can hear eight states east, and finally, after way, way too long, the light goes off. All my manic energy has drained out of me, replaced by an infinite loop of David's words: *It's lonely here. . . . It's lonely here. . . . It's lonely here.*

I drag myself back to my bag, sink to the ground, and rest my head on my knees. I allow one deep breath, then reach into my backpack and pull out my phone.

"Hey." My voice cracks. I swipe at my nose, furious that it's dripping, and try to swallow the lump in my throat. "No, no. I'm okay. I . . ." I shut my eyes for a second, "I think I need a ride. I'm sorry; I know it's late. Can you come get me?" I pause, listening. "The Tellers'."

There's silence on the other end of the phone. I talk through it. "I know what you're going to say; I'll explain everything, but can you just get here? I'll be at the end of their street. Thank you."

When Lucy pulls up, I'm leaning against a stop sign with barely enough energy left to remain upright. She lowers the passenger-side window and raises her eyebrows at the sight of me. "Need to put that bike in the back?"

I nod and she pops the trunk. A few seconds later, she darts around the side of the car with outstretched arms. "You get in. I'll get the bike." I nod again and throw myself into the passenger seat, desperate to keep myself together for a few more minutes.

Just a few minutes more.

CHAPTER SIXTEEN

Zach

Later, after our stupid family dinner, after everyone else has gone to sleep, I flick on the light in my bathroom and stare at my reflection in the mirror until all the parts of my face separate from each other and stop making sense.

CHAPTER SEVENTEEN

May

Somehow, I've made it through almost two weeks of school without being kicked out or losing my mind (at least, not entirely). I'm not going to count that night outside Za—the Tellers' house last week. It shouldn't count. My freak-out was the result of a random fault line that I plan to avoid from now on.

Speaking of avoiding things . . . I tried to drop out of drama class, but they wouldn't let me. Rose-Brady was all, *You need an elective, May, and all the rest are filled. Don't you want to graduate in June with your class?* I nodded, because I can't afford any trouble, but really I was thinking, *I DON'T GIVE A SHIT*—because I don't. What the hell am I going to do after graduation, anyway? All my college plans died the day Jordan did.

Whatever. I can just avoid *him*—the fault line. Like I said, I'm good at that. It's the only way I get through the days. Avoid my parents, avoid Miles, avoid people from my past, *avoid avoid avoid.* And now, avoid Zach.

It's relatively easy to do—today I slip into class late and

bolt as soon as the bell rings. For a second, just before I leave, I make the mistake of looking at him, and he has this expression on his face that punches me square in the stomach. I almost say something to him, but I catch myself.

What would I even say? We have nothing to talk about.

I'm heading into the cafeteria when someone taps me on the back. I'm sick of people thinking my body is public property—that anyone can reach out and touch me. I would bet my life if I were a boy, no one would try that.

Before I can even react, a squeaky voice assaults my ears. "May! I've been looking everywhere for you!"

I turn around slowly. I know that voice. I know who I'll find behind me—one of the very people I've been trying to avoid for a year. She's a persistent little weasel, I'll give her that much.

"Anne Kim." I put on my best bitch face, but she doesn't seem to notice. "Hello."

She throws her arms around me. "How *are* you? How are you holding up? Being back? The anniversary coming up? We've been thinking about you . . . about Jordan. . . . I'm sure you've heard about the memorial service I'm helping Principal Rose-Brady put together. We're going to have an assembly, talk about Madison, Jordan, all of them. Tell stories. Make sure we don't forget them."

I squirm out of her grasp and take a step away from her. "That's nice." I scan the room behind her, trying to locate Lucy.

Anne won't shut up. She never does. "We all miss Jordan so much. Him, my sister, the rest of them. During group last week, Adam—Neilson, obviously—told this story about his cousin Marcus and Jordan that was *so* touching."

I snort. I bet he did. Before the shooting, Adam was legit the biggest partier in school. He was the one who had the party the weekend before everything happened, the one where I *allegedly* talked to David. He was a legend with the guys in our grade for his ability to do a keg stand for, like, two minutes in a row. And now he's all woe-is-me, telling stories about his cousin and my brother like he used to care about them. Like he hadn't teased them mercilessly in middle school.

Anne ignores my snort and continues, "We were all so moved by it. I cried. It would have been wonderful to have you there, to add your stories. Your brother was amazing; I'm so happy I got to know him a little before—"

"Yep." I cut her off. "Yep. He was. Thanks." I glance over her shoulder toward freedom and then back to Anne. "I gotta go."

I'm about to walk away, but she catches my elbow. Goddammit, I want to punch this girl. I do a few of my therapist-advised breaths, but nope—the desire is still there inside me: I want to punch her in the face.

I struggle against her grip, and she tightens her hand on my arm in response. "May, please don't run away. We need to talk. I've been trying to get ahold of you. I wanted to ask if you would consider being a part of the assembly. Having your voice there, hearing your stories, what you went through, it would be huge. It would really help people heal."

I narrow my eyes at her. "Jesus, Anne. I thought I made myself clear this past summer, last fall, and every other fucking time you and your merry band of survivors tried to recruit me into your sorrow cult. I want *nothing to do with any of you.* Can you please get that through your thick head?"

Anne's face falls. Her lips tighten into a barely-there white line. She's so good at playing the victim. "Fine, May. You don't have to be rude. I should have known better. After you got kicked out of school, I thought, *Okay, that's unfortunate, but I can understand her anger—she's suffering like the rest of us.* And when I heard you were back, I was excited, but then everyone said you were still so . . . *mean.* And so, so angry." She shakes her head. "I thought our group might help you. We're all going through the same thing, one way or another. We all lost people that day. But most of us aren't going around being rude to people who are simply trying to offer a helping hand."

I curl my lip at her. "Do you ever listen to yourself speak? You sound like a seventy-year-old grandmother. What the hell is wrong with you?"

With that, Anne releases my arm like it just bit her, like she realized it's actually a slippery, slimy snake. She takes a few steps away from me.

Her voice shakes when she speaks again. "Fine, May. *All right.* I get it. I'll leave you alone. *We'll* leave you alone. I guess some people are just beyond help." She turns and pushes her way out the cafeteria doors.

After she leaves, I stand there, frozen, until I'm forced to move by the flow of people into the room. When I reach out to grab a tray from the stack by the entrance, my hands are shaking and my stomach is churning. A wave of shame passes over me as I remember Anne's face and the way she snatched her hand back from my arm like she was afraid I might bite her.

Maybe I shouldn't have been so mean. Anne's harmless, really. She founded her stupid support group at the end of last year for all the people who were affected by the shooting. It started out small: Anne, whose sister Madison died. Madison was first chair violin. Adam Neilson, who lost his cousin Marcus, first chair saxophone and Jordan's best friend. Peter Oppenheimer, who lost his dad, Mr. Oppenheimer, our jazz band leader. My favorite teacher. And from there the group expanded.

Now it includes like thirty other people, not that I pay attention to the DMs and texts they send me asking me to go to their dumb meetings. And when Lucy told me about the newest addition to the group, I vowed all over again to never join. Their new member is none other than Miles Catalano, my ex-boyfriend.

I heard he has some guilt about that day.

Yeah. No kidding. He should.

But he survived, just like all of those other assholes.

They survived. They're *alive.*

You'll never see Jordan at one of their stupid meetings.

After school, I'm in Lucy's car and we're heading to her house so she can get ready for the show on Friday—her first with Proper Noun and the Noun. It's hot and dry. My shirt sticks to my chest and my armpits even though we have the windows of the car rolled all the way down. Lucy's A/C stopped working last year and her dad never got around to giving her money to fix it. She gets money from her gigs, but it always ends up going to equipment or other music-related activities instead of her (as she puts it) boring-ass car. As long as it has four wheels and drives, Lucy doesn't care.

"I think you should give him a chance." Lucy's midway through yet another soliloquy on Zach; she's trying to convince me that I should keep talking to him, rather than continue with my current plan of action, aka pretending he doesn't exist. "Just come to the show—maybe talk to him. See how it goes."

I ignore her. I have my phone about four inches from my nose and am scrolling through Instagram in an attempt to send her the not-at-all-subtle message that I don't want to have this conversation. Again.

"I mean, it seemed like you actually . . . *liked* him?" Out of the corner of my eye, I can see her trying to get me to look at her. "I haven't heard you talk about anyone in . . . a long time."

I roll my eyes at my phone.

"C'mon." She nudges me with her elbow as she pulls into the short, steep driveway of her house. "May. He's a guy—a cute guy—not the devil. And you said he isn't down with the fact that his mom took the case. I bet it really sucks for him, that everyone knows—"

I cut her off. "Could you please not tell me how much it sucks for *him*? Jesus."

She shakes her head and puts the car in park. "You know, sometimes you're impossible."

I glare at her, and we sit there, silent for a minute. She sighs and unbuckles her seat belt. "Fine. Whatever, May. Don't talk to him. Could you please just think about coming to my show, though? Please? You know how important it is to me. It's my first one with these guys . . . and I've heard the venue is actually pretty decent. Like, a step up from the shitholes I played with my last band."

I pretend like I can't hear her and squint out the open window. The lawn that slopes down from her house to the street is full of tangled overgrown grass, brown and dead, like her dad hasn't been home much to mow or water it. I realize I don't know whether he *has* been home; it's not like I've been here much in the past few months.

I glance over at Lucy; she has her eyes squeezed shut, head leaning back against her seat rest. I swallow. *Fuck.*

"Fine. I'll go."

Her eyes pop open. "You'll go where?"

I roll my eyes. "Don't make me say it."

"Awww, May Day, you really *do* love me." She throws her arms around my shoulders, and I squirm under her touch.

"This doesn't mean I'm gonna talk to him, you know. I'm only going to support you."

Lucy snorts. "Uh-huh. We'll see about that."

She gets out of the car, and I hold up both my middle fingers at her back.

CHAPTER EIGHTEEN

Zach

It's the night before Conor's big show in downtown LA, and he won't stop texting me. Earlier today in school, after Matt said yet another shitty thing to me, I told Conor sorry, I love him, but there's no way I'm going to his show, but of course he hasn't gotten the message through his thick skull. Conor can be terrible when he doesn't get his way.

His latest text reads: *Bro, don't be so lame.* Like wanting to avoid another awkward situation with Rosa and Matt is lame. I love him, I'd jump in front of a moving car to save him, he's like the brother I never had, but sometimes he's so annoying.

I'm in my room, which is fit for a ten-year-old boy—maybe the last time my mom took four seconds out of her day to notice something about one of her kids. Not that I care. She's a jerk.

I lie on my back across a Transformers comforter that I've had since I was eight years old and respond to Conor's text with one word—*no.*

He's always doing this: peer pressuring me into shit I want to avoid. I shove my head under the pillow as my phone continues to buzz. I will ignore it.

I *will* ignore it.

Approximately one thousand buzzes later, I pull my head out. Twelve new text messages. *Jesus Christ, Conor.* He cannot take a hint.

I scroll through and am about to throw my phone back down when one of them catches my eye.

Lucy's friend will be there.

My heart jumps. I write back a quick response.

Lucy's friend . . . meaning May?

My phone buzzes again almost immediately.

HA! There you are. I knew that would get you to respond. Yes, duh. You ass.

I take a deep breath. May's been avoiding me since the incident during drama class last week, and after a couple attempts to talk to her, I started to take the hint. But if she's going to their show . . . and she knows that *I* might go to the show (since Conor's my only friend, although god willing she doesn't know that little detail) . . . does that mean she wants to see me?

Zach, stop ignoring me!##@!

The guy has to be the most impatient person in the world. I shake my head at my phone, but I have to admit my interest has been piqued. I can't imagine there's much chance that May wants to see me, but maybe if she's there, and I'm there, and there's rock music playing softly in the background . . .

BRO!!!!!

The buzz of my phone interrupts my reverie.

I sigh. He's not going to leave me alone until I respond.

FINE. I'll go. Now will you please shut the F up?!

He writes back a row of smiley-faced emojis and clappy hands.

Sometimes I wonder if Conor *is* actually a fourteen-year-old girl.

I open up Instagram, all casual, and click over to May's account, which I may or may not have found last week. It's still set on private. I contemplate sending a request to follow her; my finger hovers over the button for far too long, but in the end I wimp out. Maybe I'm being presumptuous, thinking that her coming to the show means something. I should just stay home with Gwen that night and do something really cool, like watch *Pitch Perfect* for the eight hundredth time.

I click over to my messages to tell Conor I'm backing out, but there's a text from him waiting for me.

YOU ARE NOT BACKING OUT!!!

I sigh and swipe out of all my open apps, drop my phone onto the Comforter from Hell, and throw my arm across my face. Sometimes I regret having any friends at all.

There's a soft knock on my door, and I bolt upright. I'm lying here with no pants on, and since I'm pretending to do my homework, there are textbooks strewn all over my bed. It looks like a tornado hit. If this is my mom home early again, she's never going to let me get away with this shit.

"Zach?" It's my dad. What in the actual F. He hasn't knocked on my door in approximately a decade.

I stop panicking, because the last person I care about impressing is my dad. I lie back down on my bed, sprawled out. No pants, legs wide. "What." I hope I sound bored as shit, because he bores the shit out of me.

He pops his head in. He's wearing pajamas. I wish I could say that's because it's eight p.m. right now, but that would be a lie. He was wearing them at four-thirty, when Gwen and I got home from school.

"Hey, kid."

Eye roll at the ceiling. "Hey." I fold my arms across my chest and don't even bother sitting up.

"Whatcha doin'?"

I roll my eyes again. "Solving Tupac's murder. What does it *look* like I'm doing?"

He pauses at my tone and clears his throat. "Uh. Well. I was just wondering if you were interested in catching the end of the basketball game with me? The Clippers are killing it."

The last time I watched an NBA game was maybe five years ago. It's so nice to have parents who pay such close attention to my interests.

"Nah, I'm good."

"You sure? It's a great game. . . ."

I prop myself up on my elbow and meet his eyes for the first time. "I said. I'm good."

He holds up his hands. "All right, all right, gotcha. Thought it might be fun. . . ." He trails off and stares at me for a second in a way that makes my skin prickle, then shakes his head. "Okay. Never mind. Sorry to interrupt." He backs out of the room and shuts the door.

Guilt swirls in my stomach after he leaves. I'm tempted to run after him and apologize, but then I think about all the afternoons he's stayed in his room with the door shut tight, all the times he's left everything up to me—Gwen, cooking, the fucking spray paint on our garage—and I don't feel so bad.

"Have a drink. Relax."

Conor stands on the other side of the tiny room where the band is hanging out backstage before their show, holding out a red plastic cup to me. And by "the band," I mean Conor: the only one here so far.

We're somewhere in downtown LA at a club, although I couldn't tell you where if my life depended on it. Conor managed to steal his dad's old rattling truck for the night, and once we got off the freeway, he drove us through the city streets like a complete madman, his equipment secured in its open bed by a couple of buoy ropes, while I held on to the dashboard for dear life. Los Angeles traffic is a nightmare, especially once you get into the city proper, and Conor really embraces it whenever he drives. Left turns through lights that have already gone red, weaving back and forth between lanes on the freeway to get three car lengths ahead of where we would be otherwise. It's like being on a roller coaster, except less safe.

"Dude, I'm too nauseous from your driving to put anything into my stomach." But I take the cup from him anyway, and sniff it. "Yo. Is this *beer*? Where'd you get it?"

He smirks at me. "Chill. You sound beyond lame right now." He motions around the room. "I mean, we're in a club, you know. When in Rome."

"I thought this was an alcohol-free club. . . . Why else would they let you guys play here?"

"Oh, little Zachy. Don't you know by now, I have my ways?"

God, he's so pompous sometimes. He settles on a speaker with his legs crossed, like he's the king of the world.

I'm about to take a sip from my cup when the door swings open. The cocky expression falls off Conor's face, fast as lightning. He waves over to me, but I ignore him. He drops his cup behind the speaker and then bolts to the door and jams his shoe under it. He stage-whispers at me, *"Hide the beer!"*

So much for the arrogant bastard act.

I pretend I don't know what he's saying. I can't help but mess with him sometimes. He's so easy.

He lunges at me, trying to grab my beer, but he can't quite

reach and keep his foot against the door. For a split second, I'm tempted to keep ignoring him to teach him a lesson about being a prima donna egomaniac, but I decide to choose the route of least resistance, per usual. I hide my cup behind the speaker I'm sitting on.

"Yoooo! Who's blocking the door?" Matt's voice rips through the relative calm. Perfect. Now I wish I'd thrown my beer at the door instead of hiding it.

I look at Conor and he shrugs like *Sorry, Zach* and moves his foot. Five seconds later, Matt barges into the room, followed by Rosa.

"Conor, what the hell? We're carrying a ton of stuff—that wasn't cool. . . ." Rosa sounds super annoyed, but when she sees me, she trails off.

Conor's eyes dart in my direction, and a flash of concern runs across his face. Then, just as quickly, it's gone. His poker face is beyond good. "Sorry, yeah. Got something jammed under the door for a sec. Sorry 'bout that."

Rosa dumps the armful of stuff she lugged into the room onto one of the ratty chairs behind Conor and perches on another one. She starts biting her thumbnail. These are the closest quarters we've been in since we broke up last year. The other times we've been in the same room, people and square footage have separated us.

Last fall, after my mom decided to screw my life up, Rosa had a big problem with her decision to take the case. Like, to the point where she wouldn't come to my house anymore.

I get it—trust me, I do—but at the same time, it's my *mom*. What was I supposed to do? Never speak to her again? Not defend her when Rosa started ranting some really mean shit about her one night after a few drinks? After that super-fun evening, I told Rosa I wanted to take a break, and then all of a sudden—*three weeks later*—there was Matt, swooping in, asking her to the homecoming dance. Never asking me if it was cool, mind you. He definitely did not give a shit.

When Rosa asked me if I cared whether she went to the dance with Matt, I said no. It wasn't like I wanted her back, and they were friends. The thing is, I didn't think she'd see him as anything more than that. Moreover, I didn't think a *friend* would do that to me—swoop in on my barely cold relationship with no regard for my feelings. Nowadays, I wouldn't be so surprised. Nowadays, I wouldn't be surprised at all.

So they went to the dance together; started dating. She and Matt had always had this chemistry, always shared these inside jokes, and had been family friends since the dawn of time. They probably bonded further over their mutual hatred of my lovely mother. Matt turned into even more of a jerk than he'd been before—or maybe I just started noticing it more.

And here we are.

One big happy family.

Matt glances around. "This is the greenroom?"

I want to laugh in his face, because it's clear he was expecting something . . . more. What a jackass. The band is playing a tiny club, not the fucking Staples Center. And considering this is the first gig they've played in almost a year, you'd think he'd tone down the diva act a little.

"It is . . . small." Rosa must feel the need to proclaim her allegiance to Matt, but her voice is shaky. She slides off the chair. "Oh gross, what did I just sit in?" She has a giant stain on her butt. I almost feel bad for her.

"Babe, lemme see." Matt takes one look and says, "All right, this room isn't gonna work."

"Jesus," I mumble under my breath.

Matt's head snaps around. "What was that?"

I sigh. "Nothing."

"No, I heard you say something. Please repeat it. I'd just love to hear what you have to say, *Teller.*" He spits out my last name like it's a curse. Which it might be, now that I think about it. "Wouldn't you, Rosa?"

Rosa glances between us like she's watching a horrible car accident she can't find a way to stop.

She shrugs.

I hate her.

I clear my throat. "Nothing. It wasn't important. I just said *Jesus.*"

"And whydja say that?"

I make a silent wish to be transported out of this room to literally anywhere else on earth, but it doesn't work. What a shock.

I shrug. "No reason."

Matt walks over and stands right in front of me. "No, I want to know."

Conor's on his feet now, watching. He always backs me up—has ever since we became friends in elementary school, and I know he always will.

But I'm sick of Conor fighting my fights.

So instead of shrinking away like I normally do, I stand up straight and lean toward Matt. I realize I have a solid four inches on him, something I've forgotten in the past few months of slumping through life.

I look down at him. "Maybe 'cause beggars shouldn't be so choosy. You know?"

His face gets redder and redder. "Beggars?" He shakes his head. "Nah, man. Who do you think you are, calling *me* a beggar?"

"Okay, enough, guys. Break this shit up." Conor is hopping up and down behind Matt, trying to get around him, between us.

Matt's really up in my face now, and part of me wants to back down and let this slide. My hands tremble by my sides. I'm pretty sure if I tried to speak, my voice would break in half. Before this year, I never had a reason to fight. I hardly had a reason to argue. Things were just . . . easy, days sliding into other days, everything lubricated. This tension is new, and I hate it, but I'm starting to see that it's not going to go away, no matter how hard I wish it. People like Matt aren't going to let that happen.

I take another step forward. My chest is inches from his, and I'm sure he can hear my heart pounding. I'm sure that if I looked down right now, I'd see my cotton T-shirt pulsing in rhythm with its beats. I'm sure I'm about to change my life with whatever happens in the next five seconds. . . . I'm so sure . . . and I'm ready for it. . . . I am. I'm ready for it.

And right as I'm about to do something—granted, I don't know what, but I know it's going to be *big*—the door swings open once again.

CHAPTER NINETEEN

May

I open the door to the room where the band's prepping, and the first thing I see is Zach and some kid in each other's faces. The second is how tiny the room is. I stop short, and Lucy slams into my back.

"Ow!" she cries. Her drum rattles to the ground. I turn and see her rubbing her arm. She glares at me. "What the hell? I need these arms tonight."

"Can you go in first, please?"

She scowls at me but doesn't argue; she knows better than to try. We trade spots and she lugs her drum into the room. I linger on the outside edge of the doorway.

"What's happening, kids?" I know Lucy can tell something's off in the room, since Zach and the other guy are standing chest to chest like a couple of douche bros, but she ignores them. She's good at this—defusing. I think she learned it from dealing with her dad's drinking when we were younger. She's done it with me so many times I've lost count. She sets the drum on the floor in the middle of the room.

The guy who's up in Zach's face turns, and I see it's the band's guitarist. Another girl, who I recognize from Lucy's audition the other night, stands against the far wall. She looks like she's trying to pretend she's not freaked out by what's happening in here. I feel for her.

Zach finally glances over at me and his eyes bug out. He slinks away from the other kid. If you tried to cut the awkwardness in the room with a knife, the blade would break.

This night is going splendidly already.

Conor sprints across the room to greet Lucy. "Luce! So great to see you. How are you? Where's the rest of your drum kit? You need help schleppin' it?" He's basically drooling on her. Standard behavior around Lucy, trust me. Her sex appeal knows no bounds. She nods and the two of them take off, leaving me stuck.

I remember that Lucy said that Chim would be here tonight. I open my mouth to mumble a goodbye, because I need to get the hell out of this tiny room, which is starting to give me hives, when my eyes land on Zach. His face is bright red. He looks so out of it and so pathetic that I can't help but take pity on him.

"Hey." All three sets of eyes land on me, and the guitarist gives me a little smile that creeps me out. Who the hell *is* that guy? What I wouldn't do to wipe that grin clean off his face. Lucy made me swear up and down that I'd be chill tonight, though, and I'm trying to honor my promise. I shake my head at him and sneer. "Not you. You." I point at Zach.

His eyes light up, and I feel even more like shit for ignoring him all week. Not that he doesn't deserve it. Or maybe he doesn't. I don't know anymore.

Zach points to himself like *Who, me?* and I nod like *Yes, obviously you, dummy, get over here.* So he does.

"Want to go see what's happening out there?" I motion to the main room behind us, where I can hear a band starting to play.

He lets out a deep breath it sounds like he's been holding for most of the night, and nods.

It's noisy in the main room. The crowd is getting thicker. The air is pungent, a mix of sweat and stale beer. In a weird way, it's almost pleasant. It reminds me of something safe, of the time before everything, when Jordan would have been by my side. Lucy started playing in her first band when we were all in eighth grade, back when he was my second brain—my *twin*—and the two of us would go to her shows and watch Lucy play, amazed that our friend was up there performing in a setting that was so different from the school band. I know he liked to go because he wished he could be a part of it—play his guitar with a real band, not just the jazz band at school. But, our parents wouldn't hear of it. They thought it would be a distraction—would take away from the end goal, whatever that was. This was before high school started, before things between me and Jordan started shifting and twisting, before it became brutally obvious to me that our parents couldn't even see me anymore. Before I realized he had eclipsed me.

Even though I have no idea where Zach and I are headed, it feels good to be out of that room. I can't take tiny spaces anymore.

I steer us around the thick of the crowd. Yet another thing I can't stand. I'd make for a stellar date.

This venue is way more packed than the ones Lucy's old band would play—those were mostly coffee shops and warehouses, where the crowd consisted of me, Chim, and a few other friends. This is the first time I've been to one of Lucy's shows since Jordan.

I feel hot breath on the back of my neck, and I jump out of my skin before I realize that it's Zach—*obviously* it's Zach. I need to chill.

"Where are we going?" He's behind me, so close that if I turned around, my nose would touch his mouth. I ignore him and keep walking until I find the wall farthest from the crowd and the stage. He lingers a few feet away, hands shoved deep into his pockets. He's so timid, and I'm taken by the sudden urge to hit him just to see what it would feel like. Just to see how he'd react.

Lucy's being ridiculous if she thinks it's a good idea for me to get involved with him. With anyone, for that matter. I'm totally and irrevocably cracked in half. Sometimes I think

I was born again that day in the band room, that the old me was murdered along with everyone else, replaced with this new person who's angry and scared and broken.

"So? What're we doing back here?" Zach sounds confused, probably wondering why he followed a crazy person into a dark corner. I don't know what to tell him. That walls are safer than empty space? That this is my first time in public in almost a year, outside of school and the band practice? That when I look at him, I want things I don't think I'm allowed to want anymore?

"We used to go to all of Lucy's shows." I pause. Take a breath. Try to decide whether I want to continue. And then I do. "Me and Jordan. He always liked going. He was all about supporting Lucy. And he loved music."

The moment I say my brother's name, I want to grab it out of the air and shove it back into my mouth. I never talk about Jordan. I haven't said his name in months. After the shooting, the media vultures took everything they could from us—our stories, Jordan's history, his school photos—but they couldn't take some things. They couldn't take my memories. My memory of our birthday in the fourth grade and the walkie-talkies we got—I made him keep his under his pillow in case I woke up in the middle of the night, scared. Of the summer we managed to get backstage to see Jack White, Jordan's favorite guitarist, and got a photo with him. Of the expression Jordan would get on his face when he would play his guitar, eyes closed, at peace.

They still call sometimes, the reporters, to ask for our comments on other school shootings, like we're some kind of experts now.

My fingers start to throb, and I realize that the strap of my purse has twisted around them so tightly that they're turning white. I release it with a shake and all the blood rushes back in so fast it hurts.

"Your brother went to Lucy's shows?" Zach's voice is so soft I have to lean toward him to hear. He's talking like he's trying to calm a scared, angry animal.

I nod. "Yeah. I don't know why I said that. Irrelevant, right?" I bark a laugh, pretend this topic doesn't shake me to my core. Pretend I couldn't care less. "Whatever. Want to go get a drink?"

Zach hesitates like he wants to say something else, but apparently he isn't as dumb as most people, because instead he just nods in agreement.

Once we move into the main area, I actually pay attention to the band onstage for the first time. Thankfully, it's not Lucy's new band, because they are really, truly terrible.

"Who the fuck is this?" I yell back at Zach.

"No clue." His lips brush my ear. They're warm. Soft. "They suck."

I allow him a tiny smile. My first tonight.

He grins back like I awarded him the Nobel Peace Prize. Totally the opposite of smooth. The kid could use a lesson in controlling his emotions.

I spot Chim across the room near the bar, waving madly in my direction.

"Uhh . . . do you know that girl over there?" Zach points to Chim, who, to be fair, does look completely bonkers right now. She has that Ilana from *Broad City* thing going on—all frenzied smiles and boingy hair. She tends to get like this at Lucy's shows. Last year, she got so excited at one that she legit puked into her water glass in the middle of a coffee shop. It was super funky and not at all cool.

"Yeah, unfortunately, I do," I yell back, and then wince. I really need to stop being such a jerk about Chim, but sometimes it's hard. We used to be close, before. We were partners in crime, and Lucy and Jordan were the ones grumbling at us to get our shit together. Now there are times when I can barely stand the sight of her, when her mere presence feels like a heavy weight on my head that won't go away. She's like a walking, talking reminder of everything I used to be.

When we get to her, Chim throws her arms around me, feeding my guilt. "May! Aren't you so excited to see Lucy play? You haven't been to one of her shows in so long." She pauses. "Not that I don't get why, because of course I get why." Her cheeks turn bright red. "No, I mean, it's so good to see you out. That's what I meant to say."

Before she can ramble on even more, which I know she will, Zach interrupts. Thank god.

"Hey." He steps around me. "You're May's friend?"

Chim's eyes light up at the sight of him. She's a serious

equal-opportunity crusher. "I am . . . and Lucy's, too. Who are *you*?" She glances at me like *What are* you *doing with a strange cute boy I've never met*? which is annoying but also makes sense since I don't think I've made a new friend in years. Not that Zach's a friend.

Now Zach's cheeks light up. "Hey. Zach. I think I've seen you around school. I'm here because Conor . . . ? The singer? Is my best friend?" He says this like it's a question rather than a statement.

"Ooooh, cool. I heard he's awesome."

Zach shrugs. "He's decent, yeah."

Chim lays her hand on Zach's arm. His upper arm is defined and boyish and not at all like mine or Lucy's or Chim's. A knot plants itself in my throat even though it's stupid. I don't care about this guy. Chim can have him. They can run away together and get married and have stupid cute little babies. . . .

"May." Chim's waving her hand in front of my face. "Did you hear me?"

"Huh?"

"What do you want to drink?" She gestures to the bar.

"Oh. Right. Just ginger ale or whatever. Thanks."

Chim gives me a thumbs-up and walks away. I really do need to make more of an effort with her.

It's so loud in here. The room is small, and with every new note they play, the band's discord threatens to deafen me. They are awful. No two ways about it.

It's super dark and the crowd's getting bigger with every passing second. People start to press up against me, around me. When one particularly aggressive guy shoves his way by me, I'm jostled up against the bar. My heart starts pounding in my ears, louder than anything else in the room. Coming over here, into this mess of bodies, was a terrible idea. But staying at home, surrounded by all those letters I can't open and can't destroy, wouldn't have been any better.

I suck in a slow breath, blow it out, but it doesn't help. I start to get dizzy. My vision blurs. I'm trapped in the thick of all these people. No way out. Not safe here, not safe at home—everywhere I go, he follows me, the stain of that day follows me—there's no escaping.

With shaking hands, I reach into my bag to find my phone. I need to text Lucy. Ask her to please, *please,* come out here and save me.

I can't find it. It's nowhere in my bag. *Where is it? Breathe, May.* I push my hair off my face, but half of it plasters onto my forehead, wet and sticky.

I'm sweating. I'm trapped and I'm sweating.

I squeeze my eyes shut to block it all out—the noise and the people—but instead Jordan's face appears, like it's painted onto the back of my eyelids. At first, he smiles at me, that little smile that's so much like my own, and I want to jump into the picture, to hold him one more time. But as I continue to press my lids shut, the picture morphs and his head explodes, and the smile melts off his face, and then I feel myself falling.

CHAPTER TWENTY

Zach

I'm standing next to May, waiting for her intense friend to return and trying my best not to get super annoyed at the dude to my right who keeps bumping into me every five seconds. My biggest pet peeve about coming to Conor's shows—other than Matt, obviously—is the total lack of personal space. Like, can't this guy take a hint and move over? Respect my boundaries? It's like I'm invisible to him.

I'm starting to get aggravated, when I notice that May's not acting normal. Not that I'm sure what her normal is, of course, but she has her eyes closed and she's teetering back and forth like she can't quite find her center of gravity. For a moment I'm entranced—she's beautiful, almost serene—but all of a sudden, her face pales.

She tips backward, and for a second I'm not sure what's happening, but then my body reacts without consulting with my brain. I bolt to her side and wrap my arm around her shoulders to steady her toppling frame. Her eyes are blank, unfocused, staring at nothing. It's freaky. A shiver goes down my spine.

"May." My mouth is centimeters from her face, but I don't want to be an inappropriate jerk and think about that right now. "Are you okay?" I look around the room for help, but no one seems to notice that there's a girl fainting in the middle of the crowd. I tighten my grip on her shoulders and see a pocket of space farther down the bar, and an open stool.

I prop her under my arm and drag her over. My arm is killing me by the time we get there, but at least she's still on her feet.

"Sit here." I pat the stool.

Her eyes have an empty expression in them. I push her onto the seat and wave to the bartender, down at the other side of the bar.

When he comes over, he takes one look at May and raises his eyebrows. "Dude, is your girl okay?" He's a typical indie kid—tight black jeans, a sleeve of tattoos, and a very LA haircut.

I lean across the bar and shout, "She's fine. Can we get some water, please?"

He pauses, considers May's floppy form, and then reaches down and grabs a dripping bottle of water, which he plops onto the bar in front of him. "That'll be seven dollars."

I stare at him for a beat, because *excuse* me—you have

got to be kidding with that price. But I don't have much of a choice, so I grumble and dig into my pockets for a ten-dollar bill.

As the bartender hands me a paltry amount of change, he says, "Dude, just so you know, management doesn't look kindly on drugs in the club," and shoots a look at May that's supposed to, I assume, convey all this *meaning.*

"She's not on drugs, man."

He cocks an eyebrow and smirks. He clearly doesn't believe me, but he also obviously doesn't really care, because a second later he turns to get the order of the girl next to me and starts flirting hard-core with her.

I grit my teeth and turn back to May, holding out the bottle. "Can you drink this?"

She's still silent. Her eyelids flutter in a strange arrhythmic way. A few moments go by, and she looks worse and worse. Her whole body is shaking, and I have to help keep her propped on the stool. She really needs to drink this water.

"May!" I yell her name just as the Worst Band in the World plays the final note of their set and quiet falls over the bar. A bunch of people turn around, but for once there's something I care about more than my pride. Still, when I start speaking again, I lower my voice. "Hey, drink this, okay?" I crack the top and shove the bottle into her hands. "I opened it for you."

She takes a tiny sip.

"Good. Keep drinking. You okay?"

She slowly drinks the water, taking tiny sip after tiny sip. After many minutes, the color in her face is more human than ghost, but she's still silent. She shakes her head.

"What do you want to do? Do you want to stay here? I think Conor and them are about to go on." She shakes her head even harder. I don't know what to do. I'm not letting her leave the club alone. I tug at the ends of my hair and decide. "Okay, let's go."

She looks like she's surprised that I'm going with her.

"Is that cool? If I leave with you?" I'm trying to come up with a polite way to tell her that I don't think it's a great idea for her to leave alone, when she nods.

"Okay, cool. Can you . . . can you walk on your own now?"

She nods again.

"Great. All right, let's go." I motion for her to lead the way. I don't want to let her out of my sight. The color has almost returned to her face now, but I don't want to take a risk.

We slowly make our way out of the club and into the warm night air. I look up and down the street, trying to figure out where the hell to go. I've spent about two hours total of my life in downtown LA, so to say I don't know my way around would be a massive understatement. The block is empty, save for a few homeless people sitting next to shopping carts down near the other end of the street. There's a shady bar next door. The blue awning over its entrance is ripped and dirty. I make eye contact with the guy sitting on a stool next to its doorway and he glares back.

I turn to May. She's behind me, shuffling her feet. Under the light of the streetlamp, she's . . . hot.

Jesus, what is wrong *with me?*

I kick myself for having such a lame thought while she's standing there miserable. I'm a jerk. What I meant to think is that she looks *okay,* like almost normal again.

"Where do you want to go?" My ears are ringing from the noise of the club, and my voice comes out much louder than I intend.

She shrugs.

"All right . . ." I pull out my phone and start googling, trying to see if there's anything worth checking out in wherever-the-fuck-we-are DTLA. "We could try to get into that bar?" I nod my chin in the direction of its entrance, and the bouncer's scowl deepens. I wince. What am I even talking about? I don't have a fake ID. *God, Zach, stop being such a douche.*

She takes one look and shakes her head. I breathe a sigh of relief.

"Okay . . . let me see. . . ." I'm desperate to come up with a plan before she gets bored or remembers that she's supposed to hate me. "There's a place Conor mentioned to me on our way here that's close. Are you okay to walk? Or should we get a Lyft?" She seems steadier, but I'd rather not have her collapse on me halfway there.

She shifts on her feet and sighs. Then she speaks for the first time since we got outside. It's like she can't quite control the muscles in her throat, because her voice rips through the night air. "We can walk!" A look of surprise crosses her face.

I pause for a beat, not quite believing her—not quite knowing what I'm supposed to do. She frowns a little when she realizes that I'm frozen, like she wants to just get a move on. Her hands are balled into fists at her sides, but they're trembling. She glares at me and then starts walking. I have no choice but to follow. I try to stay close to her, to just let her know I'm here if she needs me.

We walk most of the way in silence, past bars and rundown buildings and an eclectic mix of people: old guys in expensive suits, people waiting in line to see bands play, and lots and lots of homeless people. It's hot as hell and getting muggy. Clouds gather in the sky, and it looks like it might rain for the first time in forever. May stops several times along the way with her arms wrapped tight around her body, staring up into the sky, listless. Each time, I want to reach out—to ground her with my touch—but I don't know if that would help her or if she'd freak out and punch me in the face.

About ten minutes in, something seems to shift inside her. She looks less like she's forcibly dragging her body along the sidewalk and more like she's regaining control. She blinks once, twice, like she's focusing on the world around her for the first time since leaving the club. She stops in the middle of the sidewalk with no warning. "Zach. Where the hell are we going?"

I flush. I'm glad she sounds more like herself, although

now that I'm being forced to say where we're going out loud, I realize that the place I've chosen could be construed as sort of nerdy. But in the moment I couldn't think of anywhere else . . . and who am I kidding—I *am* sort of nerdy. "It's called the Last Bookstore."

She raises her eyebrows. "That's a real place? It sounds like something from Harry Potter."

My mouth is dry, but I manage to choke out a laugh. "Yeah, it's real." God, what if she thinks I'm the biggest loser ever for taking her to a bookstore?

She shrugs. "All right. If you say so."

I glance at the map on my phone. "It's up here around the corner."

She gives me a long look, then shrugs and motions for me to lead the way.

CHAPTER TWENTY-ONE

May

Zach and I stand in front of massive iron doors that lead into the store, and all I can think about is how when Miles and I dated, the only places he ever took me were parties where we'd get wasted and do stupid shit. He never wanted to do anything else. Back then I didn't care; I liked getting fucked-up way too much. That's what our super-healthy relationship was built on—being cool and partying. He and I would arrive somewhere together, he'd run off with the other guys on the soccer team, and we'd meet up at the end of the night to make out. Shocking that we didn't get married, huh?

Lucy tried to get me to see that a couple times, but she stopped after it led to another awful fight one night when I was drunk. I told her that she needed to stop putting her shit on me, that she'd been brainwashed by her AA cult to think the rest of the world were all addicts too. That just because she couldn't have a good time without ruining everything around her didn't mean that I couldn't.

It wasn't my finest moment.

And I was so wrong.

The inside of the bookstore is more massive than I thought it would be. It's like they took the skeleton of an old bank building and removed all the boring walls and furniture and cubicles and replaced them with books, books, and more books. There's even a giant piece of art made entirely out of books hanging up high on one of the walls. Jordan would have had a field day in this place.

Zach has been silent since we walked in. He's wearing a dazed expression, like the sheer number of books overwhelms him. We've only gotten about ten steps inside because he keeps stopping to gape at everything. About a third of my body is still icy cold and sick feeling, and I hate it and all I want to do is walk and ignore it and not let Zach see even more of the brokenness inside me.

"*Hello?* Can we please keep moving?" I cringe—I sound like a bitch. Zach's cheeks get all red, and in any other circumstance it would be adorable, but right now I just need to *go.*

"Yes. Sorry. I . . ." He trails off and then shakes his head. "This place is awesome."

I shrug. "Yeah." I guess it's cute that he's so excited, but at the end of the day, it's a freaking bookstore, not the Grand Canyon or some Wonder of the World.

I follow him through the racks. He runs his fingers over

the spines of some of the books like he's making sure they're real. To me, they just look old and dusty. I've never been much of a read-for-fun person. Jordan's copy of *The Art of War* is the first book I read outside of school in years. Jordan, he was the reader. When we were little, he would try to get me interested in the stuff he'd read—but he was always so ahead of my reading level that it was impossible for me to keep up. I finally had enough in seventh grade, when he tried to start a banned book club, and wanted Lucy and me to join. Over summer break. When we were thirteen. He wanted the first book we read to be *Naked Lunch* by William S. Burroughs. I told him in no uncertain terms to fuck off.

"Want to go up?" Zach points to a sign in the far corner for the stairs to the second floor.

I nod.

The farther we move into the store, the bigger the stupid lump in my throat grows, until it feels impossible that my voice can fit around it.

That panic that dissipated when we left the bar is back, lingering around the edges of my mind. I grip the strap of my bag in my fist, and it digs deep into the center of my palm. I don't know what I'm doing here.

I wish I had stayed in tonight. I wish I could go back to last summer: me, alone, blocking out my thoughts with the drone of the television, only coming back to reality when Lucy would come over and we'd plan another attack on Michelle Teller's house. I only came alive that summer when we were out there, fighting against what happened in our own private way. Two girls against the world. I didn't look past it; I didn't want to. My entire existence was built on those moments. I didn't deserve a future.

Now here I am, in my undeserved future, without Jordan, with Michelle Teller's kid by my side.

Lost.

I grip the rail of the staircase in my shaking hand and make my way up to the second floor behind Zach, watching the back of his shirt rise and fall in time with his breath.

CHAPTER TWENTY-TWO

Zach

When we get to the second floor, I realize that while the downstairs was cool, *this* part of the store is freaking awesome. In front of us, there's a tilted bookshelf designed to look like it has books flying out of it like seagulls.

I peek over the railing, down to the first floor. It's huge. Rows and rows of books and stacks of vinyl albums and all these people browsing: it reminds me of a long time ago when my dad was around—like, mentally speaking—and he would take me to the Northridge Mall on Sundays and let me roam around the bookstore there. Gwen was too little, and my mom was always working, even then, so the outings were always just him and me; we would spend hours together, not talking, at peace, lost in our separate worlds. Those are some of the last decent memories I have of my father.

I wander through a door and into a maze of bookshelves and then through this awesome little tunnel that's built out of books. Beyond that, there's another door, and I'm about to walk through when a hand grasps my arm. I've been so lost in my own thoughts that I jump in surprise and almost knock over a bunch of stacked books.

I turn back to see if May is as impressed as I am but she's stark white—almost as bad as she was at the bar. And here I am, nerding out, ignoring her.

Great job, Zach. Way to show this girl you aren't a jerk.

"Are you okay?" My voice cracks on the word *okay,* my worry seeping through.

She shakes her head. She looks like she might cry. Her face is crumpling, the bravery that she forced into it on our walk over from the club slipping.

"Shit. Are you okay?" I'm trying to figure out what to do. May pulls on the sleeve of my shirt and points behind her, toward the exit. *Obviously* we should leave this small, cramped space. Obviously. I'm an idiot.

I take her arm and her body steadies a little. We trace our way back through the tunnel and the maze and out into the main area, with its open spaces and high ceilings. I lead her over to a corner far away from the other shoppers, and she slides down the wall onto the floor. Her breathing is heavy. She lowers her head between her legs, elbows propped on her thighs.

Her back rises and falls, and it sounds like she's gasping for air. She needs to calm down or she's going to hyperventilate.

I sit down next to her at a total loss, before I realize that doing pretty much anything is better than nothing. I pull her to me and stroke her hair like I do Gwenie's when she wakes up from a nightmare in the middle of the night.

We sit like that for a few minutes, silent, and May's breathing slows. I lean my head back against the wall and wonder if this is all my fault.

"I'm so sorry." Her eyes squeeze together tight, and her voice sounds small and raspy. Most of her hair drapes around her head like a curtain, but some of it's caught behind her ear, so I can still see part of her face. She looks so young. Not like someone old enough to have gone through the shit that she did.

"I don't know what's wrong with me." She chews on her bottom lip. "It's just . . . I have this thing with small spaces. I don't know. I never used to, but now I can't stand the feeling . . . it's like being trapped."

I don't know what to say. It's like when Conor's uncle, who he was super close to when we were little, died in a horrible motorcycle accident and all I could do was mumble *Sorry, man* to him. So ineffective. So useless. Story of my life.

I clear my throat. "Is that because . . . because . . ." I trail off.

She ducks her head. "Yeah. That day . . . I was in the closet forever. I don't even know how long I was in there. It was so small and so dark, and all I could hear were booms and screams, and I was so sure that any second the door was going to open. . . ." Her voice catches and she trails off. Her jaw clenches.

I tighten my arm around her shoulders. There's nothing I can say that will make it better. I stare out into the main part of the store and think about how I'll never be able to forgive my mother for her part in all this. Not ever.

CHAPTER TWENTY-THREE

May

I've never talked about any of this. Not with the therapist they made me go see, not with Lucy or Grann, no matter how hard they tried to get me to open up, and especially not with my parents. And yet, right now, I can't stop myself. Zach's silence has this weird pull on me, and his arm around my shoulders has unlocked something deep inside my chest.

It's been so long since I've been touched.

"I hid in there, you know. I left all those other kids out there and I stayed in the closet and let it happen. I left my *brother* out there; I left him out there to die."

I was in that closet, searching for an extra music stand, all slow and hungover from hanging out with Chim the night before, when I heard David come into the room—heard Mr. Oppenheimer say, *Ecchles, you aren't in this class*—and then a boom and then the screams. All the screams. I tucked my head between my knees and stayed in there, in that closet. Shoved my hands against my ears and tried to block out the sounds coming from the other room, the cries, Mr. Oppenheimer's voice pleading, *Stop, please stop, shoot me instead,* more shots.

And then, silence.

The silence was the worst. It felt louder than anything that preceded it; it pressed against my entire body like a vise.

They found me in there, hours later, long after most of the other students had been pulled out of the school, long after the cops had discovered David Ecchles hiding out in a restroom on the second floor, too much of a coward to blow his own brains out like he was supposed to.

When they found me, I couldn't unball my body; it was like all my muscles had frozen in place.

They had to pick me up and carry me out of the building like that. I kept my eyes wide open as they took me through the room where the bodies had been. I knew I needed it burned into my brain, knew I deserved to have that picture carved into my mind with the sharpest instrument possible so it would stay with me for the rest of my life.

I left them all out there to die.

"You know it's not your fault, right?" Zach's voice tears me out of my thoughts, out of the play-by-play, the one that starts up at night when I forget to leave music on, when silence snakes its way through my head. The recitation of names: *Juliet Nichols . . . Madison Kim . . . Mr. Oppenheimer . . . Marcus Neilson . . . Britta Oliver . . . Michael Graves . . .*

Jordan.

When I'm stronger and more awake, I don't let most of

those names pass through my mind. Never. I block them out with all my might and what little self-preservation I have left.

"It *is* my fault." Saying those words out loud is like ripping my heart out and offering it to Zach; like handing over my most absolute truth. "It's all my fault."

Zach's eyes are worried.

"What can I do?"

I shake my head. "Rewind time?" I give a bitter laugh. "Nothing. There's nothing anyone can do."

"Look. I know this isn't the same thing, but I spent a long time letting everyone at school tell me it was my fault that my mom took this case, that somehow Gwen and I were to blame for her actions. I let them convince me of that." He leans his head back against the wall and closes his eyes. His lashes are long and black, like little butterflies landed on his eyelids and decided to make them their home. My heart skips a beat. I look away, out into the store.

A couple people walk in our direction, heading down the stairs. I should be embarrassed, sitting here with mascara streaked under my eyes, but as with most things in life over the past year, I can't summon up the energy to care.

I listen to Zach talk; I know he's trying to make me feel better. It's nice of him, even if it's fruitless. In the last few months, not many people have tried. I think everyone got tired of worrying about a girl who might punch them in the face at the slightest provocation.

Zach continues, "I decided tonight that I'm sick of it. I'm

sick of letting Matt make me feel like shit. Of letting him hold my mom over my head, like *I* did something, like I have any control over what she does. I tried to tell her not to take the case!" His face gets red. "I told her it would ruin my life. That if she didn't care about me, at least she should care about Gwenie, who was going into ninth grade . . . going to a whole new school." His hands ball into fists. "But she doesn't care. She doesn't care about us. She only cares about herself."

He takes a deep breath. "Sorry. What I'm trying to say is that I'm done thinking it's my fault. That I can control her actions. And what that asshole David Ecchles did? The fact that he's a total psycho? That isn't *your* fault."

I open my mouth to tell him that he's wrong, that it *is* my fault. I left all those people out there to die, including my twin brother. I stayed in that closet, too hungover to move, and let him die. Before I can get the words out, the lights of the store flicker and a voice overhead informs us that the store is closing in ten minutes.

Zach glances at his watch. "Whoa. It's ten o'clock." He jumps to his feet and holds a hand out. I reluctantly take it, and he pulls me up. "I think the show might be over." He pulls his phone out of the pocket of his jeans and checks it. "Fuuuuck. He left me." He runs a hand through his hair. "I'm stuck."

A part of me wants to ditch him in this bookstore. He's getting to me; I can feel it. That evil little part of me wants to run down the stairs away from him, find Lucy, and pretend that none of this ever happened. He's digging his way into my heart, and I hate him for it.

Apparently there's a tiny bit of decency left in me, because instead I say that I'll call Lucy and see if he can catch a ride with us. But after I rummage deep into my bag and finally locate my phone, I see that she's already gone too.

I tell him Lucy left. "Nice friends we have." I roll my eyes. "Whatever. We can use my Lyft account. I don't care if my parents pay for us to get home. It's the least they can do."

He's nervous. "Are you sure? I don't want to get you in trouble."

"Please. Like they give a shit." I'm sure they don't even know I'm out of the house for the first time in months. I'm sure they aren't even home to notice that I'm not there. I smirk at the thought and start down the stairs. As I walk away from Zach, the protective skin that I developed over the past year begins to regrow over me like a comfortable coat of armor. Any stupid feelings that started to creep in this evening fade with every step I take.

When we get downstairs, the store is empty, and out the front windows I see that it's pouring rain.

CHAPTER TWENTY-FOUR

Zach

When I reach the exit, May's waiting. She nods to the window. "Look."

It's pouring. In Los Angeles we so rarely see rain that it's always a surprise. When Gwen was little and it rained, she'd go outside buck naked, wearing her rain boots and nothing else, and jump in as many puddles as possible. After, she'd track muddy footprints all over the house. My mom used to have a conniption fit, but as soon as she was done cleaning up after Gwen, they'd cuddle on the couch and drink hot chocolate together.

These days, she'd be at work still. When my dad lost his job, my mom's work hours ramped up and up and up until they were all-consuming, until they took away her weekends. Until they took her away from us.

"I called a Lyft," May says.

A man wearing thick black-framed glasses and a name tag

walks over. "Hey, guys. I hate to do this, but we're locking up." He motions to the front door. "If you're waiting for a ride, there's an awning out front that you can hang under."

"All right. No worries. Thanks." I open the door and we walk out to the sidewalk.

May wraps her arms around her chest. "Ugh, it's freezing out here." She's shivering in her thin T-shirt. "It's been so hot, I didn't even bother to look at the weather." She seems worn out. Younger. More like she probably used to—approachable, not a ball of simmering rage.

It gives me the courage to close the distance between us and reach out to her like I did when we were back inside.

She flinches. "*Excuse* me?"

I drop my arm in a hurry. I suck at reading signals. "I'm sorry. I was just going to . . . Ugh, sorry. I thought maybe if I put my arm around you, we'll both be warmer till the car gets here?" My voice cracks. I sound like an idiot. What is my problem? Why can't I act like a normal human being?

"Oh, *did* you? You thought we'd be *warmer*?" She sounds a little less annoyed, and I start to relax. "For future reference, you might want to *ask* before you try to touch me. Or any girl, for that matter." She cuts me a side-eye. "Before, back in there, when I was upset, that was one thing, but this is another."

I bite my lip. "You're right. I'm sorry. I didn't . . ." I trail off. "I don't normally try to touch random girls, you know. . . ."

"Now I'm random?"

"No!" *Shut up, Zach.* "You're not random at all. You're the opposite of random. Like, unrandom. Is that a word?"

She shakes her head like she's trying not to laugh. At least my idiocy is good for something.

I continue. "Anyway, you said you're cold, and I'm sort of cold, and they say you can huddle together for heat. I'm pretty sure I saw that on the History Channel or something. So that was my train of thought. . . . I didn't mean to invade your personal space. That's not cool at all. I'm sorry."

"You already said that."

I blush. I hate my fair skin and how red it gets when I blush, like a smashed tomato. "Sorry." I roll my eyes. "I mean— Sorry. Fuck! Why can't I stop saying that?"

She's full-on laughing now. "You're a mess."

I shrug. "I haven't exactly socialized a lot in the past few months. My skills are rusty."

She laughs again and then shivers hard. "Okay, fine. Whatever. It is super cold. C'mere with that arm."

I nod and try to suppress the giant grin that threatens to pop onto my face. I wrap my arm around her shoulders and pull her close, and all of my body ignites and I'm not cold at all anymore. Not even a little bit.

The rain is coming down even harder now; the droplets shimmer in the streetlights as they fall to the ground. I've gone from babbling to mute; my brain short-circuited as soon as my skin connected with May's. She's quiet too, and I swear to god I can feel her heart beating through her skin. Her face is raised toward the night sky, her eyes closed. She is beautiful.

I take a breath and start to lean toward her. I'm not trying to kiss her; I just want to be closer to her. Her lips part and her tongue darts out of her mouth to catch drops of rain. She is peaceful for the first time tonight. I could stare at her forever.

The moment is interrupted by the sweep of headlights. A Toyota pulls over to the curb, and one of its windows rolls down. The driver calls, "You guys waiting for a Lyft? Last name McGintee?"

"Yes!" May darts away. I watch her go, trying to pull myself together before I follow her to the car.

The next morning, I wake early. Normally on Saturdays I sleep until at least ten, but this morning all I want to do is lie here in bed and think about last night. Some people (Conor) might call it obsessing, but I feel like hanging out with May shifted something inside me. I spent so long turning myself off in every way possible, letting people like Matt control me. I feel alive for the first time in months. I even got the courage to ask for her number before the Lyft dropped her off last night, and I'm way too proud of myself for it.

I pull my phone off my bedside table and see that it's seven a.m. Before I can think better of it, before I can consider that it's still practically the middle of the night, I type out a quick text to May and hit send.

What're you up to later?

I refuse to think that she didn't feel what I felt last night.

I don't care if she thinks she's broken.

I know she's not.

CHAPTER TWENTY-FIVE

May

I wake up at the butt crack of dawn. I always do now. Sleep and I don't get along, not anymore.

My nightmares last night weren't as vivid as they are sometimes, plotwise. Instead they left a trail of colors in my mind—reds and reds and more reds.

And after the colors have started to fade, my first conscious thought of the morning enters my head: *Jordan would have liked Zach.*

I don't know where it comes from. It's stupid. Not just for me, for Zach. I could tell, standing there on the street waiting for the car to come, that something was happening between us, but it doesn't matter. I don't care. That's what I told myself, over and over, last night on the way home: *I don't care.*

And now this thought, straight from my traitorous brain.

I grab my phone to see what ungodly hour it is, and a text from Zach pops up. I throw the phone back on my bed like it burned me. What is he, psychic? I cover my eyes with my hands, and a few minutes later, when I peek out, the text is still there. It hasn't magically disappeared, which is really just rude of it.

Crap.

A second later, a (2) pops up next to Zach's name. Another text. This is getting out of hand. To stop my phone from buzzing again, I read them.

The first message asks what I'm doing tonight, and the second apologizes for sending the first one so early.

I sigh, click to my Instagram, and see he's sent a request to follow me. *Jesus.* He's all up in my business this morning. There's not much to see on my account—I deleted all the dumb pictures I had posted over the last couple years of me and Chim and Miles partying together, leaving behind a few relics of Lucy playing the drums and Jordan playing the guitar. I can't help myself, though; I accept Zach and then click on his name and see that his page isn't private (who doesn't have a private account? Creeps, celebrities, and Zach, apparently). He hasn't posted many photos recently, but when I scroll down to his posts from last year, it's like the page of a very different person. There are pictures of him and Matt; him at Conor's shows hanging with the band; him with that girl I keep seeing with the band, kissing her on the cheek and making goofy faces. (Excuse me? *Who* is this girl?) In all of them, he's . . . happy. His smile doesn't have that sadness around its edges that it does now. A sadness most people would miss but that I recognize because I've seen it in the mirror, on my own face.

Goddammit. Now I feel sorry for the guy. It really isn't his fault that his mom is such an asshole. He doesn't deserve everyone's hatred. It's not fair that he has to deal with all that while I get pity and sad smiles.

I throw myself back onto my pillow and heave a sigh, then click back to his message and start typing.

Pick me up at 8.

A text bubble pops up a split second later. The guy is definitely not suave.

Great!! ☺

I could have done without the exclamation points and the emoji. There's no way this is going to end well, but when have I ever done anything that ended well?

See you then. Don't be late.

The doorbell rings at eight o'clock sharp as I'm pulling on my jeans. I haven't left my room for more than ten minutes today. I spent most of the afternoon texting Lucy, telling her about my date . . . or nondate . . . or whatever the fuck it is. She, predictably, was ecstatic. She was all like *I am taking credit for all of this. You had better name your firstborn after me.* To which I responded: *You need serious professional help.* I mean, honestly.

I'm walking out of my bedroom to answer the front door,

but my mom gets there first. *Dammit dammit dammit.* I didn't think she was home.

I rush down the stairs and find her standing in the hallway, talking to Zach. It's weirdly déjà-vu-esque, seeing the two of them there chatting.

When she hears me behind her, she turns and raises her eyebrows, a curious expression on her face. I know what she's thinking. No one but Lucy has visited me in almost a year. A hole opens up deep in the pit of my stomach. This is a bad idea.

Before everything, before last year, this would have gone differently. Jordan would have been here, smirking at my nervousness. We would have spent the hour before Zach arrived gossiping about him—going through his social media and discussing every picture in detail. My mom would have been downstairs, making dinner, drinking a glass of wine, maybe listening to some music. That's how it was when Miles entered the picture, at first. But once we'd been dating for a few months, Jordan started to hate Miles, hate who I became when I was around him, hate that I drank so much and lost myself. It got to the point that every time Miles was set to arrive, Jordan would lock himself in his room after giving me yet another sad look. He saw what was happening to me before I did. I didn't want to see that Miles wasn't good for me—that we weren't good *together*—because for the first time, I had my own life, my own friends, my own space to breathe. So I ignored it, and ignored Jordan's looks and Lucy's comments and my own goddamn brain. Ignored it all, until it was too late.

I lock eyes with my mom, standing by the door, so small these days, hunched, as if she's forgotten how to stand up straight, and she smiles at me with sad eyes. It pierces me to my core. It's like she's saying *Look at you, moving on, going out, making friends.* And I know Jordan will never be able to do any of those things, and I want to curl into myself and never open up.

I'm about to tell Zach that I can't do this, I can't go, when this wide smile spreads across his face. And something in it makes me feel like he sees *me,* instead of an angry, fucked-up girl or a warped reflection of my dead brother. So even though I don't deserve any of this, I end up in his car.

"Your mom seems nice." He sounds nervous. Of all the things he could have chosen to say. I have to hold myself back from snapping at him, being rude right out of the gate. He doesn't know. *He doesn't know.* I repeat it in my head over and over.

I must pause for an awkwardly long time, because once I manage to dig myself out of my head to respond, he's staring at me with a concerned expression. We're still parked outside my house.

I raise an eyebrow. "What?" It comes out sharp, like a snap.

He hesitates before answering. "You okay?"

I grimace. "Yes. I'm fine." I cross my arms over my chest

and grumble, "Why are we still sitting here? Are we going to hang out in front of my house all night?"

He taps his fingers against his steering wheel, drumming out a beat. "No. Of course not . . ." He hesitates before continuing, "You zoned out there for a minute. I was trying to tell you something, but it was like you didn't even hear me."

I roll my eyes. "I'm fine. *Jesus Christ.* Can we please just go?" What does this guy want from me? I gave him the wrong impression at the bookstore last night. I'm not into sharing my deep, dark thoughts with friends I've known for years, never mind boys I've known for, like, a minute. I mean, calm down, guy. Just because you saved me from some panic attacks—which, *fine,* was a decent thing to do—doesn't mean I *owe* you anything. I don't owe you a window into my damaged psyche. This isn't some fairy tale where you're going to swoop in and save me. I'm way too far gone for that shit, and I'm not ten years old. I know those stories are a bunch of crap.

I glance over at him, and he has the expression of a boy who just saw someone kick his kitten. All the fight drains out of me. I slump down in my seat and sigh. "Sorry." I push my hand through my hair. "I'm not good at this."

"At what?"

"Like, generally speaking, talking to people."

"Yeah, well. Me either. Like I said last night, I'm out of practice."

I give a little laugh. "You think *you're* out of practice? Last year I basically spoke to five people, total."

He glances at me as he puts the car into drive. "Yeah . . . Why weren't you in school until this semester?" He winces. "Is that a dumb question? Obviously it makes sense you wouldn't want to go back. . . ."

I sigh. "Look, the reason I wasn't in school is pretty much common knowledge. You could ask almost anyone from my old school and they'd be able to tell you."

He raises his eyebrows, questioning.

I sigh. "Okay, well, after the stuff that happened last year, I was really angry. . . ."

"You had every right—"

I hold up my hand, stopping him. "Let me finish, okay?"

Zach nods. He turns the car onto a side street. The road is dark and nearly deserted.

I look out my window, away from him, into the night. "Like I said. After everything last year, I was angry." I close my eyes for a moment, try to remember to breathe.

"And when they reopened school, everyone wanted to be my friend all of a sudden—people who'd never talked to me before would come up to me in the halls all *May, are you okay, how are you doing, blah blah blah*—like they wanted to feed off what happened to me, make it more their own. It was disgusting. I started getting into fights. Like, a lot of fights. Principal Rose-Brady gave me a ton of chances, because . . . well, you know. Everyone felt sorry for me.

"So yeah. I was skipping class all the time. Fighting a lot. It's not like I was just randomly kicking people's asses, though, you know. I was trying to help people. To stand up for people who needed someone on their side. That's what no one seems to understand. I was trying to defend people who needed help, even if they didn't think they did. I owed the world that much. But Rose-Brady didn't see it that way. All she saw was me punching this asshole in the face after he tried to join the shitty grief group they set up at school. . . . She wouldn't even listen to why I did it. How messed up is that?" My hands are shaking in my lap.

It's like I'm back there that day, sitting in that stupid group they basically forced me to go to, determined to mind my own business for once, to keep my head down. The second letter from the jail had arrived in my mailbox the night before, and all I wanted to do was shut my brain off and pretend none of this was happening. Then someone came into the room late and the door slammed behind them. My heart raced. . . . I almost dropped to the ground and wrapped my arms around my head. Instead I turned toward the noise, because that was what I'd started forcing myself to do—confront situations instead of hiding. Instead of hiding like a fucking baby.

I saw this guy, Jake, enter the room. He was kind of an idiot, and big. Mean. A bully. He was friends with David. No joke. *Friends.* And he thought he could just come into the room and *grieve* with everyone else? He thought he would be welcomed here? I waited for a second—waited for someone to tell him to get out. Someone to fucking *say* something.

They all just stayed silent, as usual. That's what everyone always does. They stay silent and pretend everyone's the same—that we all went through the *same thing*—that everyone in the building was affected in the exact same way that day.

And then Jake sat down, and I lost it.

It wasn't the first time I'd exploded in those months after, not by any means, but it was the most vicious. The most violent. I blacked out. I don't remember much after I jumped on Jake's back, ripping at his face with my nails, other than hands on me, dragging me back, wrapping around me tight, holding down my arms.

And then I was in Rose-Brady's office and my mom was there, somehow, and then I was at home. I never saw Jake again, and I never went back there, to that school filled with ghosts and demons, and god, I am so glad.

Later, I found out it was Chim who pulled me off him, who held me down and forced me to stop before I did something I couldn't come back from.

I never thanked her.

CHAPTER TWENTY-SIX

Zach

May's gotten quiet, and I'm not sure what to do to lighten the mood. I pull the car into a parking lot and turn the engine off. She doesn't react. She's a million miles away—her hands are balled into tight fists and she's staring straight ahead out the windshield, into the dark of the night.

I have no idea what to do, so I say in a voice that sounds way too loud and fake, "We're here!"

She jumps and blinks a few times, coming back to the present. She looks around. "Um. Where the hell are we? I thought we were getting food?" It's quiet outside the car, and the parking lot is deserted. If you squint, you can make out the dim silhouette of a playground in the distance.

Now that we're here, my plan seems stupid. I thought it would be romantic, coming to a playground at night. Like something out of one of those '80s movies I used to watch with my dad. I imagined me pushing her on a swing, her letting go of everything she's been holding on to, us having this intense, deep conversation about life. It's the sort of thing Rosa would have loved when we were together. Instead, looking out into the pitch-black night, seeing how quiet it is on the playground, how desolate, how dark, I realize my mistake. I'm trying my best not to make eye contact with May, because I'm totally embarrassed.

After a couple moments, she waves a hand in front of my face. "Hellooooo? Anyone in there? What are we doing here?"

I rub my forehead and glance over at her. "I thought it would be romantic," I mumble.

A grin flits across May's mouth. "You thought *what* would be romantic?"

"Uhhh . . . taking you to a playground at night? I thought maybe it would be different than just going to a diner and getting food. Like something out of a John Hughes movie."

"Who?" May furrows her brow.

I rub the nape of my neck. "The director . . . ? Never mind. I'm an idiot. I thought there'd be other people around, and, like, streetlamps or something. Instead it's all dark and silent and empty. . . ." I allow a smile. "It's like a scene from the beginning of *Law & Order, SVU.*"

At that, May shrinks toward the window.

"No, no," I backtrack. "I mean, just the setting—like, a dark park. Not that our night is going to go that direction . . ." She's staring at me like I have eight heads. "Oh god, of course it's not! I don't even know why I said that." *Why can't I just shut up?* "I'm so sorry. I shouldn't be allowed to speak. Never mind. Please just ignore me. If you want to get a Lyft home from here, I get it." I drop my head onto the steering wheel.

I hear a cough, and then May's laughing. Full-body, tears-in-her-eyes laughing. She even snorts.

It's awesome.

I start to snicker. "I know . . . I know. Really special of me, right? I thought this through super well."

She wipes her eyes. "I mean, I appreciate the effort, but yeah, it's a little creepy. Maybe I'm just not that romantic of a person, but I'm more into places with lights and, like, civilization." She considers me. "God, we are both such freaks. I'm glad I met you, Teller. Even if your mom is an asshole. I haven't laughed like that in years."

My heart skips a beat.

"By the way." She grins. "I got your Instagram request."

I fidget in my seat, hoping she doesn't think I was too aggressive. I know she got it—she accepted this morning. I scrolled her page all the way back to the beginning of her photos, which wasn't hard since she hasn't posted anything in the last eleven months and before that they're sparse, at best.

"Can I ask . . ." She trails off and clears her throat. "You don't have to answer if it's weird or something, but who's that girl?"

I know who she's talking about, of course. I sigh to myself.

She continues, "I've seen her around the band—she was at the drummer auditions and then at the show. I thought she was Matt's girlfriend, but then I saw this pic of you guys kissing . . . ?" She's examining her nails like she's trying to act like she doesn't care, but I think maybe she does care, at least a little.

I sigh out loud this time. I should have deleted that shit. "Yeah. That's my ex-girlfriend. She *is* dating Matt now, you're not wrong about that."

She grimaces. "Oh man. That guy seems like a total dick."

"Yeah, he's the worst. But it's sort of my fault they're together. When my mom decided to defend the shooter"—May winces—"Rosa had a big problem with it. It got to the point where we couldn't have a conversation without her bringing it up. So I told her I needed some space, and next thing I know she's dating Matt. And that's pretty much the story of my life since it all went down with my mom."

May's quiet for a moment. "Look, I'm sorry. About how I treated you after I found out about—"

I cut her off. "I should have told you instead of being so shady."

She shakes her head. "I mean, yeah, you should have—at least then my freak-out would have been in private instead of in the middle of fucking *drama* class—but I don't know that I would have handled it any better." She pauses and then says something I never thought I'd hear anyone other than Conor say: "I'm sorry that you're dealing with this. It's not your fault."

My throat constricts. I grip the steering wheel tight. It's silent in the car for a few moments. I'm trying not to cry; May is lost in thought.

Then she slaps her hands on her thighs, breaking the mood. "All right, well, there has to be something better to do than this." She gestures out her window into the black.

"I think Conor's playing some open-mike night at that new coffee shop. . . . We could go to that?" I cringe. Is it possible for me to have a life without piggybacking on Conor's?

"Oh yeah. Lucy mentioned that she's going." May smirks at me. "By the way, over/under on them dating?"

I snort. "Conor doesn't date . . . but I get the feeling Lucy doesn't either?"

"Definitely not."

"They're perfect for each other."

"Totally. Although she's usually more into girls. But we'll see, I guess." She sighs. "I nix the show option. After last night, I think I'm going to avoid crowded places for a while."

"Fair enough."

She shrugs. "Want to just go back to my house?"

Dammit, Zach, you dumbass. Way to bomb the night. I nod, trying to hide my disappointment and pretend I'm super chill with the night ending so early.

We pull up outside her house. Her family lives a few towns over from mine, not that towns really exist in the Valley, which is basically a sprawling suburb over the hill from the city of Los Angeles. I haven't spent much time over here. I never had a need, or a way of getting here, really. I got my license less than a year ago, and before that it was hard. Gwen and I depended on the school bus a lot. It's not like our parents were available to take us places.

I put my car in park and plaster on a smile, waiting for the inevitable goodbye with a sinking feeling in my stomach. Instead, she turns with a questioning grin.

"Are you planning to leave the car on while we're inside?"

"Oh . . . OH. You want me to come in?" My palms get sweaty, and my heart starts thudding in my chest.

She shrugs. "I mean, it's only been thirty minutes since you picked me up. . . . You don't have to, but I thought . . ." She trails off. "My mom's already gone out somewhere." And under her breath, "As usual."

"Your mom went out?" My voice ends with a squeak. Real smooth.

She rolls her eyes. "Calm down, nerd. I didn't mean it like *that.*"

"No, I didn't think . . . I know! I wasn't . . ." *SHUT UP, ZACH.* God, sometimes I want to throw myself out the closest open window.

She laughs. "It's fine. C'mon." She unbuckles her seat belt and swings open the car door. I sit there for a second, trying to get myself together. When I thought about tonight, I never thought we'd end up at her house . . . *alone.*

Alone. With *May.*

Fuck.

But she's standing there in front of my car waiting for me, so I swallow my nervousness as best I can and get out of the car.

I'm hyperaware of my surroundings in a way I wasn't when I came to pick her up: The three small palm trees that stand to the side of the driveway where May's car is parked. The brick path that leads up to the front door, which is painted red, and chipping at the edges. Then I notice May in front of me, the way her hair moves as she walks, and I forget about everything else and follow her inside.

Sure enough, her mom left during the half hour we were gone. May gives me a tour of the house, winding in and out of the downstairs rooms. Everything is neat and tidy, not in the sense that someone picked up recently, more like everything looks pristine and untouched. Like this isn't a place where living, breathing humans reside. Silver-framed photos hang on the living room walls, full of May and her family posed stiffly, wearing tight, fake smiles. They look professionally shot. In almost all of them, Jordan is standing behind May with his hands on her shoulders. They look so much alike.

May clears her throat and starts to speak. Her voice is so quiet I have to lean in to hear her. "After . . . the stuff that happened, my parents had this crew of professional . . . I don't know what you'd call them . . . organizers, maybe? . . . take everything of Jordan's out of the house. His books . . . his sheet music . . . anything that wasn't in his bedroom the day it happened. They had this crew come in and do a sweep of the house and put it all in storage. Except his room. They left that untouched, like they couldn't bear to go in there and move anything. And his guitars . . ." Her eyelids look heavy for a moment, but she blinks, and the moment's gone. She shakes her head.

She leads me upstairs and stops in front of a closed door.

"We don't go in there. His room." Her voice shakes with nerves. "I used to. Right after everything, I slept in there a bunch. I couldn't believe that he was gone. That I wouldn't wake up and find him sitting at the foot of the bed, looking at me like *What are you doing sleeping in my room?*" She pauses, staring down at her feet. "Then there was one morning a few weeks after . . . I overslept, and my parents didn't know where I was. My mom found me in here and . . . Jesus." She rubs her forehead. "It was like she'd seen a ghost." Her jaw clenches. "Anyway, we haven't gone in since. None of us. It's been almost a year, and this is the closest I've come to setting foot inside."

And then she reaches out and opens the door.

She's crying.

I reach out and hover my hand over her back, trying to give her something—some support—without physically touching her. I want her to know that I'm here, right behind her—that I'm here and I'm not going anywhere.

We both stand in the doorway, silent. The room in front of

us is lonely, unused, like an abandoned museum. Textbooks shoved into the shelf under the window. A half-made bed on the far wall. It's pretty obvious that no one has been in here in ages: unlike the rest of the house, which is so clean you could eat off its floors, a thick layer of dust covers the furniture. The desk, the bureau, the bedside table, all coated in gray.

May grips the wood doorframe and then leans against it like it's holding up her entire being. She's staring at the guitar that's propped against Jordan's desk. "They brought that back." Her voice is tight, coming out in chokes. "After." She blinks hard. "After . . . what happened. It was still at the school. In that room. I saw it . . . I *saw it* when they carried me out of that fucking room, Zach. I kept my eyes open, and I saw his guitar." Her tears start to fall faster, and she rubs her face hard with her palms, wiping them away. "It was lying there. Like he had dropped it, right before . . . There was blood everywhere. . . ." Her body shakes with a sob. "I miss him so much."

I close the distance between us. Put my arms around her. Pull her toward me. Say the first thing that comes into my head.

"I wish I'd known him."

May pulls away and looks at me. Her face crumples and falls again, but not in a bad way, in a way that makes me think that maybe, for once in my life, I said the right thing.

"Do you know . . . ?" Her voice breaks, and she clears her throat again and again. She's trying so hard to hold it together, and I want to tell her she doesn't have to, that she can break, that I'll help pick up the pieces, but no words come. "There were so many times I wished he didn't exist. And now that he doesn't . . . all I want is to see him one more time." She puts her hands over her face. "Jesus. I've never said that out loud. How fucking awful am I?"

"Hey. Do you know how many times I've wished my mom would just disappear?" I ask.

About a trillion. Last year, when she took the case and my life became a living hell, I spent ninety percent of my waking hours wishing I'd been born into a different family, a different life. "It's normal. I know it's hard to realize that right now, but it's normal to think that way. I promise."

"Yeah. I guess." She stares blankly into the room, like her mind is a million miles from here. "You know, the weekend before everything, he showed up at this party where I was. At least, that's the story according to *some* people." Her face pales. She rubs her temples like she has a horrible headache.

Whoa. "Jesus. That's . . ." I don't even know how to end that sentence. Goose bumps rise on my arms. I wrinkle my forehead. "What do you mean 'some people'?"

She shakes her head. "I mean"—her nostrils flare— "my ex-boyfriend. This guy Miles. He told me that. A few days after the shooting. He claimed that he saw David. With me. That we were talking." She takes a deep breath before continuing. "That night, I wasn't exactly in my right mind. I don't remember much of anything after the first hour." Some expression crosses her face, but it's gone before my brain can register it. "I was drunk. Like, really drunk. Blacked out." Her eyes meet mine, and they're narrow, defensive, like she thinks I'm going to judge her. I make sure my expression remains impassive. "It wasn't a onetime thing either. I had my first drink in ninth grade, and I liked it. Too much, probably. My friend Chim, too. The two of us were at every party, drinking, popping whatever was handed to us. My ex"—she pauses for a moment, then pushes forward—"Miles. He was part of the problem. If you talked to him, he'd try to convince you that he's this pillar of decency, but I hear things, even now—him at parties, with his fucking friends from the soccer team—it's like they think they're going to live forever." She gives a bitter laugh. "I used to think I would too."

She lets out a long sigh. "Anyway. Lucy and Jordan both hated it—the way Chim and I would get so fucked-up, do stupid things. Jordan would come with us sometimes, to parties, like he thought we needed him to babysit, which always pissed me off. Even though maybe he was right." She pauses, looks at the floor. When she looks back up at me, her eyes are glistening. "Anyway. Either he'd drive us home or we'd call Lucy for a ride. She's sober—her dad used to be this mean drunk before he got into AA—and she'd tell us we were better than all that. I never believed her. I wish I had. Stopped all that shit. Spent that time with her and Jordan, being a decent human, instead of getting mad at the two of them for trying to help. Like an asshole."

I want to say something, but I can't seem to string words

together in my brain in any sequence that makes sense. I want to say the exact right thing, the thing that will take away all her pain and her grief and her guilt, but I know those words don't exist. Instead, there in the doorway of her brother's room, I reach out and take her hand, and we stand there, silent, looking at his dust-covered furniture.

CHAPTER TWENTY-SEVEN

May

Maybe it's the way Zach seems like he's listening to me rather than just waiting to talk, but something makes me want to tell him things. I haven't talked about Jordan with anyone since he died, and tonight I can't stop. I tell Zach about the pranks we used to play on our parents when we were younger, before Jordan's extracurricular activities took over our lives, activities that I was a part of before my parents seemed to realize that I'd never catch up to him. That I'd never be on his level. It was like this unspoken, gradual thing, until finally he was the one with everything and I was the one left at home, studying in my room, looking for a way out. And then came freshman year, when Chim and I discovered how many people in our class were having parties. How many of those parties involved booze.

But sitting here, I forget all that. I talk about better times, like back in elementary school when our parents were still moderately fun and Jordan and I hard-boiled all the eggs one night after they went to sleep. The next morning, we fell on the floor laughing as we watched our dad try to crack one egg and then the next, and then the next, getting more and more frustrated and confused with each failed attempt. When we finally fessed up, my dad laughed and hugged us both tight.

I haven't seen him laugh in years.

In ninth grade, Jordan and I started playing in the jazz band together. Even though he'd been playing guitar for a couple years already at that point, I'd just taken up the trumpet. We loved practicing at night, and he'd help me when I got frustrated trying to learn new songs. He never had that issue. He could learn new stuff in a heartbeat—sometimes without even looking at the sheet music.

I forgot some of these stories until tonight, forgot that we used to have fun together, as a family. That Jordan and I used to have fun together. Even before the shooting, things had gone sour between us, and with my parents—my dad was always trying to get Jordan to do more, to push himself *harder*. My mom went along with it at first, but when my dad started talking about having Jordan apply to college early—mostly, I think, because he wanted to be able to brag about it to his friends—she finally started pushing back.

I'm not sure how much time passes with us standing here, Zach leaning against the doorframe, me close to him, arms wrapped tight around myself. It's only when my stomach gives a ridiculous growl that I realize it's getting late and I haven't eaten. I ask him if he wants some food, and we head downstairs to make popcorn.

After, we sit on the couch in the living room and just talk. I tell him family stories, memories I haven't let near my heart since Jordan died. I haven't talked this much in forever—not since the days when I'd drink too much and babble on and on into Lucy's ear.

Maybe Lucy is right. Maybe it's good to open up about things before they begin to eat you from the inside out and eventually crater your soul.

I can't believe this is the son of the person I hate more than almost anything. He was definitely home some of those times when I'd ride my bike over with a can of spray paint in my bag and write shit on the door of their garage. When Lucy and I salted nasty words into their lawn. When we left mean notes in their mailbox.

It hits me, deep in my stomach: he can never find out about any of that. I stopped going over there after the night I freaked out in their front yard. I couldn't do it anymore. He was inside. If he ever found out, he would never, ever forgive me. And I don't blame him.

I need to hide the things I did to his family forever.

Now he's here, on the brown suede couch, where Jordan used to sit, and it's surreal. That day in drama when I found out who he was, I never imagined this. I never imagined he'd be sitting next to me, listening to me talk about things I've never thought I'd say out loud.

His brown hair flops over his forehead, and these fucking *feelings* arise in my chest, and it isn't good. *It is NOT GOOD.*

I've been a ghost for so long.

CHAPTER TWENTY-EIGHT

Zach

I want to kiss her. She's sitting here next to me, telling me all these stories about her brother, and all I can think is how much I want to kiss her. I'm having yet another *Jesus Christ, Zach, you are an enormous douche bag* moment, because I know—I *know* how inappropriate it would be to do that. I can't help it. I want to anyway.

I put my hand on the couch a few inches from hers, and it takes all my willpower to stop myself from grabbing hers. I know if I do, her eyes will lose the light that's started to come back into them and we'll be back to where we were before, with lectures about inappropriate touching and bad timing.

It's a struggle, though. To pay attention to her words and look at her eyes.

It's a serious struggle.

CHAPTER TWENTY-NINE

May

I keep talking. I don't understand why I can't shut up, because for so long I could do nothing BUT shut up. Zach puts his hand on the couch, fingers splayed, and for a moment I think he's going to grab my hand, but he doesn't. And I talk and talk, and I think that maybe it's for the best.

No, it's definitely for the best.

But then my dumb hand decides to go rogue and do whatever it damn well pleases, and all of a sudden, it's inching closer to his.

When our hands touch, his eyes widen in surprise.

CHAPTER THIRTY

Zach

I'm trying to decide whether I'm reading too much into the fact that her hand is inching toward mine, and then, all of a sudden, we're touching.

CHAPTER THIRTY-ONE

May

My heart's beating so loud I'm pretty sure they can hear it on the other side of the planet. Back in my more mentally sound days, I never made the first move.

I feel naked.

CHAPTER THIRTY-TWO

Zach

I can either sit here with my hand flopping under hers like a limp fish, or I can take charge of my life for once.

Fuck it.

I reach out, slow, put my other hand on her cheek. Her skin is soft. Our eyes meet, and for once I don't need to know what's going to happen, and I don't want to hide.

CHAPTER THIRTY-THREE

May

And then he kisses me, and all the nerves in my body that I thought had died that day last year spark back to life.

CHAPTER THIRTY-FOUR

Zach

This.

CHAPTER THIRTY-FIVE

May

After Zach leaves, the house is quiet. My parents still aren't home. It's funny—I've been invisible to them since it became clear that Jordan had something that I don't, that his brain worked in beautiful, mysterious ways, that it needed to be cultivated into something great. Maybe now I just feel it more. Before they could remember that I existed in relation to Jordan. Or maybe it's because Jordan always forced them to notice me—at the dinner table, he would make an effort to bring me into the conversation, even during the last few years, when we would go weeks without really speaking.

Now, with him gone, it's all collapsed. My parents and I don't know how to relate to each other without him. I didn't realize it until he was gone, but he was the glue holding us all together. Now we're untethered, floating, occupying the same space but never touching.

I head upstairs, phone in hand.

It dings with a message. Lucy.

Tell me everything.

I roll my eyes at the screen. I think about trying to put that kiss into words and my cheeks grow hot.

And I realize that I care. *Fuuuuuck.* Guilt churns in my stomach.

He's nice, I reply to Lucy as I walk into my room.

Wowwwww. You like him!!!

It's not a question.

Yeah. I guess.

Oh MAY, I'm so happy! I can basically hear Lucy's scream of excitement from across town.

That makes one of us.

She sends me an eye-roll emoji. *So dramatic. Come to breakfast tomorrow with me and Grann? We can have those blueberry pancakes you love so much.*

I plop down on my bed and take my shoes off, throwing them across the room one at a time.

I type: *Okay.* I can't get out of it; Lucy knows the way to my heart. Grann's pancakes are legendary.

I can already picture what breakfast is going to be like, can picture the cross-examination from Lucy and Grann about the last two nights, all the questions about my *feelings.*

This is why I've been hiding under my covers for the past year. It's not right that I can move on, go back to school, start to like a boy, play the trumpet, sing, laugh, *live*—and Jordan doesn't get any of that.

He doesn't get anything at all.

In the silence of my bedroom, the suffocating weight of everything I'm hiding—from Lucy, from Zach, from Chim, from my parents—starts to press down on me again.

My phone dings and I look at its screen, anticipating another message from Lucy, but I see that it's from Zach.

My traitorous heart leaps in my chest.

CHAPTER THIRTY-SIX

Zach

It's been four days since May and I kissed, and she's all I can think about. This is the first time since my mom took the case that time hasn't seemed like it's being dragged through a field of thick liquid goo.

Nothing bothers me anymore—not Matt, not Rosa, not my parents. They've all faded into the background, their sharp edges softened against the heat of May's mouth and the feeling of her hand in mine. I'm trying my best to give her space to ease into the idea of what's happening between us—it can't be easy, given who my mother is—but it's a challenge. All I want to do is see her.

I'm at my locker on Wednesday morning, minding my own business, when Conor's grinning face peeks around the door. I ignore him, pull out my last textbook, and slam the door shut hard enough that he jumps back. He sent me about a million texts last night, trying to get the DL on what's happening with May, but I never wrote back. I want the memories to be mine and mine alone for a little while longer.

"What do you want?"

His face falls. He's like a giant puppy dog that just wants love. "You never responded to my texts last night, man! I know you're in a May-induced coma, but c'mon. Bros before—"

I shoot him a warning glance. "I'd stop right there if I were you."

He holds up his hands. "Okay, okay, I get you. I won't speak ill of your GF." He literally says the letters *GF* out loud. He's so hard to take seriously sometimes.

I glance around to make sure May doesn't happen to be within earshot. "Dude. She's not my girlfriend!" I pause, because I don't know what she is, except the person I think about more than anyone else in the world and the only person I want to talk to right now.

"Okay, well, your not-girlfriend, then." He laughs like he just said something funny.

"You know, you have a terrible sense of humor."

He rolls his eyes. "Lay off me, bro. I'm just excited for you. And once I get Lucy to say yes to a date with me, we can double. It'll be so cute. Like something out of *Riverdale*."

I snort. "I still cannot believe you watch that shit."

"OMG, it's good!"

I laugh. "You know, if all your adoring fans knew about your taste in TV and your use of ridiculous acronyms, I bet they'd reconsider your image."

"That's so binary of you, dude. Open your mind. Like, just because I'm a guy in a band, I need to act a certain way? You sound like Matt."

I glare at him. "How dare you compare me to that dickwad."

He smirks. "You asked for it. So . . . tell me about May. Do we like her? Lucy and I have a bet riding on your firstborn child—she thinks you're going to name it after her, but I'm like, nah, man, they're definitely gonna name it Conor."

I bite back a grin and punch him in the arm. It's a joking punch, but it lands hard. "Shut it." I take off down the hall, leaving him rubbing his bicep and muttering protests in my wake.

In reality, things haven't changed that much in the five days since Conor's band played, but at the same time, it feels like everything has changed—most of all, the amount of times per minute my heart beats when I know May is nearby, followed closely by how much easier it is for me to get out of my car at school in the mornings.

I see May for the first time today outside drama class, lingering in the hallway, looking lost. When she catches sight of me, her face lights up for a split second before she shutters it under her normal expression of *Whatever.* But it's a split second that will keep me going for weeks. No matter how up-and-down she might be, that expression is there, hiding under her steely exterior, and I'm the only person who gets to see it.

"Hey." I shuffle over to her.

"Hey." She blesses me with one of her rare smiles. I want to kiss her right here in the hallway, dip her over and plant one on her mouth like we're a couple in a black-and-white photograph, but instead I settle for a quick squeeze of her forearm.

"Ready for *drama*?" My tone conveys how we both feel about the class.

She smirks. "Totally. Can't wait to see Kowalski's hair today. Should be interesting, since it's raining."

I pull open the door to the auditorium. "After you."

CHAPTER THIRTY-SEVEN

May

When Zach walks up to me outside drama, my first thought is that he looks extra cute today, which is so lame. My brain is turning to total mush because of this guy. I don't remember ever being like this with Miles, even when we first started dating, but then again, my relationship with Miles was different.

Since Saturday, Zach and I haven't hung out, but we've been talking on the phone, like people did back in the twentieth century. I think I've spent more time talking on the phone in the past four days than in the entire rest of my life. Lucy's all excited, and Grann thinks Zach is the best thing ever. At breakfast on Sunday, she kept going on about the healing power of *love,* and I was like *Grann, would you please calm down?* (Except I phrased it in a much nicer way than that, because I might be a total dick to most people, but I never would be a dick to Grann.)

Even Chim is excited for me. I guess I knew she would be, if I let her, but after Lucy's show she texted me to ask who that cute boy was (her words, not mine) and I had to explain. Otherwise, she might have thought he was fair game.

Outside drama, Zach and I make small talk. I barely pay attention to what I'm saying because I'm entranced by his lower lip. A tiny part of me keeps going *Hey, dummy, this is STUPID of you, why are you getting caught up with another human being,* but then my brain replays the kiss from the other night, the feeling of Zach's hand on mine, and for the first time since Jordan died and the letters started arriving and everything went to hell, I manage to ignore it.

Zach pulls open the door and motions for me to go in ahead of him. A couple of the other kids in the class nudge each other when they see me, no doubt remembering the scene I made the other week, but I've dealt with worse. Much worse. I square my shoulders and tilt my head up like I don't have a fucking care in the world and make my way to my seat.

Kowalski's hair is on fire today. Obviously not literal fire, but the rain did not do anything to it that could be construed as positive. I catch Zach's eye and we exchange a smile that makes me feel all tingly and warm and sends the butterflies in my stomach into flight.

For the first time in forever, I dare to think that there might be a chance for me after all.

* * *

And then I get home after school, and all my optimism and dumb hope shatters when I reach into the mailbox and pull out another envelope, postmarked from the county jail.

CHAPTER THIRTY-EIGHT

Zach

I'm sprawled on the couch in my family room Thursday night, barely watching the TV in front of me, scrolling through the texts May and I have sent back and forth in the last few days, trying to figure out the perfect thing to say to her. There's this part of me, this insane part, that feels like if I can string together words in exactly the right way, I can ease some of her pain.

I'm deleting yet another sentence without sending it, when Gwen comes into the room and flops down next to me.

"What are you watching?"

I squint up at the TV and shrug. "No clue. You can change it if you want." I nod at the remote a few cushions down and she reaches out with her foot and grabs it like a tiny, cute monkey. She flips to the Disney Channel and then sneaks a glance at me like she thinks maybe I'm going to laugh at her for watching it. I make sure my face remains impassive, because I'd much rather she watch that than some of the shit that's on these days. She's growing up too fast as it is.

We're quiet for a few minutes, me playing with my phone and her watching the show.

"You know what?" Gwen interrupts the silence. I look up at her and see that she's staring at me intently. "No one's spray-painted our garage in weeks. Isn't that weird?"

The fact that my baby sister thinks it's weird that no one has harassed our family lately makes me unbearably sad for a second. I try so hard to hide it all from her: the vandalism, the nasty letters, the angry glances from our neighbors. I swallow the lump in my throat. "Yeah. True." I shrug. "Maybe people have started to forget. Not, like, what happened, but the fact that Mom felt the need to insert herself in the middle of it."

"I doubt it. Now that the trial is about to start . . ." She trails off, and I glance at her. She's staring at the television with tears glistening in her eyes, her fists balled in her lap.

"Hey. What's up, Gwenie?" I straighten and lean toward her. "Are people being dicks to you at school again?"

"Again?" She lets out a sarcastic laugh that hurts my heart. "*Again* would mean that it had stopped, ever. I'd say that people are *still* being dicks, yeah." She gives a tiny shake of her head. "Whatever. It doesn't matter."

"I thought things were going okay? Did you have a good time at that girl's party? What's her name? Emery?"

She snaps her head up, face red. "Don't ever mention that name around me again. She's awful."

My stomach tightens. "What did she do?"

"I don't want to talk about it." She sniffles and buries her face in her hands. I can barely understand her. "She invited me to that party and told me I should try out for cheerleading next year, and I thought maybe things were turning around, maybe things could go back to how they were before all this crap started . . . and so I show up to her house this past Saturday, and . . ." She lets out a plaintive sob. "And when I knocked on the door, Emery and this other girl, Jill, answered and I could hear the party going on behind them, and they just looked at me and started laughing. They didn't even say anything. . . . They just . . . laughed." She's full-on sobbing now. "And then they shut the door in my face, and I could hear them go back to everyone else and they were all . . . *laughing.* All of them. At me."

Sitting here, listening to Gwen, I want to scream at my mom. She should be here to see my little sister's pain, not off in her office, working to defend a *guilty asshole.* But whatever.

Actually, no—not whatever. I'm working on not being that guy—the *whatever* guy. The guy who always backs down and makes himself invisible.

"I'm calling Mom." I shake my head. "This is bullshit." I make a move to stand up, and Gwen throws herself on top of me.

"No, please, Zach." She knocks the wind out of me. I fall back onto the couch. "Please. Don't call Mom. Please. It'll just make everything worse. It's not even her fault, real—"

"How are you still buying that?" I interrupt. "This is *all* her fault. If she cared about us more than her stupid career, there's no way she would have taken the case. Put us through this. Don't you get that?"

"That's not true." She moves off me and crosses her arms. "She told me it's not true. She has to do this: everyone deserves a fair trial."

"Everyone? *Everyone?* The guy killed seven people in cold blood. *Murdered* them. Shot them while they pled for their lives. He killed a teacher. He killed May's *brother.* He left them all there to bleed out and die, and then he didn't even have the decency to kill himself. He stayed around and fucked up more lives. Mom isn't defending someone who might be innocent. She's defending someone who is, *without a doubt,* guilty. What the fuck is the point of that, other than for her to get publicity? She doesn't give a *shit* about us."

All the blood has drained from Gwen's face, and I realize I've gone too far. I reach out and put my hand on her arm, but she snatches it away.

"You're wrong," she says. "Mom cares about us. It's everyone else who doesn't. You're stupid if you can't see that."

I shake my head. I don't want to have this fight. "Sure. Whatever you say. Look, we're on the same side." I pause. "Just know that if you need anything, I'm here. You don't deserve to be treated like that, okay?"

She sniffs. "Yeah. Whatever."

* * *

All the anger I bury deep down during that conversation is still simmering the next day when Matt passes me in the hallway before last period and says, "Hey, Teller. I heard May basically freaked out at our show the other week," then gives a laugh, and I punch his fucking face. He looks at me in surprise for a second, holding his cheek with his hand, and then launches himself at me. He's heavier than I am, but I am *angry.* I manage to get in a couple shots at his stomach before Mr. Ames pulls me off him and drags us both to the principal's office.

To my surprise, May's sitting in the waiting room when we walk in. Matt lets out an obnoxious guffaw when he sees her, and I strain against Ames's grasp.

Ames throws us both into chairs on the other side of the room from where May's sitting and looks down at us with a frown. "Jesus, guys. What's gotten into you? I thought you were friends."

I snort and Matt shoots me a dirty look. "Little behind the times, Ames." I don't even sound like myself, and I see May listening from the other side of the room. "Haven't you heard? I don't have any friends anymore." I see Matt roll his eyes. "What? You have something to say?" I lean over to him in my chair and Ames takes a step toward me.

I hold up my hands like *It's cool, bro. All good here.*

All good here.

What a fucking lie.

CHAPTER THIRTY-NINE

May

I'm sitting on one of the principal's office's uncomfortable chairs when Zach is dragged in by some teacher. His face is flushed and his eyes narrow. When I see Matt next to him, it's not difficult to figure out what happened.

I try to catch Zach's eye from across the room, but it seems like he's deliberately avoiding my gaze. I feel bad; yesterday he said something to me about what the school is doing to mark the one-year anniversary of the shooting and I totally shut him down and walked away. And I didn't answer his texts last night. It seemed like appropriate punishment that when I arrived at school today, I got a note saying Rose-Brady wanted to see me.

Rose-Brady sticks her head out of her office and motions for me to come in. As I stand, her gaze falls on Zach, Matt, and the teacher and she raises her eyebrows. "Glenn. What's going on here?"

Mr. Ames pushes a hand through his short black hair and

sighs. "Hi, Principal Rose-Brady. Sorry to bother. I found these guys wrestling in the hallway. I think a chat with you or Principal Kalb is in order."

If I had to hazard a guess after seeing Matt's eye closer up, I'd say that they were doing more than wrestling, but the teacher seems to want to downplay whatever actually happened.

"Is that right? Hi, May." Rose-Brady's face softens when she sees me, and she steps back to let me pass into her office. I settle into yet another uncomfortable chair in front of her desk. I swear to god, the administration deliberately picked these chairs to torture the people unlucky enough to end up here.

Rose-Brady continues, "I have to discuss something with May, but it should be quick. Glenn, do you mind staying with the boys until Principal Kalb can see them? He should be back in the office any minute. My secretary's at a dentist appointment, and I'd rather not have them alone in here together after a fight."

The teacher must nod, because Rose-Brady thanks him, shuts the door, and sits down at her desk. "Thanks for coming, May."

Did I have a choice? I swallow down the words, because I'm trying out this new thing where I don't get kicked out of school.

"I wanted to just check in. I'm proud of you for staying out of trouble since you got back to school—you're obviously really trying, and I'm so happy to see it. I know every single day is hard. Trust me. I do." She pauses, wiping her eyes. "Last year, I saw you shutting yourself away, and I was so worried. So I'm pleased to watch your progress. That said, I wanted to talk to you about what we have planned to honor the victims of the shooting. As you know, it's coming up in just over a week." She looks at me, hesitant, like she's afraid I might stand up and start screaming right in the middle of her office. I dig my nails into my palm, hard. As hard as I can. Force myself to breathe. Nod. "Anne Kim and her group are helping us put together events to honor the victims, and she told me that you don't want to take part, which I very much understand—"

I feel my insides start to collapse on themselves as I imagine Anne and Rose-Brady sitting in this office, talking about me. Saying that I'm pathetic. That I can't handle anything. Well, screw them. I'm sure if Jordan were still alive, he'd be in here, helping to plan these events. Helping Anne organize.

I swallow hard and interrupt her. "I do." My voice is gritty. It sounds like I haven't talked for days.

Rose-Brady pauses. "You do?"

I nod. "I'll help. I'll participate. What do you want me to do?"

She raises her eyebrows in surprise. "Are you sure you're up to it? If you are, maybe you could give a short speech that day, talk about Jordan?" She smiles, a warm smile that makes me want to break in two. "I think it'll be good for you, getting involved with other survivors. It might help you heal."

I want to run out of her office and down the hall and keep going until I reach the ocean. But instead, I nod.

She's looking at me with raised eyebrows and I realize I'm supposed to respond.

"Okay."

She gives me a long look. "Okay. Well." She pauses. "I'm really happy to hear this. When I spoke with Dr. McMillen yesterday, we agreed that getting involved in these memorials could be very beneficial to you, but we would never force you. This had to be a decision that came from you."

I take a deep breath. What did I just agree to? Why do I keep doing this to myself, over and over?

"Great."

"Great! One thing—per the school board, we need to approve everyone's speeches for that day. Make sure they're appropriate. I'm sure you understand."

I nod.

Rose-Brady smiles like we've just had a great chat, and I press my lips together tight to stop myself from screaming.

CHAPTER FORTY

May

After I finally get out of that stupid meeting with Rose-Brady, I'm lingering by my locker, trying to delay going home as long as I possibly can. Last year, I was always busy after school: jazz band practice, choir, vocal ensemble committee meetings. These days, afternoons are empty spaces that try to gobble me alive. Usually I deal with it because I'd rather be at home than anywhere else, but this afternoon I don't want to face what I might find in the mail.

I'm so deep in my own swirling thoughts that I don't notice Zach walk up behind me. When he taps me on the shoulder, I jump out of my skin.

"Oh, man, sorry. I didn't mean to scare you. I was trying to catch you before you left. What are you doing?" He leans against the locker next to mine.

I try to shake off the jittery feeling coursing through my veins, the same one that's been thrumming through my body all day.

"Doing?" I shove a final textbook into my backpack and turn to him. The simple act of looking into his eyes helps calm my racing heart. His face is so open and trusting. "Nothing . . . Hey, what the hell happened? With Matt? I saw you guys in the office. . . ."

He flushes. "Nothing. It was stupid. Matt's a dick and I didn't want to deal with it anymore. I may have punched him, a little."

"How do you punch someone *a little*?" I give him a half grin. "Kidding. I'm sure he deserved it. That guy is a jerk."

"Yeah, no kidding."

He drums his fingers against the locker. "Anyway . . . yeah. I don't know about you, but I had a pretty shitty day. I got a week of detention starting Monday. So I wanted to see if you maybe wanted to come over? Meet my sister? Hang out for a while?" He pauses, and must see the expression that crosses my face, the one that says *No fucking way,* because he adds, "My mom won't be there. She never is. She's at work like all day and night. She even sleeps in her office half the time, since they're going to trial soon." He barks a bitter laugh, which I get. When my Dad is working on a film, he lives on set and it's like he forgets he has a family.

A thousand conflicting emotions hit me when I think about hanging out at Zach's house. *Her* house. He thinks I've never been there, has no idea I've haunted his family in the night. He's smiling at me with his big, innocent blue eyes, and I want to sink into them, I want some of that innocence for my own, so I say yes. I know it's a terrible idea, maybe the worst idea, but I say yes anyway, because that's what I do.

It'll be on my tombstone, the one right next to Jordan's. *May McGintee: Ignored Her Gut Every Time.* By then, Jordan's will be covered in moss, will be weatherworn, but mine will be fresh and new.

I find Lucy and tell her she can take my car to practice tonight and I'll pick it up from her tomorrow. She's all *I can't wait to tell Conor about this.* For a second, talking to Lucy, I trick myself into thinking this is normal and cute—our own little circle of friends, one big happy family. But then, as Zach and I walk to his car to meet Gwen, he tells me about what happened to her last weekend, and how terrible that girl Emery was. And then I remember who I am and who the Tellers are and what I did to them, and I wonder if it's not that different from what Emery did, and the feeling bursts and a familiar hollowness crawls back in.

Gwen rides in the back, silent. She's so tiny and young, with curly blond hair, and she looks like she wants to cry. My heart breaks a little for her.

Zach pulls the car into the driveway, and the outside of the house is so familiar that it's almost like arriving home. I swallow hard and plaster on a smile. I don't want to leave the safety of this car.

"Nice house! It's beautiful!" I sound way too enthusiastic, like a freaking talk-show host. Zach probably thinks I'm losing my mind. I have to pull it together.

Gwen jets out of the car, leaving Zach and me sitting in silence. He looks almost as nervous as I feel. I can't believe I'm about to do this—I can't believe I agreed. This is actual insanity, although I currently can't decide whether it's more or less insane than going home to an empty house and torturing myself by thinking about those letters. I study Zach's face out of the corner of my eye—the way his eyelashes curl up at the end, the pink of his bottom lip, his deep-blue eyes—and decide that it's less. Much, much less.

I'm about to open my car door when he speaks. "So . . . there are a couple things I need to tell you about my dad. . . ."

I pause in my exit, surprised. I've never considered Zach's dad; I kind of forgot he has one. Before meeting Zach, I didn't think about the fact that Michelle Teller had a family at all. In my head, it was always just me and her.

Zach continues, "He's a little . . . Well, the past year, maybe more than that . . . he's . . ." He trails off and squints out the window for a long moment. I stay silent. I've been there—not knowing how to explain something about my family to an outsider. "I guess what I'm trying to say is, he doesn't go out much. At all. He's . . . I don't know." He sighs in frustration. "Depressed, maybe? Or just totally checked out? Either way, he doesn't work, doesn't do much except hang around here being useless. And on top of that, we've had some people sort of . . . vandalize? Our house? Since my mom took the case? And he's been no help at all."

My blood freezes in my veins. I force my face to remain immobile.

He's looking at me; I need to say something. "That sucks." I choke out the words.

Lucky for me, Zach's way too deep in his own brain thinking about his messed-up family to consider my messed-up reaction.

"Yeah, it's been pretty brutal. I've tried to protect Gwen from the brunt of it—like, one night a few weeks ago, someone spray-painted the word *BITCH* on our garage in this freaky red paint, and it was like something out of a horror movie, all dripping red lines. It looked like blood, you know? I tried to keep her inside the house, but she ran right past me. . . . And my dad left it there for *the entire fucking day.* Conor and I had to paint over it after school." He drops his head onto the steering wheel and takes a deep inhale.

When he looks up, he gives me a sad, shaky little smile, and I want to puke on the floor of the car. I'm tempted to open my mouth and scream *IT WAS ME!* just to get it out there. But the words stick in my throat, and I know that I won't, that it would just make everything worse. All I can do is sit here next to this guy whose life I made miserable for months on end and reach out and hug him.

On second thought, the epitaph on my tombstone should read: *May McGintee: She Sucked.*

CHAPTER FORTY-ONE

Zach

It's surreal, having May at my house. Even before my mom took the case, I wasn't into having friends over. Back when Rosa and I dated, it got to the point where she thought I was embarrassed about her, because I never invited her to my house. Finally, one afternoon I gave in, and when we got to the house the kitchen was a disaster and my dad was sleeping on the couch in his bathrobe. I think that was the beginning of the end of his attempt at a career as a professional musician.

I can't believe I invited May here.

I hold my breath as we walk in the front door, bracing myself for whatever's waiting, but inside it's quiet and there are no obvious signs of my dad's pitiful existence.

We stand around awkwardly in the front hall for a second.

I figure I should speak. "Do you want a drink? Something to eat? Anything?"

May's eyes have a glazed expression, and she responds

with a weird, zombielike nod. I can't blame her: running into my mom would be terrible. I know it took a lot for her to agree to come.

I drop my book bag on the floor by the front door and gesture for her to follow me. We enter the kitchen, which appears to be in decent order, for once. No dishes from breakfast sitting in the sink, and the counters sparkle. Normally, I'm the only one in the house who cleans, outside of the housekeeper my mom hired, who comes once a month to make sure the place doesn't devolve into a total dump.

Gwen's at the counter, perched on a stool. Her face is buried in her phone, per usual.

"There's food in the fridge." Gwen's voice floats up from behind her phone.

"Wait, food? What do you mean?" I haven't been to the supermarket all week. I know we need groceries, but I've been distracted by school and May and attempting to have a life, so I keep forgetting.

Gwen finally deigns to make eye contact. "Food. In the fridge." She speaks slowly, like English is my second language.

I roll my eyes. "Yeah, thanks. I got that part. I meant where did it come from?"

She gives me a withering look. "I don't know, Zach. The supermarket?"

May snort-laughs and Gwen's face flushes with pleasure. I jab May with my elbow, trying to get her to stop encouraging my little sister's attitude problem, and she snickers again. I don't even care that they're ganging up on me—at least May has some life in her again, and Gwen looks happy for the first time all day.

I open the fridge, and by some miracle there *is* actual food in it. Like, not just the normal Styrofoam take-out containers full of rotting leftovers. Actual fresh fruit and vegetables.

I glance over my shoulder at Gwen. "Seriously, where did this come from?"

"I told you. I. Don't. Know." She sticks her tongue out at me, and then it's back to her phone.

Fourteen-year-olds are so much fun.

I give the top of her head the finger and then turn to May. "Well, it appears we're going to be able to eat something other than Easy Mac. Are you hungry?"

May shakes her head. "No. I'm good. Just some water or whatever."

I stick my head back in the fridge. "La Croix?" I hold one up for May to see and she nods. As I walk over to the cabinet to get her a glass, I mutter under my breath, "We have La Croix? What is happening? This is so weird."

The kitchen door swings open and my father walks into the room. He's dressed in normal street clothes. Not a bathrobe in sight. It's like an alien kidnapped my dad and replaced him with an ordinary person. May considers him, then turns her eyes to me, then back to him, probably wondering why I told her my dad was some sort of recluse when he's obviously a normal dude wearing khakis and an old gray T-shirt.

"Hey, kiddos." He ruffles Gwen's hair as he passes by.

He has never called us kiddos in our entire lives.

"Hey." Gwen looks up from her phone and does a mini double take. She shoots me a *WTF* expression, and I shrug.

"Zach!" He claps a hand on my shoulder. "How was school? And who's this lovely lady?" He walks over to May and sticks out his hand. "Jay Teller."

"May." She gives him a tentative smile and shakes his hand.

"What are you doing, Dad?" My voice comes out weary.

He turns to me. "What do you mean?"

This act he's putting on is bullshit. No one's fooled by it. I'm so tempted to start a fight with him, but I catch sight of May out of the corner of my eye, and I don't want her to think I'm an asshole. Instead, I shrug like I couldn't care less.

He gets all huffy, like I hurt his feelings. "What's the big deal? I went to the market earlier today. I thought we could all have dinner together tonight because—"

I interrupt him. "Sure. Whatever. Sounds good."

His eyes narrow, but he lets my tone slide. "Great. May, you'll join us?"

She starts to protest, but he won't take no for an answer. For the first time ever. Normally, he's all about that word.

He insists that we all sit in the kitchen while he fixes us a snack. As he's chopping vegetables, he asks May question after question, so many that it's embarrassing. It's like he's never met a friend of mine, like he thinks he needs to put on a show to make sure she'll come back. I want to yell at him to stop, to shut up, to leave us alone, but instead I silently pick at my food, and when I can't take it for one second longer, I excuse myself to the bathroom, leaving May behind.

CHAPTER FORTY-TWO

May

What in the fuck am I doing here?

The question has been running through my head since I walked into the house. With every passing moment, I'm getting more and more wound up, more and more trapped in my lies. More and more worried that I'm going to slip up and say something and Mr. Teller is going to figure out who I am.

I don't know why I keep saying yes. Yes to hanging out with Zach, yes to coming over, yes to dinner, now yes to helping Zach's dad set the table while he peppers me with questions.

Do I like school?

How did Zach and I meet?

They're normal questions, but something about the way Mr. Teller asks them sounds like he's reading out of a parenting manual, like this stuff doesn't come naturally to him. I try to keep my answers short—tight. *I'm new at Quincy Adams. I was homeschooled.* I leave the time before that out. My last name out. My answers are vague. Filled with blank spaces I babble to fill.

"Do you like drama class?"

Why do adults feel this incessant need to fill the air around them with *noise*? Does Mr. Teller actually care if I like drama class? I doubt it. This sort of chatter is the worst; I never had to make shitty small talk with Jordan. We were different, but we still had that weird twin thing. We could sit in silence for hours and somehow understand each other anyway. I guess that's what happens when you share a womb with someone for nine months.

I shrug. "It's okay."

"Just okay?" He smiles at me like he thinks he *gets* it.

I press my lips together in an expression that may or may not resemble a smile and reply, "Yup." I really need him to stop talking. Stop asking me these questions that are starting to get more and more specific—more and more directed toward things I don't want to talk about with anyone, and especially not with him.

Zach walks back into the room, presumably to save me from this painful conversation, but before he can say a word, there's a noise outside in the driveway. Zach jumps a little and turns to his dad.

"Is someone here?" He sounds tense.

His dad puts another fork and knife and napkin on the table. That makes five place settings. I count: *Me, Zach, Gwen, him . . .*

Oh my god.

I hear it now: the unmistakable sound of a car door slamming.

Mr. Teller claps his hands, delighted. "That's what I was trying to tell you before, in the kitchen. I thought it would be nice if we had more family time, so I told your mom I'd shop and cook if she could make it home by dinner, and . . ."

He keeps talking, but I stop listening.

Zach's face has gone stark white. "Mom?" He gags on the word. He turns to me, panic clear in his eyes.

My brain fuzzes. A giant glass wall slams down between me and the rest of the world. My head detaches from my body and floats up to the ceiling. A voice says *I have to go to the bathroom* in a strange, high pitch. It can't be me—I've always been an alto. But then someone who looks a lot like me bolts out of the kitchen and down the hall. It's like a robot has taken control of my body.

Once I get to the bathroom, I'm breathing hard. In the mirror, my face is wrong. More like Jordan's than ever. Like our shared features are eating away at my individual ones. I sink down to the edge of the tub and drop my head into my hands, trying to remind myself that it isn't real, to breathe, just *breathe.* I don't want to have a panic attack in the middle of the Tellers' house.

There's a knock on the door, and I can't even summon the strength to tell him to go away.

"May?" Zach's voice, through the door. "Are you okay? I am so sorry. I had no idea. . . . Can I come in?"

I nod into my hands. My body has frozen in this position.

He waits a second, and then: "I'm coming in, okay?" Through my hands, I see the door open, and then his shoes. He sits down next to me. "Hey . . ." He hesitates, and then he puts his hand on my shoulder. "Is this all right?"

I nod, and a sob fills the room. It sounds like the cry of an injured animal.

"Look, we can run out the back door right now if you want. You and me. I don't care what they think. Fuck them. I mean, *Jesus*. My mom is never here, and she picks tonight to come home. . . ." He trails off. The heat of his hand on my shoulder pins me in the moment.

My heart thuds in my chest so hard I swear my ribs are going to break. "There's a back door?" My voice shakes, but at least I'm able to speak. At least I recognize it as my voice.

"Yes!" He sounds so eager to fix this, and a wave of shame crashes over me. I made his life such a hell with my dumb, immature vandalism. I bet his mom didn't even see any of the messages I left. I bet Zach cleaned up his family's mess, again.

I realize I don't want to run out the back. I don't want to be the cause of yet another situation Zach is forced to deal with.

I pull myself together as best as I can. He's watching me with such tenderness that I want to cry. No one but Lucy has cared about me like this since Jordan died.

"It's okay. I can do this."

He makes a face. "May . . ."

I shake my head. "I swear. I'm okay." I put my hand over his. "It's not like she has any idea who I am, right? I'll just pretend I'm some random girl you know from school and leave it at that."

He grimaces. "You don't know my mom very well. . . . She never just lets things lie."

I force a laugh. "Your mom doesn't know *me* very well. Why do you think Rose-Brady kicked me out last year? After they carried me out of that closet, I promised myself I'd never let people intimidate me or back me into a corner ever again." I wipe my eyes and put on my best resting bitch face. "I'm good. Let's go." I stand and hold out a hand for him.

When we walk back into the kitchen, Michelle Teller is there.

Michelle Teller.

Here.

In front of me.

I want to cry.

She's standing in the kitchen, talking to Zach's dad. They sound tense. I realize with a jolt that I've never seen her in person. She looks different than she does in photos. Smaller. Less like the Antichrist's little helper and more like a normal, tired, overwhelmed mother. It's unsettling.

She greets me with a wan smile and a hello, like I'm just

another one of Zach's friends. Like I'm anyone. Like I'm not about to explode all over her kitchen floor. I force a hello out of my mouth. A *Nice to meet you.*

Nice to meet you, Michelle Teller.

The biggest lie I've ever told.

Then Zach's dad is all *Well, everyone, time to eat!* All jolly and shit, like we're just one big happy family. He doesn't seem to notice that his wife looks exhausted. That his son looks like he wants to scream.

I can't even imagine what I look like.

We all sit down at the table. Michelle Teller sits at the head, her husband at the other end. Zach has taken the chair between his mom and me, like a human buffer. There's an awkward pause after we're all seated, a small silence that digs into my core and twists my stomach into a knot, and then Zach grabs a bowl and passes it to me. I take it from him, thanking him with a voice that's barely more than a whisper, and then hand the bowl to Mr. Teller, who dishes himself some food. Small talk starts. I train my eyes on my plate and force myself to eat the food in front of me, which is decent. I'd probably enjoy it, if I weren't about to projectile vomit all over the floor.

Moments pass. They chat about . . . stuff. I can't hold on to their words. The beat of my heart in my ears is too loud. I stare down at my plate wearing my best fake smile, the one I hope says *I am just a random classmate of your son's and there is nothing to see here.*

But, as is my luck, my invisibility doesn't last long. I've taken only a couple more small bites of food when I hear: "So, how do you and Zach know each other?"

My breath catches. I look up from my plate. *She* is staring at me, expectant. A parent asking her kid's friend a normal question. I don't know if I can do this—have an actual, real conversation with this woman. She's connected to David in a way I can't totally comprehend—she's breathed the same air as him, sat across a room from him, looked him in the eye. A silence stretches between her question and my response, a painful silence that starts to eat through my skin and gnaw my bones.

Zach jumps in, trying to deflect her attention from me. "We know each other from school, Mom."

"Ah." She sounds surprised. She takes a couple deliberate bites off her plate and then turns to me again. "It's just . . . you look so familiar. I thought I knew all of Zach's friends. Have we met before?"

I shake my head. It's beginning to seem quite possible that my voice has failed and I've been rendered permanently mute.

Zach responds for me again. "She's new, Mom."

My stomach flips. I wanted to get through this dinner without Michelle Teller finding out any details about me at all.

"Where did you go before?" She tilts her head like she's really looking at me for the first time.

"Before?" My voice squeaks out, all high-pitched.

"Before QA? Where did you go to school?"

I start to speak—"I was homeschooled"—but Zach's voice tumbles over mine.

"She went to Carter."

My mouth drops open, because *What the fuck, Zach?* but when I glance at him he looks so shocked at what just came out of his mouth that I can't summon up the energy to be mad. This moment feels inevitable. She was going to find out. I knew it the second she walked into this house.

Something flashes across Michelle Teller's face, but she composes herself before I can decipher it. She raises an eyebrow. "Oh? You went to Carter?"

I nod.

She furrows her brow. "What did you say your name is?"

I swallow. Zach's hand finds mine under the table.

"May?" My name catches in my throat.

"May." She purses her lips. "That's not a very common name."

I shrug. A lump of terror churns in my stomach.

"What's your last name, May?" She narrows her eyes at me.

"Hey, Mom." Zach intervenes again. "Lay off."

She cuts him off with a look.

"McGintee?" I choke on the word.

"McGintee?" She glances at Zach to confirm. All the blood has drained from his face. "Did she say McGintee?"

He nods.

Gwen and Mr. Teller are silent. The entire table has

stopped eating. Everyone is watching Michelle Teller and me like they're waiting for an explosion.

"As in Jordan McGintee? As in his twin sister?" she says in a strangled tone.

When I hear my brother's name, I spring to life for the first time since dinner started. Who does this lady think she is, throwing his name around like it's hers to say?

"Yes. Jordan was my brother." My voice is shaky, which pisses me off. I force myself to meet her eyes.

"I'm very sorry for your loss, May." Her words sound cold but the look she gives me runs counter to them. She looks devastated. Worried beyond belief. Like she has no idea how to handle this situation.

Well, good—that makes two of us.

She turns to Zach's dad. "Did you know about this?"

"No. I had no idea."

Fury bubbles up farther into my stomach with every second that passes. How dare she act like I'm not welcome in her house? She should be throwing herself at my feet, groveling for me to forgive her for defending that piece of shit that murdered my brother.

She heaves a sigh and says to me, "I'm sorry. I really am. This is an unusual situation, to say the least. I wish someone had given me a heads-up. . . ."

"I didn't think you'd actually decide to come *home,*" Zach mutters.

She glares at him and then turns back to me. Smiles a

toothy crocodile smile. "We'll just have to be careful to avoid talking about the elephant in the room and we should be okay, legally speaking."

I dig my nails into my palm, hard. "Great. Fine by me." The last fucking thing I want to do is discuss *anything* with her.

After that, dinner collapses into an awful, awkward event, even worse than before. I retreat into my own head, the world fuzzing, the words around me muffled by the anxiety coursing through my body. Zach's dad attempts to make conversation, cracking little jokes, trying to make light of one of the most fucked-up situations in the history of the world. A pain grows in my stomach, making eating impossible, so I gulp down glass after glass of water, just to have something to do.

After dinner, Zach drags me into the living room.

He looks like he might cry. "I am so sorry. I don't know what came over me. I don't know why I said that about Carter. What is wrong with me? She asked, and . . . I don't know. I don't know what happened. I'm so sorry."

I shake my head and shut my eyes against his face, his words, the light of the living room. After a moment, I open them. I'm too tired to be upset. I'm too tired to be much of anything right now.

"It's okay." I make a halfhearted attempt at shrugging. "It was bound to happen." And it was. The moment I agreed to come here, I set this on course. Zach didn't force me here. I agreed. "I just want to go home."

"I'll drive you," he says.

I nod in thanks. "Can I use the bathroom first?" All I want to do is leave this house and never ever return, but I drank about a gallon of water at dinner and now I think I might pee my pants.

"Sure. I'll be here."

I'm leaving the bathroom when I hear hushed voices coming from the kitchen. Michelle Teller and her husband. She sounds exhausted. I linger for a second in the hallway, out of sheer morbid curiosity. What does this woman, who I've thought about every day for months, talk about with her husband when they're alone?

"How could you not have known?" She's speaking softly, but the words are clear as a bell.

"How could *I* not have known?" Zach's dad sounds incredulous. "He's *your* client! This is *your* case. Shouldn't you have all the faces of the victims memorized?"

"I do, Jay. I know all the faces of the *victims*. . . . They visit me in my sleep. When I close my eyes, they're all there." She pauses. "But that girl survived. And there were reasons behind her survival that maybe even she doesn't know."

My stomach twists.

There's a beat of silence, and then he responds, "What does that mean?" He sounds confused. "This is the first friend Zach's made all year. I know it's awkward, but you talk to opposing counsel all the time in your cases, so what—"

She interrupts. "Nothing. I shouldn't have said that. You know I can't talk about the case with you."

"Jesus, Michelle. You're the one who brought it up!"

There's a noise behind me and I whirl around. Gwen's standing down at the end of the hall. She doesn't even seem to register me, just her parents' angry voices floating toward her.

The expression on her face punches me in the gut: her sad eyes, her turned-down mouth, her pinched eyebrows—they all look so familiar, so much like what I see on my own face in the mirror.

When Zach drops me off at home, all the lights are off and the mail is still tucked in the box. I want to ignore it, but I can't.

I find it exactly where I knew it would be, under a pile of catalogs and a few bills: another thick envelope from the county jail.

Zach's mom's words run through my head: *There were reasons behind her survival.*

Reasons.

I need to know what he has to say.

I rip open the letter.

THE LETTER

Dear May,

I don't understand your silence. I hope you're getting these letters. Can you please come visit me? That's all I want, May. To hear your voice. To see your face. It's so lonely in here—the only thing that keeps me going is the thought of seeing you again.

The last time I saw you, that day, when I opened the closet door, you wouldn't even look at me. Then I had to go because they were coming to get me. I never got to tell you what I needed to say.

I used to watch you during class. Math, English . . . you were always so nice. You were the only one who actually heard me. Do you remember that one time when I asked four goddamn people if I could borrow a pen because I had forgotten mine, and you were the only one decent enough to give me one? Everyone else lied and said they didn't have any extra or pretended they didn't hear me. Like I didn't even fucking exist. But you knew I existed. You always knew.

You saw me, May. You talked to me and knew that I mattered, even when everyone else tried to pretend I didn't.

We're better than all of them, May. They live little, shallow existences, happy in their ignorance, but we aren't like them. I know you would have gone out with me if you could have. I totally understand why you couldn't, especially after our conversation at that party at Adam's house.

You were so lonely. That night when we sat outside, talking. So lonely. I understood that—I've always been lonely too. Know that I'm here for you, May, no matter what. Not like Miles. That guy never saw you like I do. I SEE you. I know what you want and what you need. I'm sorry he's still out there and that he sees you all the time. He doesn't deserve to.

Look, May. It's been almost a year since I started writing, and I haven't gotten any response. You have *to respond. I know you think about me all the time, the way I think about you. I have something important I need to tell you. If you read my last few letters, you already know that. If you didn't, why not? Why are you ignoring me, when we both know how much we mean to each other? Since I don't know how else to get you to visit me here, I will say that what I need to tell you is about Jordan, and that day. Does that make you curious enough to come? I know this place is disgusting and not worthy of you, but I'm here.*

I hope you come. I miss seeing you. You're on my approved visitors list; all you need to do is show up.

Yours always,
David Ecchles

CHAPTER FORTY-THREE

May

Hours later, I'm still curled into a ball on my bed with the comforter wrapped tight around me. It's not helping to keep out the cold. The house is dark and silent like it always is.

I'm alone.

All the letters have been pulled out of their various hiding places, envelopes ripped open, pages read, and now I'm trapped on my bed, surrounded by a mountain of notebook paper with words scrawled onto them that I'll never be able to scrub from my brain. I wish I could dig into my head and get them out, pour bleach in there to remove the stain.

I am going to be haunted by his words for the rest of my life.

I used to avoid David Ecchles at all costs. We all did. He had gotten in trouble sophomore year for a poem he wrote in English about Columbine—it ended up getting him suspended from school. Everyone knew he was strange—scary, even. Then, at the beginning of junior year, my AP History teacher, Mr. Taylor, asked me to tutor him. I didn't have much of a choice—there was no real reason why I couldn't. And it wasn't terrible; I was surprised by how he knew a ton about the battles of World War II, about what weapons were used when and where. He was awful at writing papers, though.

After about a month of tutoring, he asked me out twice, and of course I said no because I was dating Miles, and because David was *David*, and after that he got weird. Really weird. I started seeing him around school in places he shouldn't have been. I finally told Mr. Taylor I couldn't help him anymore—I made up a lie about being too busy with band stuff—and after that the only place I remember seeing him was in class.

Until, at least according to that asshole Miles, that night at Adam's party.

That weekend before the shooting was like any other back then. Lucy and I got into an argument about whether I should go to Adam's party. I told her to stop being such a fucking judgmental old lady, that she wasn't any fun.

Later that night, when I was about to leave the house to meet Miles, my mom stopped me in the kitchen, a frown on her face. *Why isn't Jordan going with you? You two never hang out anymore. You used to be so close. What's going on with you guys?*

And suddenly, I needed a drink more than anything. Suddenly, all I wanted was five hundred drinks, enough to drown out her voice, enough to drown myself in.

Jordan was upstairs in his room listening to music, this M83 song he was obsessed with, and the absolute last thing I wanted was to go invite him to come with me and have him watch me like a hawk at the party, be judged for drinking too much, and be forced to leave early because he was bored.

I couldn't stand the thought of it. Of his face the next morning in the hallway outside the bathroom we shared, looking like it always did after nights like that, his expression asking me *What is happening to you, May? Who are you?*

A hard, mean pebble formed in my gut, and I growled at my mother, *I'm going alone. All by myself. I'm allowed to have my own life—my own friends. I'm sick and tired of my loser brother always coming everywhere with me.*

In response, her eyes widened, but they were trained on something behind me in the doorway. I whipped around and there he was, watching us. His eyes locked on mine and I tried to form words, to squeak out an apology, but before I could, he turned around and left the room, and then I left the house, and three days later, he was dead.

In my bedroom, on my bed, in the present, a sound splits the silence, and I realize that it's coming out of me, that I'm screaming.

I run into the bathroom, and everything I've eaten today spills out of me into the toilet.

After I'm empty, I drag myself back into my bedroom and see the letter lying on my bed, taunting me.

There's so much I can't remember, so much I don't know. All the questions I've pushed out of my head over the past year swarm in at once: Did I see David at that party? Did we really talk? Did Jordan call out my name before he died? Why didn't I leave the closet to save him? Did he forgive me for how I'd treated him? The thought of David's knowing something about Jordan that I don't makes me feel like he's stolen another piece of my brother from me. He's already taken too much.

I reach for my phone and go to my favorites. I call my top contact.

Even though it's late Friday night, she answers on the first ring. Like she always does.

Forty minutes later, Lucy sits on my bed, a letter gripped tight in her hand. The other letters are scattered around her, like she's sitting in the eye of a hurricane. She finishes reading another one and looks up at me, eyes wide.

"You've been hiding these for, what, a year?" She motions to all of them. "There are so many. I cannot believe you've been letting this guy harass you for so long. . . ." She tries to hold my eyes, but I look away, at the wall, anywhere but at the letters or at Lucy.

"Hey." She reaches out and grabs my limp hand. "Hey. Don't ice me out." She pushes back against the headboard. "I don't pretend to know how you feel about all this. I mean, I guess I thought I sort of understood, because I loved Jordan too, but . . . I think I was wrong. I don't know. I really don't." She trails off and rubs her forehead, all weary. "I thought you were healing . . . starting to rejoin us in the world. You stopped drinking, you're back in school. Zach seems like a good guy. But Jesus. This is bad, May. It's very, very bad."

I cross my arms tight across my chest and stare at the floor, blinking back the tears that keep filling my eyes. Something sharp digs into my palm, and I realize I'm gripping one of the letters so hard that the paper has cut my finger.

I watch the bright red spot of blood bubble up through my skin like it belongs to someone else.

All of a sudden, I'm furious. How dare she judge me: Lucy, with her perfect face and her perfect AA meetings and her perfect grandmother. Lucy, who has no idea what it's like to have a brother, no idea what it's like to hear him die. I whip my head up. She has a look of pity in her eyes and I want to wipe it right out.

"What would *you* have done with them?" I growl.

"Fuck. I don't know. At the very least I wouldn't have let them pile up without saying anything. All those times . . . all those times I asked how you were doing. All those times my *grandmother* asked you, and you just acted like you were okay, like everything was okay. All that time, you were hiding all of . . . this." She shoves the letters toward me with disgust.

I snort. "Oh, okay. You think you would have handled it better? So easy for you to say. You were on the other side of the school during the shooting. You can talk *alllllll* about how hard it was to go through it, but you didn't really, did you? None of you fucking did—not you, not Chim, not Miles. . . . not even Anne, who everyone thinks is such a *survivor.* You want to talk about surviving? Nine people walked into the band room that afternoon, and guess how many were still breathing when they left?" I'm shaking. Tears fall hard and fast down my face and I don't care. "Two. Me. And this asshole." I hold up a handful of the letters, throw the pages at her. I want to rip them apart, rip everything apart, tear it all away until there's nothing left but raw, bloody pulp.

Lucy tries to put her hand on my shoulder, starts to say something. I know she's trying to get me to calm down, but I am sick and tired of being told to be calm.

"No." I shove her hand away. "Do not touch me. I asked you to come over because I needed your help, because I need to figure out how to handle this, but all I get is judged. It's bullshit. Don't you care about how it might make me feel?"

Lucy takes a deep breath and lets it out. She closes her eyes for a second, like she's dealing with an irrational child. I'm about to open my mouth again to keep ranting, but she speaks first.

Her voice is deep and low. "Are you serious? You have got to be kidding, asking whether I care about how you feel. All I've done for the last year is care about how you feel. What about me, May? Jordan was like a brother to me. I loved him." Tears fall from her eyes. I've never seen Lucy cry. "I *loved him,* and you never acknowledge that. Even when he was alive, you didn't acknowledge it; during freshman year, you started acting like I was a traitor when I'd want to hang out with him. Like I wasn't allowed to be close with both of you, like I had to *choose*.

"It's like you think you're the only one who lost something—some*one*—that day, whose life was changed forever. Like no one else was in that building. Like no one else thought they might die. That entire time, we had no idea what was happening—the fire alarm kept blaring and everyone was huddled under desks, crying and watching the news on our phones, and I kept texting you and Jordan and getting no response. Don't you get that what happened *broke* my *heart*?" Her mouth sets in a thin, hard line. "It's not fair, May. You don't allow anyone else the tiniest amount of room to grieve . . . and if we try to, you judge us for how we're doing it."

"No—" I open my mouth to defend myself, to tell her how wrong she is, but she ignores me and keeps talking.

"I even committed crimes for you, to try to help you feel better. You think I can afford to get caught vandalizing shit? It would fuck up my college chances forever. You know my dad isn't some fancy producer. We don't have a huge house like you do; my family can't afford to send me to college wherever I want to go. These days my dad can barely hold on to a job, not that you would know anything about that, since you haven't asked me about myself in months. But I didn't let any of that stop me. I was trying to be a good friend. I didn't even complain when you flaked on my birthday party last summer. I knew it was hard for you to get out of the house, to be around people. . . ." She pushes herself off my bed and stands up, arms crossed.

"I miss you, May. I've missed you for a year—missed you singing, missed you laughing, missed hearing your trumpet. Sometimes it feels like that fucking monster took both of my best friends that day." She shakes her head. "Can you please admit that this is out of control? You have to tell your parents about these letters. You have to stop letting this guy mess with your head—stop letting him have power over you. Can't you see that?"

I'm shaking with anger. I cannot believe the one person in this world I thought I could still trust would say this shit to me—would judge me like this. I'm frozen on my bed, still as a statue, and when she tries to touch me, I fling her hand off my arm with such violence that she jerks back in surprise.

She closes her eyes for a beat, and when she opens them again she looks so, so sad. "I'm going to leave. Please, though, tell someone about these. An adult. Your parents. These letters . . . This is so fucked-up. You have to do something. This guy is obsessed with you. Look at all these letters. He's not going to stop until you *do* something—until you tell someone who can help. This is *sick*. Don't you see that, May? Don't you?" She looks at me imploringly, and when I don't respond, she sighs. She gathers her coat and purse, and all the while I stare at my feet, refusing to look up until the bedroom door shuts behind her.

CHAPTER FORTY-FOUR

Zach

When my phone rings midday Saturday and I see that it's May, I sit up in bed and check myself in the mirror before I answer, like she can see me.

"Take it down a notch, Teller," I mutter. I flop back down on my stomach, propping myself up on my elbows. I've been sprawled here since Conor dropped me off an hour ago. He dragged me to the mall earlier because he wanted to buy a new shirt. I think he's trying to impress Lucy.

"May!" I practically yell her name into the phone. I cringe. I sound so fucking lame I'm tempted to hang up. I clear my throat. "How are you?"

There's silence on the other end and then a sniffle. "Hey." Her voice is thick, like she's been crying. I'm quiet, trying to figure out what to say. "Are you there?"

"Yes. Hi. I'm sorry." There's another sniffle from her end of the line. "Hey, are you okay?"

"I'm fine." She coughs a phlegmy cough. She's obviously lying.

I don't know how to respond. With Rosa, it was easy. She always wanted me to know every single thought that passed through her head, good or bad, and even though that was beyond exhausting at times, she was never a mystery. May is another story.

Her voice cuts through my thoughts. "Can you come over?"

"Right now?" I cringe as the words leave my mouth. Will I never learn to think about what I'm saying before I say it? "I mean, yes. Definitely. When? I'm there." Now my words are tumbling over each other like they can't figure out how to leave my mouth in the proper order. May lets out a bark on the other end of the line. At least my awkwardness is occasionally useful.

"Now would be great, if you don't mind."

"No! Yes, I mean. Wait, no—I don't mind." I shake my head and force myself to shut up for a second to control my verbal diarrhea. "I'll be there soon."

When I park outside May's house, it looks so dark and quiet that if I didn't know better, I'd think no one was home. I ring the bell and she answers immediately, like she was sitting on the other side of the door waiting for me.

Her face is swollen, red, puffy, like she's been crying for hours.

My eyes widen. I knew from the call that she was upset, but this—this is way beyond what I was expecting. I open my arms just in time for her to fall into them.

"Hey. *Hey.*" I stroke her hair, and for once in my life I'm pretty sure I say the right thing: "Are you okay? What happened? How can I help?"

Thirty minutes later I'm sitting on her bed, surrounded by the most fucked-up letters I've ever seen. We haven't spoken a word since we got to her bedroom and she pushed them toward me. I tried to ask her what they were, but she shushed me and motioned that I should read. Now I'm silent for a very different reason.

"What do you think?" Her voice catches on the word *think*. I can't bring myself to look at her. These letters are . . . I don't even know if there's a word that's strong enough to describe what they are. *Horrible* doesn't have the right ring. *Awful* is too weak. *Sickening* might be the closest.

"Have you told anyone about these?" I cringe. I sound so judgmental.

Her face shutters. "No." She starts to scoop the papers into a pile. I'm losing her. The last thing I want is to lose her.

"Hey." I grab her hands to stop her from her busywork.

"I'm sorry. I didn't mean for that to come out like it did. I'm a dick."

She laughs, but it's forced.

"This is all . . ." I'm at a loss for words. I know if I say what I want to say—*fucked-up beyond belief*—it'll be the end of the conversation. My heart's pounding fifty miles a minute. This is so far above my pay grade it's not even funny. I brush a stray hair off her forehead and think about what I'd want to hear if I were in her position. Who am I to say that the way she's dealt with these letters is wrong? I have no idea what I would do. "It's just a lot to process. Let me start over. Please?"

She nods. She seems so small, and it hurts my insides.

I close my eyes for a second to compose my thoughts. When I open them again, I say, "First off, can I ask you why you never told anyone about these?"

She flushes. "I don't know. When the first one arrived, I couldn't believe it was actually . . . real. Like, how did he get to me? He's in *jail*. You're not supposed to be able to *do* that when you're in jail." She shakes her head. "I was dumb. I didn't realize that it's *easy* to do things in jail if you know the right people. But with that first one, it's like I didn't even want to think about the fact that it existed, so instead of saying anything, I shoved it into the back of my closet." Her mouth is set in a line.

"But they kept coming?"

She bites her lower lip. "Yes. They kept coming. And coming. And your mom never stopped him." Her mouth is set in a line.

"Did she *know*?" I sound skeptical. I can't help myself. There's no way my mother knew about that shit and didn't try to stop it. I might have major personal issues with her, but I have to admit that she's really good at her job.

She looks at me like I'm an idiot. "Why wouldn't she? He's her fucking client."

I can't believe I'm about to defend my mother, but here we go. "Yeah, but I doubt she knows everything he does. If there's one thing I know about my mom, it's that she's obsessed with following the letter of the law."

The expression on her face gives me the chills. She purses her lips. "Do you think that fucking matters, Zach?" She growls my name. "She *should* have known. She should have done something. She should have done her job. She should have protected me. Someone should have protected me." Her voice has been growing louder and louder, and on that last word, it shatters into a million pieces and she starts to sob. "Did you read the last one?"

I nod.

"I never read them before tonight. I hadn't even opened them. But last night, when I read that last one, about Jordan, I just . . . I need to know. What he's talking about? Does he really know something about Jordan? Did Jordan tell him something?" She pauses, takes a ragged breath. "Look, you wouldn't understand. The weekend before my brother died . . . I was an asshole to him. A total fucking asshole. He probably hated me. And then he was gone. We never made up. If David"—she chokes on the name—"knows something—*anything*—about what Jordan was thinking before he died . . . if it was something about me . . . I have to know." Her hands are clenched into fists and her fingers are losing their color. She looks up at me with wide eyes full of sorrow, and I know that I'm going to help her, no matter how bad an idea I know this is. "Zach, why did he leave me alive?"

I take a deep breath, sensing that this is one of those moments I'll remember forever, one of those moments that will stick in my brain, that will split my life in two. And then I ask:

"What do you want to me to do?"

CHAPTER FORTY-FIVE

May

The morning after I call Zach, we're in the car heading to the one place I never would have thought I'd be going: the fucking Twin Towers jail in downtown Los Angeles. I cannot believe this is my life. There is something very wrong with it.

Everything in me is balled into a tense knot: my stomach feels like it's trying to escape my body and run down the freeway, back home.

After we decided to go last night, I googled the Twin Towers jail. It has the honor of being named one of the top ten worst prisons in the United States. All I know about jail and prison is from *Orange Is the New Black,* and I'm pretty sure the place we're going is nothing like that.

It was surprisingly easy to make an appointment to see him. Scarily so. I guess as long as you're on someone's approved visitors list, they don't care who you are. I read that there are eleven thousand inmates at the two jails downtown, so I guess I shouldn't be surprised that it's that simple.

With every mile we drive, the knot in my stomach grows larger. Soon it's going to swallow my entire body, and all that will remain will be a pulsing mass of anxiety. I haven't heard from Lucy since our blowup Friday night. This is the longest we've gone without speaking in years. But I can't think about it right now; if I do, I might implode. I can't imagine my life without her.

"What?" Zach looks over at me with raised eyebrows, and I realize that I just said Lucy's name out loud, like a total freak. I flush.

I shake my head. "Nothing. Sorry, I'm just stressed." I haven't told him about the fight.

"It's okay." He hesitates, then grabs my hand. It takes all my willpower not to snatch it back. He's helping me; I like him. I want to be normal; I want to be a girl who's in a car with a boy who likes her, driving to a normal destination. That's all I want.

But I know better than most that you can't always get what you want.

Or even what you need.

"So, what's the plan?" Zach is trying his best to be chipper, which is hilarious, given our current situation. "When we get there . . . do I come in with you? Is that allowed?" He pauses. "Look, I'm not trying to be your mom or anything, but I don't think it's a good idea for you to go in there alone." A tiny part of my brain snorts and thinks, *If you were being like my mom, you wouldn't even be in this car,* but I'm too distracted to say it out loud.

Instead I reply, "You read his letter. I have to go alone. That's the only way he'll talk to me." I sound like a robot. Zach's face is tense, his forehead creased. I remind myself that the reason he's involved in this mess is because of me, and that I should be nice to him even though my default mode is Evil. "Look, I appreciate your coming with me. Trying to protect me or whatever . . ." I trail off. Draw a shaky breath. I can't find the energy to continue. The landscape flies by outside the car, the palm trees that line the freeway zipping past in a streak of green.

We're getting closer.

I dig my nails into my palms, and the pain reminds me to get it together. I need to do this. I owe it to Jordan. I need to hear his last words, even if they come from the mouth of the monster who murdered him.

Zach's silent, driving.

"I'll be fine," I mumble. I square my shoulders like I've done so many times this past year and try to trick myself into believing my own bullshit.

He presses his lips together and I can tell he wants to say more, but he nods. "All right. I'm here. If you need me."

I nod.

We're quiet the rest of the ride.

* * *

About twenty minutes later, we pull up outside the complex. It's made up of two jails in downtown LA: Men's Central and Twin Towers, where David is. From the outside, the two towers look nondescript. They don't look worthy of their names, of what's inside them. Just a couple squat, ugly, medieval-looking gray buildings. The most startling thing about them is the lack of windows. You'd never guess that inside is a maze of hallways, thousands of inmates, and terrible living conditions. You'd never guess that inside is my brother's killer. Even though I've been getting envelopes postmarked from this complex for almost a year, I never thought about it as a real place until the other night. I had no idea any of this was here.

After we park, we sit in the car for a minute, silent and still. Zach keeps trying to catch my eye, but I can't bring myself to look at him. I've been pulling at the cuticle of my thumb over and over since we got off the freeway, and it's starting to bleed. My hands are a mess of scratches and torn skin.

I'm pretty sure I'm going to scream.

This is the anger I've been running from this entire year, the shit that got me kicked out of school. The fury that leaked into my body that day is rising in me. How dare this freak bribe me into visiting him? He doesn't deserve to have Jordan's final words; they should be *mine.*

Zach whispers, "Are you okay?" and I know I can't sit here any longer, wordlessly screaming into the black void of my own head.

I need to get a grip if I'm ever going to make it out of the car and into the jail. The minutes are ticking by, and we're getting closer to my appointment time. I need to go.

I switch myself to autopilot, like I did in the days after the shooting, after they carried me out of that tiny closet that had become my home, past abandoned bags holding buzzing cell phones. That was the worst thing: the cell phones I could hear buzzing as news of the shooting spread and parents started calling.

"Yes. I'm okay." I reach over and open the car door. Step out into the dark parking lot. Force a smile in Zach's direction. Close the door. As I walk away, I hear him say that he'll be here when I'm done, but I can't turn back to acknowledge it. If I do, I'll never make it out of this garage.

Everything is a blur once I leave him. My body takes over and my mind shuts down.

I fumble trying to open the door to the visitors' intake building because my hands are shaking so bad. Finally, a uniformed woman takes pity on me and swings it open from the inside.

I am going to throw up.

Somehow, I make it to the front desk and slip my ID through a tiny hole in the bulletproof glass.

Bulletproof glass.

The gruff man behind the counter shoves a clipboard in my direction and motions for me to sign it. I scribble something that looks vaguely like my signature, and then he barks at me to go sit down and wait. *Go sit down and wait.* Like this is just a normal day, a normal place.

Like I'm a normal person.

I drag myself over to the bench, limbs heavy, like they're made of concrete. Collapse on the bench next to a sobbing woman. My eyes are dry now.

As I wait, a thousand thoughts pummel my mind.

What did Jordan say before he died? Why couldn't David just tell me in one of his fucking letters? Why did he have to force me to come here?

I think back to that night—the night of the party—but it's this blank space in my brain that I can't penetrate. I remember getting to the party, drinking with Chim, glaring at Miles from across the room, and then . . . nothing. Whatever memory used to be there was obliterated by a black hole of alcohol-induced amnesia.

The room starts to tilt. I drop my head in my hands. I can't do this. I need to get up and go. What was I thinking coming here? Lucy was right.

And then the decision is made for me. They're calling us, all the people in the waiting room, telling us to put our phones in the lockers that line the far wall, to form a line by the opposite one; it's time.

help.

I sit on a cold metal stool in front of a thick Plexiglas window and a black phone.

I shiver.

* * *

A loud alarm sounds, and on the other side of the window, men start to shuffle in.

Even if they weren't handcuffed, there'd be no mistaking them for anything but prisoners. Their gait, the dead look in their eyes, the unhealthy tinge of their skin—all those things give it away.

And then I see him.

And then he sees me.

And then he smiles.

Tears prick at the corner of my eyes, but I cannot—I WILL NOT—let them fall. He doesn't deserve to see me cry.

He picks up the phone on his side of the window. He stares at me. I'm frozen. I can't look away.

I want to die.

Why won't anyone help me? Why am I alone?

I'm in the closet and the gunshots have stopped and there's an eerie silence, a silence that's thick and black, and I'm wrapped in a ball on the ground, my arms wrapped tight around my legs, and it's all I can do to keep my voice inside my body, but I can't let it out because then whatever is out there will come for me. And I have to be silent and I have to be quiet and my throat is raw from holding it all in; my entire body *aches* from holding it all in. And then the door slowly swings open and light pours in and it seems so wrong to see light again. I should be forced to live here in this blackness, in this silence, forever, since I stayed in here and left them all out there with that gun. All of them.

Jordan.

And then I'm screaming his name and I only stop because a face pokes into the closet and for this awful, heart-wrenching second, I think it's him—it's Jordan—but then I see that it's David Ecchles, who I tutored, who asked me out on dates, who I saw in the hallways, and it takes me a second to put it together: David Ecchles is the boy with the gun and the boy with the gun is David Ecchles, and then the scream I've been holding in my throat rips free and it's loud and it hurts and I'm pretty sure it slices my skin deep, so deep that I'm bleeding straight into my guts.

And then he smiles this horrible, toothy smile, and says, "Hey, May. You look pretty today," and shuts the door again.

And I scream and I scream and I scream and I scream and I scream.

* * *

He's wearing that same smile now.

A scream builds in my throat, but I can't let it out. They'll kick me out of here, and I've made it this far. I have to get what I came for. On the other side of the window, David Ecchles motions for me to pick up the phone. My hands are shaking violently in my lap, and I ball them into tight fists and finally they still enough for me to reach out and grab the phone.

CHAPTER FORTY-SIX

May

"Hello, May."

He leans forward in his seat and puts his palm against the Plexiglas between us. His eyes are glassy; the whites are yellowed from lack of sun. They look reptilian in the fluorescent light. I lurch back, almost fall off my stool.

"I didn't think you'd come. No one ever comes to see me."

I'm silent. My throat is dry. My brain and my body disconnect. I'm still breathing, my heart's still beating, but I'm not really here.

"You're my first visitor, did you know that? My parents and my sister won't even take my calls. I think they hate me." His voice catches. The sick feeling in my stomach expands. He doesn't deserve to be upset. He doesn't deserve to have feelings.

The partitions on either side of me narrow my view. He's the only thing I can see.

I swallow. My head aches. I grip the cold phone and force my mouth open, force air down my throat.

"Ple-ease." My voice breaks on the word. What a dumb word. What a dumb asshole I am for having said that word. To *him*. My body shakes. I clear my throat. "I'm here because of your letters. That's the only reason." I'm pitiful. Light glares from the ceiling; my armpits sweat through my shirt. My stomach lurches. "In your letters. You said you had something to tell me. About Jordan. You said he told you something, that day."

David bows his head for a moment. His hair is tangled and unkempt. He looks up at me, and I recognize the wild, empty expression in his eyes from when he'd stare at me in school. "I'm sorry, I'm so sorry. I said that to get you to come visit me. I didn't want to disappoint you, but I didn't know how else to get you here." He's talking fast, his words tumbling over each other, like he's out of practice.

"What?" My voice is small. A high-pitched buzzing starts in my ears. I try to stand, but my knees buckle under the weight of my body and I land back on the stool, hard. "What do you mean?"

He's quiet for a moment, and then: "You're looking at me like I'm a monster." He sounds sad. Bile leaps into my mouth. He shakes his head. "I didn't think you'd be so scared of me. I lie in bed at night, and the memory of your face is the only thing that keeps me going. Our conversation that night at the pool. You, sitting there all alone, crying. It was fate that I was there to help." He pauses. "You know, I only went to that party to see you."

"That party." This room is stifling. I'm struggling to breathe.

"Yeah—the one Adam had? I'd been planning everything for months—I couldn't stand it anymore, any of it: The way people walked right by me in the halls like I didn't matter. Oppenheimer always picking on me in music class. My dad—I had to show him that I have balls, that I'm not a fucking crybaby." He growls that last word. His lips pucker and turn white. "I was going to wait a couple weeks." He barks a dry laugh. "But after we talked, it all made sense. . . . It was like everything fell into place. It all came together." He pauses and looks down for a moment, and when he looks back up, there are tears in his eyes. *Tears.* "Sometimes I can't believe I did all that stuff. It's like . . . Who is that person? Was that really me? I don't know. All these thoughts get twisted." He shakes his head. "But then I remind myself of our conversation, and it all gets easier to manage in my brain."

My eyelids flutter and my heart skips a beat. "We didn't talk at that party." My voice is flat. "We didn't." The last part comes out as a whisper, a lie that I can't quite give up.

On the other side of the Plexiglas, David looks confused. "Yes, we did."

The buzzing in my head grows louder. *We did.*

He continues, "You remember. That night. We sat out by

the pool. You were crying. Miles was inside somewhere, getting drunk or doing something stupid. You said your parents never cared about you—you felt like you were invisible. You said you hated your brother—you wished he would just disappear."

"I never said that." *I never said that. I didn't. I didn't.*

A memory flickers at the corner of my brain.

Did I?

"So I made him disappear for you . . ." His voice is getting louder. "Tell me you remember, May. Tell me you're kidding. I thought you'd be happy that he's finally gone. You're free."

"No. I didn't— I'm not—" I choke on the words. My heart is rattling my rib cage and my breaths are choppy and short. I remember Miles's words: *I saw you outside, talking to that psycho. You guys looked like you had a lot to say to each other.*

I hadn't believed him, not really. Or maybe I had, but I'd buried that belief deep in my core and ignored it, and ignored it, and ignored it, until I thought it had gone away.

But it's right here in front of me, eyes flashing.

"No. No. No . . ." I'm shaking so hard that my stool rattles against the linoleum floor. "That's not what I meant. That's not what I meant at all." I force myself to stand. "I need to leave." I look around for a guard, someone, *anyone* to help me. *Help me.* Tears blur my vision. I'm frozen in place. My knees buckle, and I'm forced to grasp the edges of the partition to keep my body upright.

"Please. May. Wait." David reaches toward the Plexiglas

again, and it's like I'm back there in that closet, back there in the dark, and then that light peeks through and I think it's Jordan's face, but it's not, and it never will be again.

My world turns black.

Zach and some giant man help me into the car. I'm limp. Floppy.

We're driving.

Zach tries to talk to me, but his words don't sound like English. I can't concentrate enough to hold on to any of them.

My stomach roils. "Fuck." I'm going to be sick. "Pull over."

"What?" Zach throws me a questioning glance and registers the panic on my face. "Shit. Okay, okay. I need to find a spot . . . somewhere safe." He glances in the rearview mirror and then over at me. "Hold on." He twists the wheel sharply to the right and we skid onto the shoulder of the freeway, going way too fast.

He slams to a stop on an embankment and I jump out of the car, put my head between my knees. I retch, but nothing comes out. I haven't eaten since I spilled the contents of my stomach into the toilet on Friday night. Tears stream down my face.

All I want is to be the girl I was last year, even though I was a mess, even though I was a shallow idiot who never considered the consequences of my actions. I want to be in my room, annoyed at Jordan because he's spent the last four hours practicing his guitar without stopping. I want to be at one of those stupid parties with Jordan by my side, him bored, but refusing to leave until I agree to go with him. I want to be at the dinner table, not able to get a word in edgewise because my parents only care about what he has to say.

The one person at that table who cared about what I said was Jordan. And now he's gone. The person who I shared a womb with, who I grew into a human with, who only ever wanted to be my friend, is gone.

Forever.

Because of me.

Zach comes to where I'm bent over, hands on knees. He puts his hand on my heaving back, but it feels way, way too heavy. It feels like the weight of everything I've done in the past year, everyone I've harmed, so I shrug it off. A hurt look crosses his face, but I'm too far gone to care.

CHAPTER FORTY-SEVEN

Zach

May won't answer my calls. Since our visit to the jail, things have been tense. I waited in my car for what felt like hours before finally heading inside to find her. I had a feeling something terrible had happened.

When I got in there, they had her propped up like a scarecrow on a bench in the waiting area. She was really out of it. It was scary. A guard from the jail and I had to help her into the car because she couldn't walk. The whole way home, I kept trying to get her to talk to me about what happened, but she barely spoke.

When I dropped her off at her home, she got out of the car without a word and went inside.

At first, I figured she just needed time to process everything, but it's been three days of silence now. She wasn't in drama yesterday; I don't think she's been at school. Today's the anniversary of the shooting, and there are a bunch of events and a big assembly that she's supposed to speak at along with some other kids from her old school.

I look for her all morning, and after fourth period I find myself walking down the hallway where all the Carter kids have their lockers. It's eerily hushed, which makes sense, considering. There's a table set up with a serious-looking woman sitting behind it and pamphlets strewn across the top. As I pass by, I see they're all about grief. A couple people huddled in a corner, a guy and a girl. She's crying, and he's trying to comfort her. His arm is around her shoulders, and she's leaning into him.

I grimace. That's what I should be doing for May right now. What I should have done the other night. Not even as a person who's sort of dating her. Just as a friend. I should never have let her get out of my car without making sure that she was okay. That, at the very least, her parents were home. That she wasn't alone.

I catch sight of Lucy's head of brown curls on the opposite end of the hallway, moving away from me, and I run to catch up. She's chatting with a girl I recognize from Conor's show, the one May introduced me to at the bar.

"Lucy!" I'm out of breath. "Wait up."

She glances over her shoulder and sees me. I must look like a total mess, because she raises her eyebrows and stops. The other girl stops too. They appraise me, arms crossed, eyebrows arched. It's very intimidating. I have to force myself to speak.

I clear my throat. "Hey." I can't read their faces. "I'm trying to find May?"

The girls glance at each other.

Lucy speaks. "Have you talked to her today?"

I swallow and shake my head. "Sunday was the last time I heard from her?" It comes out like a question.

Her eyes widen. She shoots another glance at her friend.

The friend speaks. "Hey. Zach, right?" She sticks her hand out, all formal, which is weird, but I shake it because I am nothing if not unfailingly polite. "I'm Chim. We met at Lucy's show the other week. You haven't heard from May?"

"Not since a few days ago. Do you guys know where I can find her?"

There's a pause, and the girls silently communicate.

Lucy says, "I haven't talked to her since last Friday. We sort of . . . had a little bit of an argument. I was trying to give her some space to cool off. Have you seen her at school?"

"No. She wasn't in drama yesterday. She won't answer my calls." I'm getting actually, for-real worried now.

"But you saw her on Sunday?"

I nod, and am about to tell them what we did, but realize how fucked-up it sounds. "Yeah, we hung out. I haven't heard from her since I dropped her off."

Lucy narrows her eyes. "What did you guys do?"

"Do?" My voice squeaks.

"Yeah. On Sunday. What did you guys do?"

"Nothing much."

She closes her eyes for a second, looking pained. When she opens them, she says, "Let's cut the bullshit, okay? You saw the letters."

My mouth falls open, but I pull it shut and try to compose myself. How does she know?

She sighs. "Look, Zach. The fight May and I got in? It was over those letters. She showed them to me, and I kind of freaked. I feel bad about it, but it's also really messed up that she's been hiding them for this long. . . ." She shakes her head. "Whatever. That's irrelevant. She called you after I left, didn't she?"

I flush. "How do you know?"

"Look, I don't mean this to sound insulting, but she doesn't have very many people to talk to these days, especially people she trusts."

Out of the corner of my eye, I see Chim bite her lower lip.

I make a decision. "Yeah. Fine. She did." I'm getting defensive, but Lucy's acting like I was May's second choice, and it rubs me the wrong way.

"What happened after she showed them to you?"

My nostrils flare. "Nothing." Lucy's glare makes my hair stand on end. "Okay. *God.* She said that she needed to know what her brother had said—that she needed his last words—so . . . so"—I lick my lips, summoning the courage to say the words—"I went with her to the jail."

Lucy's eyes widen. "Excuse me, *what?* You did *what?*" She starts hitting me with her books and I duck, trying to protect myself with my arms. "You went with May to *prison*? To see that fucking *freak*? Are you deranged? Are you a total moron? Why in the world would you do that?"

She's still hitting me, and it hurts.

I yelp. "Hey. Hey! Stop!"

Chim pulls her back. Lucy's red in the face and breathing hard.

"Thank you. *Fuck.*" I rub my upper arm and glance around the hallway, and sure enough, people have stopped to stare. Great. Cool. Fantastic. I start to feel my skin prickle like it has so many times over the past year due to unwanted attention and take a deep breath. *Who cares?* Who cares that everyone is staring, per usual. What's important is May. I turn back to Lucy, who's still glaring at me. "Look, I thought going there might help her get some closure. I was trying to be a good friend." I squint at the wall over Lucy's head. "I thought . . ."

"That you could save her?" Lucy is fuming.

"What?"

"You thought you could save her. Admit it. You weren't doing this for May. You were doing it so you could play out some bullshit Prince Charming fantasy you have."

"No, I—"

She talks over me. "I bet. I just *bet* you were thinking about May when you took her to see her brother's *killer.* Totally something you do for someone you care about." She glares at me, eyes flashing.

Chim puts a hand on Lucy's arm. "Hey. Both of you need

to calm down. I know you're worried, so you're blaming the messenger"—she looks at Lucy, then turns to me—"and I think we both know that you were trying to be that guy to May, but I get it. You like her, you were trying to do what she asked."

"No. I was trying to be there for her, since no one else was." Lucy and Chim wince, and I feel like a jerk.

I run my hand through my hair, starting to understand the degree to which I fucked things up. On Sunday I was so focused on making May happy and giving her some sense of closure that I didn't consider the consequences. What it would be like to come face to face with the person who murdered your twin.

Lucy takes a deep breath and closes her eyes. I'm worried that she's going to start screaming at me again, but when she opens them back up, some of the anger has drained from her face. "Okay. I get that it wasn't intentional—you weren't *trying* to fuck her entire world up. Fine. Fine. Whatever." She sighs. "Let's move on to more important matters, like where in god's name *is* she?"

My heart sinks. "I haven't been able to get ahold of her. Maybe we should go by her house?" I thought about doing that last night, late, but I talked myself out of it. I didn't want to be pushy, overbearing, too in-her-face. Now I regret it.

Lucy holds up a finger as she rummages through her bag. "Her parents still have a landline. . . ." She pulls out her phone and taps the screen. Holds it to her ear. "It's ringing." A few seconds later, she shakes her head. "No answer. Just the machine. Shit."

I feel sick, deep in my guts. If anything happened to May, it's all my fault.

I look at Lucy. Her eyes are rimmed red. "Let's leave right now, go to her house. We can take my car. She has to be there. Where else could she be?" I say.

Lucy gives a limp, weary shrug. All the fight has drained out of her. Her eyes are lifeless. "Sure. Whatever. I guess it can't hurt. Let's go."

We're almost at the doors to the school when a voice calls from behind: "Hey, guys. Are you on the way to the auditorium for the memorial?" We glance at each other and then slowly turn around.

Mr. Ames stands in the middle of the hallway, arms folded across his chest, eyebrows raised. He definitely knows we were not headed to the assembly. *Fuck*. The assembly. Where May is supposed to talk. She's going to get kicked out of school again if she doesn't show.

"Mr.—" I'm searching for an excuse for why we have to leave school, but he cuts me off.

"I know, guys. I know this is a rough day for us all." He gives Lucy and Chim a sad smile. "Let's all walk together?"

I look at Lucy and I know we're thinking the same thing: there's no way May would want us to tell the school if there was something wrong.

So I nod to Mr. Ames, and we all trail behind him as he walks toward the auditorium.

When we get into the room, we shuffle into a row of seats halfway to the front.

I'm so tense I'm shaking. All I can think about is May walking away from me when I dropped her off the other day. The way she shut down after we left the jail. The fact that I had to go into the building to find her, because she was too far gone to make it out herself.

Where the hell *is* she? Why did I leave her alone?

CHAPTER FORTY-EIGHT

May

Memories well up in me, each one more vivid than the last. Jordan on our sixth birthday, sitting with me in front of our cakes. He got a Superman one and I got a Minnie Mouse one and we both loved them so much and our mom was so happy, and our dad didn't yell once that whole day.

The first time Jordan played a guitar, in fourth grade, he surprised us all—he was so good. Naturally talented, unlike most of the other kids—unlike me. He picked it up so fast, and he was writing his own music before sixth grade began.

When we were thirteen, and our dad made us both apply to the Stanford Summer Arts Institute. The dismissive look my dad gave me when the emails arrived and only Jordan was accepted.

Freshman year, finally able to join a band at school together. Jazz band was great at first. Great until it wasn't. Great until it was yet another place where Jordan excelled and I did not.

Me, last year, too drunk to stand upright, leaning against the wall outside our house fumbling with my keys, trying to get them into the lock. Jordan was behind me waiting, and after a few seconds passed he told me to hand over the keys, and he did it himself. I don't remember much else about it except that I didn't thank him—I never thanked him. I just acted like he was in my way as I shoved by him into the house.

I open the door to the auditorium, crowded by these thoughts. The last time I was in here was with Zach. His face flits across the edge of my mind. I shake it away. I can't let anything distract me from what I came here to do. I grip my notebook tight between my hands and walk toward the stage.

I spent the last few days alone, hiding in my room. I was tempted to raid my parents' liquor cabinet, to drown out the thoughts in my brain like I used to, but it was better punishment to keep myself sober and aware. To not let myself forget.

I haven't been to school in days. I couldn't go. I could barely put on my clothes to get here this afternoon, and the only reason I did is because I have some things I need to say.

Principal Rose-Brady catches my eye as I approach the stage and beckons me over. I'm ready for this. I have it all written down in my notebook—the perfect speech. The one they all want to hear. I was supposed to show it to her yesterday, but I was out. *Sick*. I perfected my mom's phone voice years ago.

Behind her, there's a small group of people lingering around the microphone stand, Anne at its center. The guy standing next to her turns toward me, and I realize that it's Miles.

A banner hangs over their heads. IN MEMORIAM. The faces of the dead plastered on either side of the words.

I turn away before I see Jordan's face.

"May. I'm glad you came even though I know you haven't been feeling well." Rose-Brady ushers me over to the edge of the group and holds out her hand. "I just need to look at your speech quickly." I grimace at her but comply. I hand over my notebook. It's clean and new—I bought it just for this most fucked-up of occasions.

Rose-Brady flips through the pages, skimming the words. After a few beats, she looks up with a pleased expression. "I have to say . . . I didn't quite know what to expect, May, but this is lovely. This speech is approved." She gives me a smile, and then turns to the group, clapping her hands. "All right, guys. We're starting soon. Everyone ready?"

I force a stiff, fake smile onto my face and nod along with the rest of them. Nervous chatter rises from Anne's merry band of mourners, but I swallow hard and try to ignore them. I can't get distracted. There's too much at stake.

As I wait for everything to begin, Anne comes over and tries to act like we're friends. Her normal MO. She says hi and puts her hand on my arm. It takes all my willpower not to shove it off and then shove her off the stage.

Thankfully, Rose-Brady grabs the microphone a moment later. It screeches as she taps it, saying, "Testing . . . testing . . ." A couple kids snicker in the front row.

She motions for us to line up behind her like a bunch of stupid ducklings. Out in the audience, everyone's talking and whispering. The energy is almost . . . excited.

It's sickening.

It's like they're getting off on this shit.

It reminds me of the media after the shooting, how they were all like *It's so awful. . . . What a tragedy,* but under their caked-on makeup their eyes were full of glee. What a thrill to have something of national importance to talk about on their crappy local news shows.

I stand on the stage watching everything move around me, but totally disconnected from it all. Nothing seems real. Rose-Brady gives her speech first, and then Anne. I don't hear a word. People in the front row start to cry. On either side of me, I hear sniffles. I clench my hands into fists by my sides.

I'm so wound-up that I jump when a hand touches my shoulder. Rose-Brady stands in front of me.

"It's your turn, May," she whispers. She squeezes my shoulder. "I know this is hard."

I press my lips together and nod.

I clutch my notebook to my chest as I walk up to the microphone, my heart beating a wild rhythm into my ears. Under it, the rest of the world is muted. I set the notebook down on the stand in front of me and open it. From stage right, Rose-Brady gives me a thumbs-up. I almost start to laugh.

My notebook is full of black ink and bullshit. I don't need to read what I'm about to say, and I'm definitely not going to read the words written in here—all the fucking platitudes everyone wants to hear. I know what I'm going to say; I've recited the words so many times in my head that I've started dreaming them.

I clear my throat and it echoes through the crowded auditorium. I squint into the bright lights and see Zach sitting a bunch of rows back, flanked by Chim and Luce. What the fuck? They're all whispering furiously to each other. If I had to guess, I'd bet they're talking about me.

I force them out of my mind. I take a deep breath and begin.

"Hi, everyone. My name is May. May McGintee. My brother, Jordan, died. He was my twin. You probably knew him as that genius kid. The one who took the PSAT and got a perfect score as a seventh grader. But he was more than that. He loved so many things—all kinds of music, indie bookstores, hanging with his friends—but playing the guitar was his passion. He loved it. He would practice for hours, with his friends from the jazz band, with me"—my voice breaks—

"and even alone in his room. His guitar was *part* of him. It was more who he was than anything else at all." I swallow hard. My fingers shake, and I grip the sides of the stand tight, trying to calm the fuck down. That first part is exactly like the speech I showed Rose-Brady.

I take a deep breath and push forward into the stuff that matters. The stuff that isn't in that dumb notebook.

"Whatever. That's what they want us to say—they want us to recite a bunch of trite memories about the people who died so we can all move on with our lives, right? We can pretend we did our part, remembered the people who died, because we all recited these memories and all agreed to pretend the same thing: *Oh, wow we were all so great to each other, before; everything was so fucking great.* But that's bullshit. I'm here to tell you all the *truth* about how things were before." My voice catches, but I plow through it. "I was a terrible sister. A terrible, awful, *shit* sister." My voice trembles on the last word. I want to puke all over the microphone. I look up. I expected a gasp at this last part, but people mostly look confused. Some even look bored, like they're wondering when they can get out of here and get on with their lives. Out of the corner of my eye, I see Anne and her cohorts nudging one another, like *What the fuck is that crazy girl doing now?* Rose-Brady, who was deep in conversation with her co-principal when I began to talk, is now paying full attention to what I'm saying. I don't have much time left.

I hurry to continue. "That last year, all we did was fight.

I abandoned him over and over again, and one last time that day. The day of the shooting, I stayed in that *fucking* closet and listened while he died. While they all died. I stayed in there because I was a coward." My voice cracks. "No, I *am* a coward. And I deserved to die more than any of them."

Rose-Brady's next to me now—*May, stop. May. Give me that microphone. May, don't do this.* She can't do anything, though—she can't put her hands on me—not if she wants to keep her job. So I continue.

"I told David Ecchles stuff about my brother that I never should have said out loud—to anyone. I told him that I hated Jordan. That I HATED him. And then David murdered all those people because of me. Do you see what I'm trying to say? That's why I'm still alive. This is *all my fault.*"

I pause, trying to catch my breath. It's coming out in gasps. Tears are falling fast down my face, cutting jagged lines on my cheeks. Through them, I catch a glimpse of Lucy, halfway out of her chair, the teacher next to her tugging her back; I see Zach already on his feet next to them.

Rose-Brady has disappeared from my side. The pages of my notebook are damp under my sweaty hands, my head is pounding, but I force myself to stay here. They all need to know that *I* am a monster. That I deserve to be punished.

To my left, Rose-Brady reappears, flanked by two school resource officers. They're coming toward me, fast. My stomach drops at the sight.

I grab the microphone and pull it closer to my mouth.

It makes a loud *SCREECH*. People sitting in the front rows cover their ears. "Do you all hear me? I killed him! I killed my brother. I killed all these people. *I* did this." I'm trying to get it all out—I'm talking so fast that I'm stumbling over my words. Some small part of my brain recognizes that I'm losing it. I don't think I'm getting across what I want to get across, and my mouth can't seem to find the words I practiced over and over again in the bathroom mirror.

One of the resource officers is next to me, pulling on the microphone cord, trying to take it away, but I hold it tight in my hand. My throat is raw. Everything hurts and nothing will ever be okay again.

Rose-Brady drops to the floor below the stage, and she must find the outlet where the microphone is plugged in, because it cuts off, plunging the room into silence.

Then the school resource officers are on me and one of them takes the microphone out of my hand and the other puts his hand on my arm, gently trying to pull me away, more gently than it seems like he wants to be, and I'm sure Rose-Brady told them to do that—to be gentle with me—but I don't want them to be. I deserve to have them throw me down on the floor, to handcuff me and take me away, so I struggle against his grasp, and as I struggle, his hand squeezes my arm tighter and tighter and tighter.

All of a sudden, Zach and Lucy are in front of me. Lucy is trying to get the guard to let me go, screaming *You can't do this; get your hands off her!* but he ignores her and tightens his grip on my arms. I go limp. I'm sobbing. I can't hold myself upright for much longer.

The room is in chaos—kids in their seats, holding up their phones, probably recording this shit—but I don't care. It doesn't matter. I hope they are. In front of me, Zach reaches out to me—*May, it's going to be okay*—his voice reassuring and kind, and he's stupid for wanting to help me—stupid for caring about me. I'm broken. It's no use. I can barely get my voice out of my mouth, but I manage to say the one thing I never thought I'd let myself say out loud. The thing he deserves to know.

It was me.

He doesn't hear me at first. Or he ignores it. It doesn't matter, because I say it again.

It was me.

This time he pauses, tilts his head like he doesn't understand what I'm saying.

"*What* was you?"

Your garage. Your lawn. All those times. You forced to clean up the mess.

My voice doesn't sound like my voice.

I gulp air into my throat.

It was all me.

This time I know he hears me, because his face folds in on itself and he steps back, away from me. Looks down at the floor. The guard still holds my arms, waiting for Rose-

Brady's instructions, and his grip is the only thing keeping me upright.

When Zach looks up, the light in his eyes has gone out.

It hits me in the stomach, deep—the disgust, the revulsion, everything I deserve and everything I've always feared I am, reflected back at me.

And then he turns and walks off the stage.

He's gone.

I drop my head down on my chest, sobbing, legs trembling under me, threatening to fold.

Someone touches my arm, soft, gentle, and I think maybe it's Zach, maybe he came back, but when I look up it's Lucy, always Lucy, and then the world pitches into black.

The next thing I know, I'm in Rose-Brady's office, fluorescent lights flickering above my head, and she's sitting at her desk, frowning at me. Lucy sits next to me, holding my hand.

I can barely concentrate as Rose-Brady talks. She says that the rest of the assembly has been canceled. That I took away all those people's opportunity to remember what we've lost. That she understands that I'm still grieving, but so are other people. That she wishes I had come to her in private instead of doing what I did.

All I keep thinking about is when Jordan and I were younger, around six or seven, and I was scared of the dark.

Jordan never was. He was always so much braver than me. Never afraid of silly things. Every night, I would lie in my bed, too scared to move, until I couldn't take it anymore and I would bolt out of my room and into his. He would be sleeping, but he'd wake up and see me, and without a word he would scoot his body over toward the wall as best he could and make space for me in the bed. I would climb in, and we would cuddle together for the rest of the night.

As we got older, he tried to make our dad pay attention to me, encouraged me to try out for the band, took care of me, night after drunk night, and all he ever wanted in return was to be my friend, my brother, my twin. I ruined that. I ruined everything.

Lucy squeezes my hand tighter and I realize I'm whimpering, tears streaming down my face, soaking the front of my shirt.

Then Rose-Brady says my parents are on their way, and my brain clicks off and I sink down in her hard-backed office chair and I wait for whatever comes next.

CHAPTER FORTY-NINE

Zach

I can't sleep.

Much earlier, after I got home from school, after that awful, horrible day, all I wanted to do was sleep. I wanted to close my eyes and never wake up.

Instead I'm lying on my bed with all my clothes on, even my shoes, staring up at the ceiling. It's nine p.m. and I've been lying here for hours, staring.

I'm turning May's words over and over in my head, trying to fit them back together, like maybe if I rearrange them in just the right way, they'll mean something different. But they won't—of course they won't. *It was me.* There's no two ways about it. *May* was the person vandalizing our house—the person who made my life miserable for months on end. And she lied to my face over and over and over again.

Was she just getting close to me so she could get to my mom? Using me for some psychotic revenge on my family? It's pretty obvious that she never cared about me at all.

There's a knock on my door. It takes all my energy to hold back a scream.

"What?" I growl.

"Zach?" My dad pops his head into the room. "Just seeing if you want to watch something with me . . ." He trails off. "You okay, kid?"

I press my mouth into a long, thin line. "Yes. I'm fine. I'm always fine."

He hesitates in the doorway and then comes farther into my room. I squeeze my eyes shut. Can't everyone just leave me alone?

He sits down on my bed. "Want to talk about it?" He's acting like this is normal. Like we're best buddies. Like I'd *want* to talk to him about anything at all.

"Nope." I open my eyes and glare at him.

"C'mon. Might make you feel better." He nudges me.

I move away from him and cross my arms. "Stop."

He sighs. "Shit. Zach, man. I'm trying, here. Can't you throw me a bone?" He reaches out again. I shove his hand off my arm.

"Get. Off."

"Hey . . ." He reaches out a third time, and deep within the center of my being something snaps.

I grab his fingers and look him straight in the eyes. "I said, *get off me.*" He flinches out of my grip with a hurt expression, but I don't care. I just don't care.

"What are you even *doing* here? You pick today of all days to act like you care? Where have you been for the past year? The past five years? Trying to start a stupid band like you think you're *my* age? Hiding out in your fucking cave, forcing me to clean up your mess—forcing me to take care of Gwen. I've made the two of us dinner, driven her to school *every day.* Cleaned up the horrible shit that people wrote on our fucking garage." Bile rises in my throat at the thought of the garage and who those *people* were. I refuse to cry in front of my father. Instead, I grab my phone. Stand. "I can't deal with this right now."

"Zach—" He reaches for me again, but I move too fast. "C'mon. Zach!"

He's still calling my name as I walk out of my bedroom, down the staircase, and out the front door.

A short while later, I pull up to Conor's. I texted him on my way over, and he's waiting outside as promised, holding a brown paper bag by his side. The house looks worse than the last time I was here. The weeds in the front yard have all grown back since we pulled them out a couple months ago.

He waves as I pull to the end of the cracked asphalt driveway and park. I slowly get out of the car, the weight of everything pressing down on my shoulders.

"Hey." He chin-nods in my direction and hops onto the

hood of my Jeep. Usually I'd yell at him, tell him to stop denting my car, but right now I'm too exhausted to care. He opens the bag he's holding and pulls out a six-pack.

"Stole these from my dad." He sounds younger than usual. He always does when he's at home. It's like the magnetic field of his house tears away the persona he's created.

I raise my eyebrows and glance over at the front door but know better than to ask any questions, like *Is your dad passed out on the couch?* We've been through this before.

I climb up onto the hood of the car and settle in next to him, wincing as the metal dips beneath my weight. He hands me a beer.

"You okay, man?" He nudges me with his shoulder. After the assembly, he found me staring into space, slumped against a wall of the emptied auditorium, and forced the whole story out of me. The jail visit, May's disappearance . . . what she said to me right before she was pulled away by the resource officers.

I take a long sip from my can. The beer tastes terrible. I swallow it and take another gulp.

"I dunno." I shrug. "I'm . . . I've been better. . . ." I trail off. The air is filled with noise from the nearby airport, small commuter jets taking off and landing. All those people on board, living lives totally different from mine. Leaving here. What I wouldn't give to trade places with them.

"I just feel like an idiot."

"Why?" Conor says.

I shake my head. "Don't be like that. You know why. I trusted her. I thought . . . I thought she *got* me. I brought her to my fucking house! I don't bring anyone to my house, except you. I thought that maybe, for the first time in forever, someone saw me. Like, *me,* not my fucking mom."

The balloon of anger that's been floating in my midsection since earlier today, slowly leaking, finally bursts. I throw my beer across the driveway, can still half full. It lands and explodes. Conor, god love him, doesn't react.

I continue, "But then I find out that *all she saw* was my mom. It's such bullshit. I can't believe she came over, acting like she'd never been to my house before, all the while casing the place."

I expect Conor to be sympathetic, but instead he snorts. I glare at him and he holds his hands in front of his chest. "I'm sorry! I'm sorry. I'm not laughing at you. But, bro, *casing* your house? Really? May doesn't seem like the type."

"She didn't seem like the type who'd *vandalize* my house either!"

He shrugs. "True, but when she was doing that, did she know it was your house?"

I squint out into the night and grab a new can of beer out of the bag. "You mean, before we met? I guess no. . . ." I grunt the words out.

"Since you guys started . . . whatever"—he waves his hand vaguely in the air—"has anything been spray-painted on your house? Any shitty letters left in your mailbox?"

I clench my teeth. "No, but . . . she came over! She was *inside* my house! She acted all innocent, like she'd never been there before. She sat at the dining room table and had dinner with my parents!"

"Dude. You need to chill." He says it offhandedly, like he assumes I'll just go along with him without argument. I'll just *chill.*

I slam my fist on the hood of the car, and he jerks back in surprise.

"I'm tired of chilling. I'm sick of being this pushover who lets everything roll off his back. I have a month of detention 'cause I'm sick of letting Matt rub the fact that he's dating my ex-girlfriend in my face, and I don't even care. Who just puts up with that shit for as long as I have? What sort of person am I, letting them try to make me feel like I'm nothing? He was supposed to be my friend." I stop talking, hands shaking, insides turning. It's a new feeling. It's a *feeling.* "All those people at school, they were supposed to be my friends. May was supposed to be my friend. My mom was supposed to be . . ." My voice breaks. I stop speaking.

We're silent for a while, sitting there on the hood of my car, staring into the blackness of the yard, and then Conor reaches into the bag and pulls out another beer. He hands it to me without turning my way, and I take it and bump his shoulder in thanks.

CHAPTER FIFTY

May

My parents let me go straight to bed when we get home from the assembly. I'm in no condition to talk. No condition to hear about what I did wrong, because I already know—I did everything wrong.

Everything.

I wake up the next morning early, because my body and my brain won't let me sleep. I don't want to open my eyes. I don't want to breathe. I don't want to be here anymore.

I lie in bed, unmoving, under the heavy covers, until the sun starts to peek through the curtains. Until my bladder won't let me anymore.

So I get out of bed.

* * *

I stumble into the hall and toward the bathroom, trying my hardest to be quiet. I don't know if both my parents stayed here last night. I don't know what they're thinking. The car ride home with my mom was awful. She wouldn't look at me. She drove silent, crying the whole way.

When I get out of the bathroom, the door to their bedroom is open. My breath catches. Some tiny part of my brain recognizes that I haven't seen that door open in months. It's always shut tight, just like Jordan's.

"May."

My dad's voice floats out the open doorway. He's here, for once, not wherever he's been for the past year at night. I don't even know if my parents are together still. I don't know anything, and I haven't had the mental capacity to ask.

A sudden sharp pain in my stomach almost bowls me over.

"Can you come here, please?"

I want to say no. I want to leave. I want to run.

Instead, I walk toward their door, because I have nowhere else to go. No one to call to my rescue this time.

Lucy is gone.

Zach is gone.

Jordan is gone.

A whimper escapes from my mouth.

Inside their room, my mom sits on the bed. My dad paces back and forth in front of the fireplace on the far side of the room. Neither of them looks like they've slept. They're wearing the same clothes they had on yesterday.

My dad looks over at me, and I swear to god he doesn't recognize me at first. For a second, it's like he's seen a ghost. His face pales and then he coughs, and the moment is gone. His expression snaps shut and his eyes narrow.

"May." My name sounds like a curse coming from his mouth. "What the *hell* was that about yesterday?" He's talking low; his voice is tight. "What were you thinking, hiding those letters from us for so long? Telling those people that *you* killed your brother? The prosecutor is furious." He runs a hand through his hair, and when he speaks his voice has softened. "Why didn't you tell us about the letters? We could have done something. We could have stopped it." His voice cracks. He stops pacing for a moment. Clears his throat. Turns toward the fireplace and grips the mantel. After a few seconds he turns back to me. "Instead you just let him do this to you? Why would you do that? Why would—?"

"I don't know." My voice explodes out of my mouth before I can stop it. "I don't know, all right? I don't know." The tears have already started. Fucking traitorous tears. I bite the inside of my cheek so hard I taste blood. Ball my hands into fists at my sides. I'm so sick of them ignoring me. I'm so sick of them acting like I'm not worth anything. The one who isn't special. The one no one sees. "When exactly was I supposed to tell you? After Jordan's funeral, when you ran off halfway through the wake because you had to deal with some bullshit emergency on your set? During the four seconds that I see Mom every week? Should I have shoved a note under your

bedroom door? Not that *you* would have seen it. Do you even sleep here anymore? Do you even *live here* anymore?" My dad flinches.

"You don't understand," I go on. "You don't understand *anything.* My entire life, you've never tried to understand me. Once you realized that I wasn't smart like Jordan, that I was *normal,* you treated me like I was nothing. You never asked about my grades, about my life. It was always about him." I'm screaming now. My voice scrapes along the inside of my throat; it hurts, but I keep going.

"You never saw me. You barely knew I existed. But you wanted me to *tell* you about this? Would you even have cared?"

My mom starts to cry. I think I hear her say "Of course I would have," but it's so quiet and low it might be my imagination.

My stomach lurches, but I swallow down my guilt. My entire life, my role in this family has been in the background. I've spent my whole life making myself small. I spent my entire life thinking I didn't deserve anything else, because I wasn't smart enough; I wasn't talented enough; I wasn't *enough*.

After I stop yelling, we're silent. My mom on the bed, her fragile frame shaking with sobs. My dad stands in front of the fireplace, stone-faced. All the energy drains out of me, leaving me wobbly and raw. I sink down to the carpet, pull my knees in tight, put my head down on them. I whisper into them, "I'm sorry," over and over again, like I think Jordan can hear me, like if he could, he would care.

Then my dad's cell phone dings with a text, and he makes a sound like a grunt. "Of course we would have, May. *Christ.* Look, the prosecutor just texted me. They want those letters, now. We need to hand them over." He pauses. His voice softens. "I'm sorry you're upset. I'm sorry you don't think we gave you a good life. We tried our best."

I pick my head up off my knees. There are dark bags under his eyes, he looks exhausted. He looks like he's aged forty years in the past ten minutes.

I nod. Drag my body up off the ground. Say in a monotone, "Okay. I'll go get them."

I leave the room without a glance back, go into mine, and pull the letters from under my bed, where I stuffed them four nights ago, before Zach and I went to the jail. *Four nights.* It seems like a lifetime. I find a shoebox in my closet, place them inside.

When I walk back into my parents' bedroom, my dad holds out his hand and I put the box in it.

I expect a sense of relief. I expect to feel . . . well . . . *something.* Instead, there's the same hollow emptiness. The same tightness in the middle of my belly. The letters might be physically gone, but their words are seared into my brain forever.

My dad takes the box, tells us he's going down to deliver it to the prosecutor now, tells me some bullshit about how he hopes someday I'll see that he was doing the best he could for Jordan.

He walks out of the room, leaving me and my mom behind.

CHAPTER FIFTY-ONE

May

I haven't left my house since the conversation with my parents. It's been a week. No joke, Lucy has called my phone sixty-seven times. I'm not sure how many times she's tried the house phone, because my mom had to unplug it. Again. Just like after Jordan. My mom informed me that after my speech went viral, people from all over the country started calling. Reporters, crank callers, angry assholes, fans. *Fans.* That gives me the creeps—fans, just like a serial killer.

Which, I guess, I sort of am.

Zach hasn't tried to get in touch with me. Not once.

I shouldn't be surprised. I shouldn't be, but somehow, I am. I keep thinking that out of everyone, he should understand why I did what I did. He hated his mom too. But every time the thought crosses my mind, I remind myself of the words I sprayed on their garage, the lawn I salted and ruined, the constant thought he had that someone was out to get his family, and I'm reminded that I'm the worst person who has ever lived and I know that Zach will never speak to me again.

I wake up late in the afternoon, sticky with sweat, my brain still tangled inside a nightmare. I hear low voices murmuring from downstairs, and I pull my pillow over my head to block them out.

There's a knock on my door a few minutes later, and I hear it open.

"May," my mom whispers. I pretend I don't hear her. I pull the pillow down farther onto my head.

She lingers for a few moments longer, and then the door shuts quietly.

I take the pillow off my head and roll over, face toward the wall. I'm trying to convince my body to go back to sleep, when the door opens again. Footsteps cross the room and a cool hand brushes the nape of my neck.

"Oh, May Day." It's Lucy. "I've been trying to call you." She strokes my head. It's the first human contact I've had in a week. Something deep in my midsection begins to relax, and it feels like a betrayal.

"Stop." I grunt out the word and shuffle my body closer to the wall. Lucy draws back, leaving a cold, empty spot where her hand was.

"May. Jesus Christ. You scared the shit out of me the other day. Please—you can't do that again." Her voice cracks in a way I've never heard. I finally relent and roll to face her, just in time to see her face crumple. It stabs me right in the middle of my heart, because Lucy *does not cry.* "I can't take it—I already lost one of you. *We* already lost him." She sniffles and then takes a deep breath and lets out a sigh. "I'm sorry. I should have been there for you—at the jail, after the jail. Those letters . . . it wasn't fair of me to judge you for hiding them. I can't imagine what I'd do in your place. I was trying to protect you. I was worried. This whole year, you've been looking for a way to blame yourself for what happened . . . and then to have that asshole tell you that . . ." She shakes her head.

"I know things between you and Jordan weren't great . . . at the end." She puckers her lips and squints at my wall before continuing, "Look, Jordan told me something a couple weeks before the shooting that . . . I don't know . . . I never shared with you. You were always so shut down whenever I tried talking about him, and I never wanted to push it. . . ." She coughs. "Jordan was planning to apply to college, but not one of the ones that your parents wanted him to go to. Not some Ivy League or Stanford. He wanted to study guitar at Berklee in Boston. He was trying to create the life *he* wanted—not the one your dad kept trying to push on him." She laughs—a little, sad laugh. A laugh that contains multitudes.

She lapses into silence, staring at the wall above my immobile form. I can't bring myself to move—to speak. I'm pinned under the weight of her words.

Finally, Lucy breaks the heavy silence. "May, please know

it wasn't your fault. You didn't say anything that any normal person wouldn't say. You didn't pull the trigger. You didn't kill your brother. You aren't culpable because you stayed in that closet. You aren't to blame. Your parents didn't handle shit right, for so long. Your dad—acting like Jordan's future was some status symbol that he could flaunt—ignoring you . . . It was fucking toxic." Her mouth dips into a frown. When she speaks again, her voice is low. "Do you know how many nights I've thanked the universe for the fact that you're still here?"

Tears run down my nose. I'm frozen in place on my bed. I want to scream and yell and hug her and disappear, all at once.

She continues, "Look. I can't stay. Grann drove me here, but on the condition I didn't bother you for too long. She's worried. We all are. Chim wanted to come with me, but Grann said that one of us was enough for the time being. I mostly just wanted to bring you something—I'm going to leave it on your desk, okay?" She stands and walks across the room. I hear her put something on the desk. "Will you call me, once you've looked at it?" She pauses, waiting, and then says, "It's okay. You don't have to answer. I love you. I'm here for you, whenever you need me. Okay?"

The door closes behind her and I roll to face the wall, crying myself back into oblivion.

* * *

When I wake next, it's dark outside. My alarm clock says it's seven p.m. My heart aches. The ghost of Jordan is everywhere in this house, swimming through me with every breath.

As I stir from my sleep, I notice how stuffy it is in here. Like no fresh air has come in for days. Suddenly, I can't stand it: the bedsheets twisted around my legs, the clothes I haven't changed in days.

I throw off the sheets and sit up. A small bit of moonlight filters through the window. In it, I see a shoebox on my desk. A piece of notebook paper sticks out of its side. I sit on the edge of my mattress for a few minutes, staring at it. I don't know if I can take any more surprises.

I stand and walk over to the box and grab the piece of paper. It reads: *He knew how much you loved him.*

I open the box and it's filled with photos—hundreds of them. Jordan, Chim, and me, sitting at a table at one of Lucy's shows. I remember it so clearly—Chim had just told us the dumbest/most amazing joke ever about a grasshopper walking into a bar, and for the rest of the night Jordan and I teased her mercilessly. In the photo, Jordan is mid-laugh. I forgot how he looked when he laughed; he threw his entire body into it, no holding back.

Another photo, from our sixth birthday party. We're sitting in front of a cake, and Jordan's blowing out the candles. I'm looking at him with this expression of absolute, pure love on my face. I remember when I felt like that about him, like no matter what, it was the two of us, in it together.

It takes me a solid hour to look through all the photos. By the time I'm done, I'm a total mess, snot running from my nose, tears trailing lines down my face, but something inside me has lifted. Something that's been tearing at me for a year. Longer. Something that started when Jordan and I grew up and apart, got bigger when I started partying and lost myself, and took over my whole soul after the shooting. Somewhere along the way, I forgot what is true: Jordan and I loved each other—before anything else, that was the absolute truth of my life.

I'm still staring at the photos when my phone rings.

It's Lucy.

"Did you look at them?" she says to my *hello.*

"Yeah." I swallow hard. There's a lump the size of the Mount Everest in my throat.

"I went through all the old photos on my phone and on Grann's phone, and your mom sent me some, and I printed them all out. . . . I wanted you to *see* it, May. To be able to hold the proof in your hands. That you were happy. That Jordan was too. That you loved each other. You need to remember history as it actually happened, not as your brain is trying to get you to see it. Not how that asshole is trying to get you to see it."

"I still said that to him. I still did that—"

She cuts me off. "May, you were fucking *drunk.* Anyone could have said that shit about someone they loved who was annoying them. You weren't the person who turned drunken words into something so awful. You didn't tell him to do anything. You didn't do anything but *survive.* You survived, and that's okay. Jordan wouldn't have wanted you to come out of that closet; he wouldn't have blamed you for staying in there. He would have wanted you to live. Fucking *live,* May."

Tears are streaming down my face, and I can barely speak around the lump in my throat. "I can't—I've tried. . . ."

Lucy doesn't let me get away with that—she never has. "You haven't—and you can. You *can.* If you don't want to do it for yourself, do it for me. For Jordan. For everyone and everything we've lost. I love you, May. Jordan loved you. Please. *Try.*"

A small moan escapes my mouth. I think about the photos—about all the moments Jordan and I had together and all the moments we won't have. I want nothing more than to dive back into the safety of my bed and never emerge, but I know Lucy's right. Jordan would have hated seeing me this way: a ball of pain and anger and regret.

I swallow hard, then force the words out of my mouth, the words that I never thought I'd say in relation to myself again. "Okay. I'll try." My voice is small but clear.

"You promise?"

I nod even though she can't see me. *"Yes."*

Lucy sniffles on the other end of the line. "I love you, May Day."

"I love you too. I really do."

"I know."

We say our goodbyes and then I sit up, wipe my face with tissues. My tears have finally subsided, at least for the moment. I take a deep, shuddery breath and swing my legs over the side of my bed. I pick up the box that Lucy left for me, tuck it under my arm, and walk out the door and into the hallway.

I stand in front of the door to Jordan's room for a minute, the moment imprinting in me deep, all the way into my bones, and then reach out and turn the knob. I push open the door. His scent still lingers here. His guitar sits under the window across the room, next to his desk. The trees outside cast black shadows over it; I squint through the dark of the room to bring it into focus. What I want more than anything in the world is to have my brother appear. To see him sitting at his desk, wearing a little smile. I would walk over to him, give him the biggest hug I've ever given, tell him how sorry I am—how sorry I am for *everything*—how much I miss him—how much I love him.

I will never stop missing Jordan.

I walk into his room for the first time in almost a year, and over to his bed. I run my hand down its length, remembering, and then lie down in it, breathing in and out, whispering over and over *I love you.*

I must fall asleep, because I stir awake when someone sits on the edge of the mattress. I roll over and see my mom, watching me with a sad smile. She reaches down and brushes the hair off my forehead, like she used to when I was little, and then motions for me to scoot over. She lies down next to me and wraps her arms around my back. We sleep like that until morning, in Jordan's bed.

CHAPTER FIFTY-TWO

Zach

All of a sudden, I'm like a celebrity at school. After the assembly, word got out that I'd been hanging with May over the last couple months, and now every day some dick is like *Teller, what was it like making out with a crazy chick?*

And then there are the freshman girls who are all soppy about it, sighing loudly when they see me in the hallway, convinced that May and I are some fucked-up version of Romeo and Juliet. Even Gwen is buying into that crap, telling me I should call May and forgive her.

It's like history is rewriting itself right in front of my very eyes.

As usual, the one person who's treating me like *me* is Conor.

I've gotten good at remembering to plaster on a fake smile as I walk through the halls. The only time I let my guard down is during class, while the teachers drone on and on about some subject or another and my mind drifts. To May. Always to May.

I can't help but wonder how she's doing—this whole mess can't be easy. From what I hear, she's been put on leave from school indefinitely because of the stunt that she pulled. That's what people are calling it: a stunt, like she decided to give that speech for attention or some bullshit. The thing I've learned most of all this week is how little people care about the truth.

I've locked eyes with Lucy and Chim in the halls a few times, but I can't quite bring myself to stop them, to say hi. Every time, I look away first.

I'm dragging myself through the days.

Conor has a show tonight and he's trying to convince me to come, but he's crazy if he thinks that will happen. We're riding home in my car together—me, him, Gwen. Gwen's in the back typing away on her phone. Conor's going on and on about his show, but I can barely hang on to any of his words. The occasional nod or grunt has appeased him thus far, thankfully. He's borrowing my car after he drops us off at home to pick up a new drum set or something. I couldn't care less.

"Yo, watch out!" Conor grabs my arm, and I slam on the brakes in the nick of time. I almost drove through a red light. Seconds later, a truck barrels through the intersection where we would have been.

Fuck. I take a deep, shuddering breath and close my eyes.

When I open them, Conor's watching me with a concerned expression. He shakes his head. "Zach . . . what the fu—"

I cut him off. "I don't want to hear it."

"You almost—"

"But I didn't, right? I didn't. We're fine." Gwen peeks her head between the two seats.

"What's going on?" She's been so engrossed in her phone she missed the whole thing, thank god.

"Nothing." I shoot Conor a warning look to keep his mouth shut and he glares back. I know I'm going to get some major shit for this.

Sure enough, we get to my house, and as soon as Gwen hops out, Conor turns to me with an expression that I've never seen on his face.

"Dude. Get your head out of your ass. You almost killed us back there." He sounds so serious it pisses me off.

"No, I didn't."

"Um, yes. Yes, you did. Didn't you see that truck? It would have slammed into us—"

"But it fucking *didn't,* did it?" I'm gripping the steering wheel so hard it hurts. "We're fine."

He shakes his head. "Not sure you're fine."

"I am *fine.*" I spit the word out.

He heaves a heavy sigh and then shrugs. "Fine. You're fine. We're all fine. Whatever, man. Moving on." He pauses. "Will you do me a favor, though, and please come to this show tonight?"

He's relentless with this fucking show. "Fine. I'll go if it'll stop you from harassing me any more. Jesus Christ."

He smirks like he always does when he gets his way.

"Good. It'll do you some good to get out of the house."

I'm opening my car door when a thought occurs. I turn back to him with narrowed eyes. "May's not going to be there, right? This isn't some ridiculous scheme to try to get me to talk to her?"

Conor makes a face. "Seriously? First of all, I'm not one of those freshman girls who think you guys are star-crossed lovers. Second, do you think she wants to go out in public so soon, after everything? Pretty sure not."

I almost ask him all the questions that have been running through my head—what's happening with her status at school, how has she been doing—but I stop myself.

It's not my business anymore.

"I'll pick you up in a couple hours." Conor smirks. I roll my eyes and hop out of the car. He slides into the driver's seat and takes off, backing out of the driveway at top speed. His driving always gives me a mild heart attack. The fucking nerve of him, giving me that lecture. Dick.

The downstairs of my house is empty, so I head up to my room, intent on throwing myself on my bed and drowning my sorrows in shitty emo music while I wait for Conor's return. But I'm barely settled on my bed when there's a knock on the door. I throw my head back against my headboard and groan, but it's not like I have any place to hide.

"Yeah?"

I expect it to be my dad. Instead, my mom's salt-and-pepper hair pokes through the doorway, and all of a sudden I wish I'd stayed in my car and driven away with Conor.

"Hi." She looks nervous. I've never seen my mother look nervous.

"Hi." I sound weary. I am weary. I'm tired of all of this—of my life being jerked around by other people. Of my absolute lack of ability to do anything about it. Like I said to Conor, I'm sick of being such a pushover. With that thought, I sit up straighter and look my mom dead in the eye. "What do you want?"

She winces, only for a split second, but I see it. "Do you mind if I come in?"

I shake my head. "Fine. Sure."

She tiptoes into my room, grabs the chair from my desk, and drags it close to my bed. She takes a seat on it and clears her throat. "I came home from work early today—"

"Congratulations." I interrupt her.

She gives me a tight-lipped smile. "Okay. I get it. You're angry. Can I continue? I didn't come in here to argue. I'm sorry I haven't been here much this week; we're ramping up to the trial and things have been nuts."

"No different than any other week," I mutter.

"Zach." Her voice is sharp like a slap, but I don't care. I keep going.

"Yeah, Mom. You know it's no different than any other week. The fact that you haven't been here. You're *never* here."

Her cheeks flush. Her lips have disappeared into a thin

line, and I know—I just *know*—that she's about to lay into me for being a jerk to her. But after several moments of tense silence, she nods. "You're right. You have every right to be upset. I know this year hasn't been easy on your or your sister. I hope you know that wasn't my intention when I took this case."

I shake my head in disgust. Like she cares.

As if she just read my mind, she says, "I care."

She's looking at me like she used to when I was little, before she started working eighty-hour weeks and I never saw her. Before my dad stopped being a functioning human being and I had real, actual parents. I bite my bottom lip to keep it from quivering.

"Do you remember when you were about ten years old? I had just started working at the firm, and they put me on an awful case."

"I remember that you missed my baseball games that season."

She frowns and nods. "Yes. I did. I'm sorry. I know I missed more than a few, over the years." She continues, "Do you remember any details about that case?"

I shake my head.

"I was defending this guy—he wasn't much older than you are now—who'd been accused of something he didn't do. A rare thing, when you're a defense attorney." She lets out a harsh little laugh. "He didn't have much money. . . . I worked it pro bono. And he was found guilty. To this day, I can remember his face, his mother's face, when they took him away."

"That's awful," I say. And I mean it, but I don't understand her point.

"Since then, I've been doing my best to make sure everyone has a fair trial, whether they are guilty or not. I always see little bits of humanity in my clients—little bits that represent things I see in myself. In you." Her eyes are sad.

"You've always been an idealist—a perfectionist," she continues. "It's one of the many things I admire about you. I know you think I never should have taken this case. I know it feels like that would have been the right thing to do, especially given the harassment that our family has dealt with because of my decision. That said, one of the reasons I became a lawyer—one of the reasons I still *am* a lawyer—is because I truly believe that everyone deserves a fair trial. I'm not going to let anyone tell me I can't do my job. And I know you and Gwen are strong enough—brave enough—to deal with whatever those people throw at you. Maybe you think it's not fair of me, putting you both in that situation to begin with, but I have convictions too."

She pauses for a moment. "As you get older, I hope you can remember that people aren't just the sum of their mistakes. The world isn't black-and-white—the best thing you can do for yourself is to look at the spaces between those poles, to see that extremes aren't useful to anyone. Your dad is starting to realize that, but for years, he couldn't. Not about himself, or about anyone else. You remind me of him sometimes."

I tense at the mention of my dad. "I'm *nothing* like him."

She nods. "I get it. I know it hasn't been an easy few years with him."

I mutter, "Understatement."

"I know a lot of things have fallen on you that you shouldn't have had to deal with. Helping out around the house, driving your sister places, all of it. I appreciate it more than you know, Zach. And your dad does too." She sighs. "He's been trying, though. I know it feels like it's too little too late." She takes a deep breath. "But I think you deserve to know—he's suffered from depression for years."

My jaw clenches. I knew that; of course I *knew* that—but this is the first time I've heard it said out loud. I don't like how it makes me feel: a churning mix of guilt and anger and worry and fear. I squint down at my hands, limp in my lap, blinking hard.

"Hey." My mom's hand wraps around mine for a moment, and I look up, surprised. Her eyes are worried. "This is hard to talk about, isn't it?" I shrug. She shakes her head. "We should have talked about it more, over the years. *I* should have. Trying to balance everything—work and bringing in money for our family, and you guys, and your dad . . ." Her eyes mist. It's the closest to crying that I've ever seen her come. "I'm sorry if I haven't handled it well. If he hasn't. But you have to understand—depression is a beast. He's still there, under it, and now that he's finally getting some help and taking the right medication . . . I'm sure you've noticed he's been trying to engage more?"

I nod, reluctant to agree, but thinking back on all the knocks on my door over the past month, the times he's popped his head into my room. The times I dismissed him.

My mom leans back in the chair and grows quiet, and in the silence, I realize this is the most we've ever discussed my dad.

"May was the one who vandalized our house all those times." The words are out before I can stop them.

She raises her eyebrows. "May? Your friend who was here for dinner?"

I nod.

She clears her throat. "Ah. She told you that?"

"Yeah." My voice sounds rough and gravelly. "At that memorial assembly. She gave this speech, and then when I tried to go help her, I guess she decided she needed to come clean or something? I don't know. I haven't talked to her—I'm not *going* to talk to her." I growl the last word; I sound angrier than I even thought I was.

She pushes a hand through her hair, a tired look in her eyes. "Look, Zach. I'm not going to try to tell you that you shouldn't be angry. I know it was a breach of trust on her end. But please keep in mind that that girl—she's been through hell. I hope you remember that. I hope you can see it. I saw the video of the speech she gave, and it sounds like she blames herself for everything—even though she doesn't have any reason to. The weight of that can do strange things to a person."

I shrug. "Still."

She raises an eyebrow. "Still?" She leans toward me again. "Look, I'm the person who took this case. She wasn't trying to hurt you—she was trying to hurt *me*. I'm not saying what she did was right, but I'm also not saying that it was unforgivable. At least, not in my mind. That said, I hope you're careful with her. She has a lot of healing to do yet."

"I'm not talking to her." I cross my arms tight against my body.

"I know you might not want advice from me, but I think you should reconsider. I bet she could use a friend right now." She pauses. "As could you, I think."

I shrug.

We're both quiet for a moment. I lie back on my pillows, look up at the ceiling, trace constellations in the stars above my bed with my eyes. My dad put them up years ago. They used to give me comfort as I fell asleep at night—the light from them, the familiar patterns.

My mother breaks the silence. "I'm sorry I haven't been a better mother."

"Mom—" As usual, my first instinct is to protect.

She puts up a hand to stop me. "You don't have to say anything. I know I haven't been an ideal mom. I hope you can understand it when you get older—the things that pull you in different directions. Especially as a woman and a mother . . .

it's not easy to find a balance." She shakes her head. "I'll try to be better, to do better, to be present for you and Gwen more often. As for your father . . . maybe give him a break sometimes, okay? Watch some basketball with him. He's had a hard few years. And he desperately wants to be your friend."

I hold back my initial response, which is to make a shitty comment about everything she just said, and nod instead. I don't know if anything has really changed between us, but this is the longest conversation we've had in years, and even through my stubbornness, I can tell she's trying.

When Conor gets back an hour later, I'm ready and waiting to go to the show.

CHAPTER FIFTY-THREE

May

It's weird. Since the other night, my mom and I have been talking. Like, actually *talking* in a way we never have before. The morning after we woke up in Jordan's bed, something shifted between us, and it was like she saw me for the first time in years. She told me she had spent the better part of the last year holed up in her office, trying to hide from the world because she felt so guilty. She knew that all the expectations she and my dad heaped on Jordan had started to drive a wedge between him and me, and she feels responsible for the fact that the two of us had drifted so far apart toward the end. She wishes she had stopped pushing Jordan, only thinking of the future and his potential, and instead seen who he was as a person and appreciated the present. I guess my dad hasn't come to the same conclusion, because apparently he's moving out. Moving out—officially. I can't say I'm surprised.

And then my mom told me it's about time I tried to live

again. Just like Lucy said. I told her I would consider it, as long as she did too.

My mom and I are eating dinner together, which hasn't happened in forever, when Lucy texts.

Come to my show tonight.

My mom looks at my buzzing phone and raises her eyebrows.

"Sorry." I move to switch it off, and she shakes her head.

"It's okay." She smiles. "Who was that?"

"Lucy. Who else? Her band has a show tonight, I guess."

"Are you going?"

I widen my eyes and shake my head so hard I'm surprised it doesn't fall right off my neck. "No!"

"Why not?"

"Mom. You know why not." The video of my speech is out there on the Internet, making the rounds, although the numbers have started to slow on YouTube, thank god. The other day, my mom watched it, finally. She said that no matter what *anyone* says, what happened wasn't my fault.

Still, Rose-Brady told my mom that the board won't make a final decision about my status at school until everything gets much, much calmer. She's apparently fighting for me, though—again—which is more than I deserve.

There's no way I can go out in public right now.

No. I respond to Lucy.

A text bubble pops up immediately.

Yes.

No.

May, get your ass out of your bed.

Lucy, leave me alone.

Never.

I look up, and my mom's smiling. I realize that it's because I'm smiling. I haven't smiled in over a week.

"Go." She reaches out and takes my hand. "It'll be okay."

"What will?"

"All of this—all of us. We will be okay. I promise."

Another text from Lucy dings on my phone: *Zach will be there.*

I swallow. Look up at my mom. "Zach will be there."

She smiles. "*Go.*"

I look down at my phone, hesitate for a second, and write: *Fine. I'll go.*

Lucy's response is instantaneous. *Yes!!!! I'll pick you up in 20.*

"I have to change!" I shove my chair back with more energy than I've felt in weeks, then pause. I can't leave my mom here all alone right after we've come back together.

She sees my hesitation. "It's okay. I promise. Go."

I swallow and nod. "I miss him, Mom."

Her eyes fill with tears. "Oh, honey. I miss him too. Every second of every day."

* * *

Lucy picks me up, and it takes me several minutes to realize that her drum set isn't in her backseat.

"Luce, where's your stuff?"

"Huh?" She glances back, and for a second, I swear she doesn't know what I'm talking about. "Oh, yeah. My drums. Um, Conor took them for me. I had to get something fixed earlier, but I didn't have time, so he did it for me."

I give her a weird look. "Okay . . ." She's been shifty and vague since I got in the car. We lapse into silence for a while. The burned-looking landscape of Los Angeles rolls by, the green of the palm trees bright against the beige of the underwatered grass. I think about Jordan and my mom and Zach and what I could possibly say to him to make him understand.

We turn onto a long road, heading up into the hills of Topanga Canyon, and I glance over at Lucy. "Where are we going?"

"We're almost there." Her half answers are starting to freak me out. Outside the car, the night is dark. There are no streetlights. We're bumping along some half-paved road to god knows where.

"Luce, where are you taking me? I'm serious. I can't handle any surprises right now." My entire body is tensing back up. I can't believe I let her talk me into leaving the house. This was a mistake, just like most things I do. When will I learn?

She glances over, and I must have a petrified expression on my face. She decides to take pity on me. "I told you. I have a show."

"In the middle of nowhere?" I can't believe she would do this to me, and right now, of all times.

She shakes her head. "Chill. Just trust me, okay?"

We pull into a steep driveway, and when we get to the top, Lucy manages to wedge her car into one of the only spaces left. There are a bunch of cars up here, at least fifteen or so, parked haphazardly on the gravel outside a barnlike structure. It looks like a hobbit's house. "This is where you guys are playing?" I raise my eyebrows at her, skeptical.

She bites her lip and breaks eye contact. "May, don't freak out, okay?"

My heart sinks deep into my chest. "What?" The word comes out flat. Short. Scared.

She squints out the windshield, avoiding my glare as she speaks. "Look. Here's the thing. This is Anne's uncle's house. He lent it to her for the night. I wasn't lying—the band is playing, but this is also sort of . . . an unofficial memorial. Since the one at school didn't exactly go as planned."

My face is burning. "Anne's uncle's . . . ? Lucy. What in the actual fuck. Why would you bring me here?" My voice starts to rise.

She sighs and has the audacity to roll her eyes at me. It makes me want to punch her. "C'mon, man. Can you just go with it? Please? For me?"

My stomach clenches. I'm not even that upset she lied to me; I'm more terrified that I'm about to be confronted by a bunch of people who hate my guts. If someone asked me earlier today to come up with the thing I'd want to do *least* tonight, this would have been right at the top of the list. Lucy should have known not to do this.

I shake my head back and forth. "I can't go in there. No one wants to see me. They're probably all waiting to throw shit at me. Take me home. Or get your shit and get out of the car, and I'll drive myself. Either way, I'm not going in there. That's all I know. There is no way I'm going in there."

She reaches over and grabs my limp hand out of my lap. She holds it up against her heart. "I promise you, they do want to see you. Can you please just trust me? I would never put you in a bad situation. You know that, I think."

Tears prick at the edges of my eyes. I try to blink them away, but a few escape and roll down my cheek. Traitors. I catch them with my tongue and suck them hard into my mouth.

I'm silent for what feels like forever. Thinking. Looking out at the barn. Trying to decide whether I can do this.

Whether I can be brave.

Finally, I nod. Because it's Lucy. Because Zach's in there somewhere. Because I know Jordan would have wanted me to try.

It's about fucking time I started trying.

I unbuckle my seat belt and get out of the car. As we walk into the house, I try to keep my head down. The inside looks like a giant yurt. The living room furniture has been pushed back against the walls, and a bunch of my classmates mingle in the middle of the room. Across the room, I see Conor and a couple other guys from the band setting up their gear.

The first person we run into is Anne. Of course it's Anne. She's by the doorway, talking with a girl I recognize from school.

"Hi, guys." Anne nods at Lucy, then turns to me. "May. It's good to see you." She sounds sincere.

I bite down on my chewed cheeks and take a deep breath before responding. "Yeah. You too."

"I'm glad you came. I think it's important for us all to take some time to heal together." She pauses. "Look. I know you think I'm the most annoying person on the planet, but I have to tell you something. No one blames you, May."

"Okay," I reply. It's the most pleasant exchange we've ever had, but I don't believe her.

Anne's mouth trembles. "After your speech, our group had a meeting. I know you don't have any interest in being a part of it, but—May, you should have heard the stories. The guilt you feel—it's normal. We've all been carrying it." A tear runs down her cheek. She blinks hard and swallows. When she speaks again, her voice is small. "You need to hear this. It's not easy for me to say—to remember. The week before the shooting, I told my sister I wished she'd never been born. I never said I was sorry. And then she was gone. You weren't the only one who did shitty things. No one blames you."

I look at the floor. The carpet is scuffed and worn. I look back up, into her eyes, and nod. "Thank you." My voice wavers. I know this isn't an easy gift she's giving to me; it's one that hurts and breaks her heart, and I appreciate it more than she'll ever know. I reach out and put a hand on her arm. She clasps her hand over mine.

"I don't know if you know this, but in the past couple years, Jordan and I became pretty good friends. We were lab partners, and he was so freaking funny." She gives a little laugh. "I really miss him. I really miss all of them."

Another thing about Jordan I didn't know. How much was there about my brother that I didn't see because I was too intent on him staying the person he had always been to me? How much did I miss by resenting him? Those nights when I thought he was tagging along after me to parties because he wanted to feel superior. When I look back on it now, I see it so differently. I remember all those times he made sure I didn't drink too much, the times he would hide my Solo cups full of vodka from me even though I would get so angry at him. The times he and Lucy would collect me and Chim from parties and drive us home, and then Jordan would help sneak me in through the front door so our parents wouldn't hear. He was doing it because he cared. Because he knew that I was losing myself. Because he loved me.

My throat tightens and I swallow hard to hold back the tears that threaten to spring into my eyes.

Lucy, who's been chatting with the girl standing with Anne, turns back to us. "Sorry to interrupt, guys, but I have to go help set up." She looks at me. "You coming?" I nod.

Anne and I exchange wobbly smiles, and then Lucy leads me toward the makeshift stage.

As we push through the crowd, I make eye contact with Brian, Jordan's friend. He's walking through the crowd on the other side of the room. My heart skips a beat in my chest, as it always does when I see him, but for the first time I hold his gaze. His eyes widen for a second, like he's surprised that I'm not running away, but after a beat they grow sad. He smiles and raises his hand in greeting, and it flashes through my head that he's a leftover, just like me. Jordan's gone. Marcus is gone. He's the only one of their trio who's still here. I smile back. I wave. I mouth "I'm sorry." He nods, and before I can say more, my view is blocked by a group of people shuffling up to get closer to the stage.

Lucy leaves me and heads up to the stage to get organized. I wander over to the wall on the left side of the room. I'm hiding, but I'm also watching, for once, instead of being trapped inside my own thoughts. Chim arrives with a couple girls I used to be friends with at Carter. Seeing her face makes my breath catch in my throat. The photos Lucy brought over the other night triggered things I'd buried deep down inside myself, and they reminded me that I've missed Chim—that there was more to us than drunken nights and hangovers. She's my oldest friend in the world now, and somewhere along the way I forgot that we used to have fun together before drinking kidnapped our friendship and turned it into something else entirely. She spots me and waves. I wave back but stay where I am. I know the two of us need to talk—really talk—sometime soon, but this is not the place.

I notice that on the stage Lucy and Conor keep bumping shoulders. At first, I think it's accidental, but then I notice how he watches her when she's not looking, and I know he's smitten. Poor guy.

Across the room, Anne directs traffic coming in the front door. The seven photos from the school memorial hang from the wall on the other side of the room. I see Jordan's face, and for the first time, looking at it doesn't make me want to scream.

When I turn back to the band, Zach has appeared on the other side of the stage. He's staring at me like he's seen a ghost. I'm about to wave, to go over there and say something—anything—but before I can, Conor grabs the microphone.

"Thank you, everybody, for coming out tonight. It means a lot to so many people that you're here. I think Anne wants to say a couple words?"

Anne walks up and whispers into Conor's ear for a second. He nods and she steps back off the stage.

Conor puts his lips to the microphone. "Okay. No speeches tonight. She just asks that you guys remember to meet out back after the show. Cool. Thanks."

He turns to the band, now poised and ready behind their instruments, and nods.

As the first note hits, Lucy catches my eye. I recognize the song immediately: "Wait" by the band M83. It was Jordan's favorite song before he died. He would play it on repeat in his room, over and over, until I swear I heard it in my dreams.

I start to cry.

Lucy has a look of deep concentration on her face as she plays, and in the moonlight she's so beautiful. So . . . Lucy.

For the first time in a year, I think that maybe, one day, I'll be able to get up there and sing with her again. Lucy and my mom are right—it's time. It's time for me to start living again—time for me to do something to remember Jordan. He always protected me; he was always there for me, even when I was pushing him away, and now it's my turn to protect his memory, to do something to honor him in a real, significant way.

After the band finishes playing, everyone shuffles out into the backyard. I try to find Zach in the melee but don't see him anywhere.

I wander out, following the stream of people, and find myself on the back patio, face to face with Miles. He sees me and stops, all nervous, like he doesn't know what to expect out of my mouth, like I'm this loose cannon he's afraid of. I can't really blame him.

"Hey." I speak first.

He nods at me, still silent, hands shoved deep into his pockets, eyes on the ground, avoiding my gaze.

I take a shuddery breath. "I'm sorry."

He glances up, surprised.

God, this sucks. Being a human. Expressing things other than the anger that has been eating me from the inside for so long. I force myself to speak again. "I've been awful to you." I shake my head. "It wasn't fair. It wasn't your fault." I take a deep breath. Say the words that so many people have been saying to me for so long. The words I'm finally beginning to think could actually be true.

"It wasn't anyone's fault but his," I say.

Miles is silent for a beat. The chatter of our classmates envelops us, and for a heartbeat it feels like we're standing in a space apart from everyone else, like we're back at the beginning, before everything ate away at us and turned us into monsters. We're not the same people we used to be; no one here is. We'll never be those people again, but I think maybe, just maybe, there's hope that some of us will become better people than we were before.

Finally, he speaks. "Thank you." He looks like he wants to say more, but someone calls his name from across the yard, and the moment passes. Before he walks away, he glances over at me. "You okay?"

I bite my lip. Nod. For the first time in forever, I might not be lying.

Miles leaves me standing there, alone again. I walk farther out into the yard and see that there are hundreds of white balloons spread out on Anne's uncle's huge sloping lawn. Anne's in the distance, leading a few of my classmates from Carter around, barking orders, back to her old self. I smile at the sight.

They're all carrying helium tanks, helping people fill balloons for their launch. When they're full, the balloons look like doves. Anne explains that once the doves reach a certain height, they break apart and biodegrade into the atmosphere. I hang back, watch the first doves float into the air, beautiful and strange.

"Hey, May." Zach's at my elbow, holding two balloons. He looks uneasy.

All the things I planned to say to him fly out of my head when I look at him.

"I'm so sorry—" My voice catches. There's a lump in my throat the size of the world. I lock eyes with him, trying to convey everything I'm feeling—everything I've experienced—everything I was and am and will be—with my gaze. I want him to know that I never would have done what I did had I known him. I want him to know that I'm not as angry anymore.

"I know." His face softens. "I am too. I get it, though, I think. Finally. My mom had to help me understand. . . ."

I open my eyes wide in surprise.

He shrugs. "I know. I didn't expect it either."

The moon comes out from behind a cloud, bright and bold, illuminating all the flying doves. As they rise, it becomes harder and harder to tell that they aren't real—that they're nothing more than shells and air.

"I thought maybe we could do this together?" Zach holds out one of his balloons. I take it from him, and my vision blurs with tears.

The last time I was around most of these people outside of school was at a very different party, under very different circumstances. I'll never stop regretting that night and what I said. I'll never stop regretting how Jordan and I ended, but there's a tiny flicker inside me that's beginning to grow—a small part of my brain that thinks maybe Lucy's right, that Jordan did know how much I loved him, that he always knew.

I just wish I could have said goodbye.

Side by side, Zach and I hold our doves up in the gentle, warm breeze. I silently recite the seven names I'll never forget: *Madison Lee. Marcus Neilson. Mr. Oppenheimer. Juliet Nichols. Britta Oliver. Michael Graves.*

Jordan McGintee.

Zach takes my hand, and together we let go and the doves float up, up, away into the night sky.

AUTHOR'S NOTE

I started writing this book a year before **Parkland** (Alyssa Alhadeff, Scott Beigel, Martin Duque, Nicholas Dworet, Aaron Feis, Jaime Guttenberg, Chris Hixon, Luke Hoyer, Cara Loughran, Gina Montalto, Joaquin Oliver, Alaina Petty, Meadow Pollack, Helena Ramsay, Alex Schachter, Carmen Schentrup, Peter Wang) and **Santa Fe** (Jared Conard Black, Shana Fisher, Christian Riley Garcia, Aaron Kyle McLeod, Glenda Ann Perkins, Angelique Ramirez, Sabika Sheikh, Christopher Stone, Cynthia Tisdale, Kimberly Vaughan). Eighteen years after **Columbine** (Cassie Bernall, Steven Curnow, Corey DePooter, Kelly Fleming, Matthew Kechter, Daniel Mauser, Daniel Rohrbough, Dave Sanders, Rachel Scott, Isaiah Shoels, John Tomlin, Lauren Townsend, Kyle Velasquez). Five years after **Sandy Hook** (Charlotte Bacon, Daniel Barden, Rachel D'Avino, Olivia Engel, Josephine Gay, Dawn Hochsprung, Dylan Hockley, Madeleine Hsu, Catherine Hubbard, Chase Kowalski, Nancy Lanza, Jesse Lewis, Ana Márquez-Greene, James Mattioli, Grace McDonnell, Anne Marie Murphy, Emilie Parker, Jack Pinto, Noah Pozner, Caroline Previdi, Jessica Rekos, Avielle Richman, Lauren

Rousseau, Mary Sherlach, Victoria Leigh Soto, Benjamin Wheeler, Allison Wyatt). I could go on and on, take up pages upon pages, listing all the schools where mass shootings have occurred. Naming their victims. In total, as of this writing on May 9, 2019, almost 250 people have died in school shootings since Columbine. According to a recent article in the *Washington Post,* **228,000 students** have experienced gun violence at school in some manner. School-related violence has increased by 19 percent since the twenty-first century began. Schools are now regularly equipped with metal detectors and security, and practice active shooter drills. As May McGintee says in this book, "Now they are one and the same, the frightening places and the daily places." This is our reality.

I wrote this book for all of you who are faced with this reality, day in and out. I wrote it for the people who have lived through the shootings that are mentioned above and the many other shootings that aren't. The leftovers. The *lucky ones,* who are haunted by what they've faced and by what they have yet to face. The human beings who are collateral damage of these shootings, who have had their lives ripped out from under them, split open, used for media fodder, and then forgotten when the world moves on.

These people have had their personal memories splashed across the front pages of newspapers and discussed on twenty-four-hour news channels, and have then been left to pick up the pieces of their lives, somehow, some way, just like

May and Lucy and others in my book—left to try to find a new normal once the dust has settled, if *normal* is even an applicable word in this context.

The world needs to remember survivors and their families. The effects of these shootings can reverberate for years. So, to all the kids who can't move on because your pain is still with you and always will be—I see you. You are not alone.

Speaking of mental health: the shooter in my book is specifically referred to as *psycho* in multiple instances, throughout. And it's important to remember that the majority of people with a mental illness are *not* violent. After mass shootings, political rhetoric often centers on the mental health of the perpetrators, simplifying a complex issue in a dangerously reductive way. The role that the unique gun laws in the United States play in these incidents cannot be discounted or ignored. I would also be doing a disservice here if I didn't note that our country is in desperate need of better, more affordable mental health services, for all of its kids.

I wrote *The Lucky Ones* for those who have gone through horrific events like these, and for those who fear that they might endure a similar fate someday. For those who have made their way through painful, heartbreaking times and managed to find their way through to the other side. May's story is one of pain and fear and loss, but also one of hope.

Without hope, we are lost.

Liz Lawson

RESOURCES

The Lucky Ones is a work of fiction, but many of the events depicted within weigh heavily on the minds of teens, young adults, and their families every day. If you or someone you know needs help, please don't hesitate to contact one of the resources below. These organizations are there to help.

If you or someone you know has been through a school shooting:

Coalition to Support Grieving Students
grievingstudents.org
877-53-NCSCB (877-536-2722)
info@grievingstudents.org

Substance Abuse and Mental Health Services Administration
samhsa.gov
1-800-985-5990
Text TalkWithUs to 66746

If you or someone you know suffers from post-traumatic stress disorder (PTSD):

PTSD Alliance
ptsdalliance.org
888-436-6306
contact@ptsdalliance.org

The National Child Traumatic Stress Network
nctsn.org

If you or someone you know suffers from depression:

Teen Lifeline
teenlifeline.org
1-800-248-8336 (TEEN)

National Alliance on Mental Illness
nami.org/Find-Support
800-950-NAMI (6264)
info@nami.org
Text NAMI to 741741

If you or someone you know has substance abuse issues:

Substance Abuse and Mental Health Services Administration
samhsa.gov
800-662-HELP (4357)
1-800-985-5990
Text TalkWithUs to 66746

Addiction Center
addictioncenter.com/teenage-drug-abuse
855-706-9275

If you or someone you know needs grief counseling:

The Dougy Center, The National Center for Grieving Children & Families
dougy.org
866-775-5683
help@dougy.org

If you or someone you know is suicidal:

Suicide Prevention Lifeline
suicidepreventionlifeline.org
800-273-8255
Text 273TALK to 839863

ACKNOWLEDGMENTS

I've been sitting here staring at a blank page for approximately twelve hours now, trying to come up with some fascinating words about my Process and trying to make sure I don't miss anyone I should thank. (Twelve hours might be slightly overstating things, but maybe not by much.) I finally decided I should start writing—'cause just like writing a book, if you never start, you can never finish. WORDS OF WISDOM, GUYS.

First and foremost, I am truly one of the lucky ones. I am honored and blessed and amazed every day that all the people named below came into my life and that I was lucky enough to keep them in it . . . and, man. I'm not sure *lucky* is a strong enough word.

This book wouldn't be a book without . . . a lot of people. It takes a village—NAY! It takes a city—a country—a *world* to make a book. So many pieces have to come together!

To start, my fantastic, funny, brilliant editor, Krista Marino, who fell in love with Zach and May right away. I feel so fortunate that my first foray into publishing was with you. You are hilarious and wise, and I have loved getting to know you over the past year. Thank you for chatting with me about everything and making me laugh, even when it was hard. To Beverly Horowitz, Barbara Marcus, Judith Haut, Alison Impey, Monica Jean, Felicia Frazier, Elizabeth Ward, and the rest of the fantastic team at Delacorte Press and Penguin Random House: thank you all so much for all the hard work you've put in on my book baby. For having me in to the office and giving me such a warm welcome. It's appreciated more than I can properly put into words.

Likewise, to my badass agent, Andrea Morrison, thank you for believing in me, my book, my writing. Thank you for always being a calming force in response to my slightly . . . panicky emails. Thank you for accepting and appreciating my thought process and the fact that I don't love to bow to the status quo without serious conversation. Your encouragement, editorial skills, responsiveness, and all-around badassery is always appreciated. I feel very, very, very, very, very lucky to have ended up with you in my corner. Thank you also to the team at Writers House, particularly Amy Berkower, Erica McGrath, Erin Patterson, and Carolyn Kelly, all of whom gave terrific and much-appreciated notes on this book.

And to Writers House in-house editor extraordinaire Genevieve Gagne-Hawes: without you, this book would NOT be a book. Or, rather, it would be, but it would still be sitting on my computer, twenty thousand words shorter, lacking much of what's in it now. Not to mention, I might not have even *written* this book if it weren't for the fact that you pulled me out of the slush pile and requested a full of my previous manuscript. Even though that ultimately ended in a rejection, your beautiful, heartfelt, enormously encouraging response to my writing gave me enough hope to keep trying. Thank you. Truly.

Sincere thanks to all the authors who blurbed my book, for your time, for your words, and for reading! A particular thanks to Erin Hahn, Karen McManus, Kathleen Glasgow, Laurie Elizabeth Flynn, Kelly Coon, Courtney Summers, and Brigid Kemmerer for the advice, guidance, and synopsis help along the way.

To all the early readers of this book in its various iterations: My husband, who reads everything I write and picks me up when I wander into his office halfway into writing a manuscript and collapse on the couch moaning that I have no idea where I'm going or where I've been. My parents, who I'm pretty sure I harassed to read it when it was like ten pages long and then again at ten pages, and then again at a hundred (you get the point). My aunts, Barbara and Kathy, who were kind enough to read a draft along the way. My sister, who reads all my stuff because I force her to (kidding . . . sorta). My cousin Sarah, who also is forced to read all my stuff. And all my friends who read it before it went to copy edits: Janet Geddis, Leslie Grumman, Jess Lorton, Galloway Allbright, Harper Glenn, Jennifer Sommersby, Jeff Bishop, Tayna Guerrero, Jenn Moffett, Alechia Dow, Shannon Takaoka, June Hur, Eva Gibson, and Suzanne Park.

To all my friends who are like family—I love you all. And thank you in particular to Anne Marie McGintee for letting me steal your last name for my book. May appreciates it.

To Joanne Kowit, Rhonda Steinberg, and Graham Lockett for putting up with all my school-policy-related questions (and to Graham—thank you for helping me settle on the correct 2020 terminology for barfing).

To my therapist. Without you, there wouldn't be a book. Without you, I don't think there would be much of anything I have now. (Therapy is *really important*, guys! Take care of your mental health!)

I know I already thanked some of the following people above, but they need to be thanked again, separate from their skills as early readers.

My parents—man. I keep telling myself that these won't be

sappy acknowledgments and then I get to this part of them, and it's like . . . tears. I hear so many tales of people's families not supporting their writing, and so I know how lucky I am, in so many ways, to have been born with you two as my parents. You've always encouraged me—from early days till now—to follow my dreams. Thank you for always answering my calls (even when it's like the seventh one of the day). Thank you for bringing me up to question things and to think rationally. I could write a book-length thank-you note to you, but I don't think I'm allowed to do that, so instead I will just say that I love you very, very much.

To my sibs and in-laws: Joel & Kate Lawson. Tori & Nick Gregorios, Shannon & JC Cameron, Kristen & Levi Solmose, and Joel & Joanne Kowit—I am a lucky woman to have you all in my life.

To Brenda del Cid: You are amazing. We are so lucky you came into our lives! Thank you for giving me the peace of mind to be able to concentrate on work and writing rather than worrying about my child. We LOVE you.

And last but zero percent least: My Kowit boys. Reed and Jackson. You are my heart.

Reed: Thank you for always believing in me. You gave me the time and space and love and hope I needed to write and to keep on writing. You talked me through the enraging times and were always by my side. You are the kindest man I know.

Jackson: I hope that someday you'll hold this book in your hands and say *This is what my mom did when I was little.* I love you so, so much.

ABOUT THE AUTHOR

Liz Lawson works in the entertainment industry as a music supervisor for film and TV. She lives in Los Angeles with her family. *The Lucky Ones* is her first novel.

lizlawsonauthor.com
@lzlwsn